I0743193

MAN MADE GOD 001

By Brandon Varnell

Art by Lonwa

To see Brandon Varnell's other works, or to ask for permission to use his works, visit him at www.varnell-brandon.com, facebook at www.facebook.com/AmericanKitsune, twitter at www.twitter.com/BrandonbVarnell, Patreon at https://www.patreon.com/BrandonVarnell, and instagram at www.instagram.com/brandonbvarnell.

If you'd like to know when I'm releasing a new book, you can sign up for my mailing list at https://www.varnell-brandon.com/mailing-list.

ISBN: 978-1-951904-09-8

DEDICATION

This page is made in dedication to my amazing patrons.
Without them, my characters would never get lewded by so
many wonderful artists:

Aaron Harris
Alarinnise
Alexander Rodruiguez
C.L. Holgrahm
Chase Corso
Dominic Q Roddan
Edward Lamar Stephenson
Emery Moore
Feitochan
Forrest Hansen
Jacob Floores
Jason Grey
Kevin
Lucid Fayte
Matthew Wallace
Max A Kramer
Micheal Moneymaker
Micheal Z Lively
Nicholas
Phillip Hedgepeth
Rafael Eriksen
Sean Gray
Seismic Wolf
Starwarscout Jon
Syed Hamdani

Thomas Jackson
Travis Cox
William Crew

CONTENT

A FATED MEETING

Fayte Dairing was wearing the baggiest clothes she could find: A large beige jacket that hid her body from view, which went over a long black dress that hid her legs from sight, and black boots with fur lining the interior. Finishing her outfit was her veil. The veil adequately covered almost her entire face. In fact, everything except her eyes were hidden behind it.

She did her best to ignore the people attempting to see past her veil. She was glad it was cold outside. The winter air in New York City forced everyone to wear jackets and coats, which meant her current attire didn't appear all that strange.

She never took her veil off in public anymore. She had learned a long time ago that showing her face to others could incite all kinds of trouble.

Of course, even without her face being shown, people still looked at her like she was a curiosity. Even now, surrounded as she was by hordes of individuals, every set of eyes in the vicinity was on her.

"Hey, who is that lady? Why do you think she's covering her face?"

"I don't know who she is. I've never seen someone in that getup before."

"Is she crazy?"

"Maybe she's a babe and is hiding her face because people will become too enamored if they see her true appearance?"

"She could also be hideous under that veil. Maybe the reason she's hiding her face is because she doesn't want people to feel disgusted by her presence."

"Are you an idiot?! Look at how pretty her eyes are! How can someone with such beautiful eyes be ugly?"

"Maybe she has scars all over her face. You don't know."

Fayte felt like sighing, but that would have accomplished nothing. It would only consume more energy. Like everyone else present, she was here for a reason.

The line that she was standing in was long, traveling from the front of the store all the way to the end of this street and beyond. This store, which had just opened a few hours ago and was owned by a company called Mystique Incorporated, sat on the corner of Francis Lewis Boulevard and Hollis Avenue. Next to it was a supermarket. On the other side of the street was a store selling mobile phones, a Starbucks, and several restaurants.

She had come early this morning to be one of the first in line. It seemed, however, that she had underestimated how determined other people were to be first. There had already been over one hundred people when she arrived. Now only eighty-eight people were standing in front of her, which meant she would still be standing in line for quite some time.

With nothing to do but stand there as the line moved at a snail's pace and put up with the people trying to peer through her veil, Fayte thought about the issues she was dealing with.

In any other case, on any other day, she would have never been caught standing in a line for anything. She used to have servants who would have done this for her. However, now that she'd been disowned, she had no other choice but to stand in this line and wait her turn. She refused to allow her shoulders to slump, but it was a near thing. The pressure of what she had to accomplish, and the consequences should she fail, was nearly overwhelming.

"Waaa! It's so warm!"

"Of course it's warm. That's why it's called hot chocolate."

"I know that."

"How are your hands? You aren't cold, are you?"

"Hee-hee. I'm fine. The chocolate is warming them up."

For whatever reason, the two voices speaking up caught her attention. Fayte looked up and sought out the source. Maybe a dozen yards from her was a young man and a young woman. The man looked to be around the same age as Fayte herself, while the girl appeared maybe a year or two younger.

She was not the only one who found themselves staring. These two had caught the attention of everyone nearby. Even those people who had been trying to peer through her veil were now looking at the pair.

Fayte could understand why.

The young woman was, quite frankly, adorable. Her skin, whiter than freshly fallen snow, had a light shade of pink dotting either cheek. It was not from makeup that made them that way. Fayte could tell her blush was natural. Her small nose was cute and her pink lips were stretched into a refreshing and pure smile. Bright blue eyes peered out at the world, revealing a breathtaking innocence that Fayte could not believe existed in such a cruel and merciless world as this one. This girl was prettier than a doll. Even being dressed in a thick jacket and her legs covered in a blanket could not mask her virginal and innocent beauty.

However, even though Fayte and the eyes of almost every person was on this young woman, it was not because of her otherworldly appearance.

She was sitting in a wheelchair and was hooked up to a MELSS, a miniature external life support system, a device used to keep people who possessed a terminal illness alive.

In this day and age, there were few diseases that were not curable. Everything from AIDS to cancer had a cure. Among the many diseases on this planet, there was only one disease that did not have a cure.

No one was willing to go near the young man and young woman. In fact, as the young man pushed the pretty young woman along the sidewalk, everyone made sure to give them a wide berth. Fayte felt a pang of pity in her chest as she looked at them.

After studying the girl for a moment, Fayte turned her attention to the man. The fact that he remained by that young woman's side was enough to give her a passing interest in him. Anyone else, even the girl's family, would have avoided her like the plague. But he remained by her side. His dedication toward this young woman made her feel respect for him.

The moment she laid eyes on him, Fayte froze.

The young man pushing the young woman's wheelchair was no less beautiful than the girl.

His masculine face looked young and boyish, containing the charms and energy of someone who had entered adulthood not long ago. He had blond hair and green eyes. Unlike everyone else who was bundled up for winter, including the young woman in the wheelchair, he was dressed in skinny black jeans and a white collared shirt. The shirt stretched across the muscles of his chest and broad shoulders, and the clearly defined muscles in his arms flexed as he pushed the wheelchair. Many of the women standing in line stared at him and sighed.

"Look at that man. He's so dreamy."

"Mhmm. I wouldn't mind having him push my wheelchair."

"It's too bad he's with that girl though. I mean, she has—"

"Don't say it! There's no need to be rude."

"It really is a pity. She's so pretty. If she wasn't… you know… those two would make the perfect couple."

Fayte couldn't deny that last woman's statement. Those two really did look like a match made in heaven. Both were beautiful in their own right, and it was clear from the way the young man was staring at the young woman that he was completely smitten. Even she could not help but sigh at the loving expression on his face. It really was tragic since the illness that girl had was clearly the only fatal disease doctors hadn't been able to cure.

None of that was what had caught Fayte's attention.

It was the way the man walked.

Having been raised in high society, Fayte had learned to be observant of others. She had spent many hours studying people and learning about what kind of person they were from simple observation. It was this ability to deduce someone's intent from their mannerisms that had landed her in trouble to begin with.

This young man walked with a deadly grace. She meant that in the most literal sense of the word. It was the kind of grace she would expect from the fae folk of legend, but there was an intent to it that made her think of an expert assassin. More than that, however, the way he walked was something she was intimately familiar with.

She was 100% certain she knew who this man was. And if he was who she thought he was, then he might be the key to solve all her problems.

Fayte's heart rate sped up.

Despite being near the beginning of the line, Fayte stepped out and followed after the young man and the young woman in the wheelchair as they slowly left the area.

"Hey, hey! Is that idiot really stepping out of line now? She's only a dozen people away from entering!"

"Who cares? One less person means that much less time to purchase the new game. Do you know how long I've been waiting for *Age of Gods* to come out? Ever since it was announced two years ago! That's how long! I don't want to wait anymore! I can't!"

Fayte ignored the peanut gallery. Who cared what they thought? She walked at a brisk pace, following the two as they walked through the streets. It was quite easy. Everyone who laid eyes on the young woman went out of their way to avoid the pair. She only needed to travel behind them. The only difficulty was in not allowing herself to be seen. She honestly felt bad about intruding on them like some stalker, but she was desperate.

The pair did not enter the subway. The young man eventually stopped in front of a car that was parked on the roadside. It was a state of the art vehicle meant for two people. Long and sleek, painted with a glossy black finish, the car was obviously not something a normal person could afford.

The young man pressed a button that automatically opened the passenger door, which revealed a chair that was fully reclined, explaining why the car was so long despite being meant for two. He lifted the girl from the wheelchair, carrying her in his arms like a gallant prince carrying a princess. The scene was so picturesque that she almost forgot what she was doing. As the young man set the young woman on the chair and buckled her in, Fayte used her phone's camera to discreetly snap photos of the car's license plate number.

The car soon sped off, but Fayte no longer paid attention as she accessed her call list from her phone. She only had one contact on her friend's list now. She'd erased all the other ones. She pressed on the name Su.

"Fayte?" a soft and meek voice came from her phone's speaker.

"Hey, Su," Fayte said in a gentle tone. "I know you are being tutored right now. Sorry to bother you."

"You could never bother me." Su became a little more animated as she spoke. *"But what are you calling for? I thought you went out to get the new game system for* Age of Gods. *"*

"I was, and I still am, but something really important just came up. Listen, do you think I can ask you for a favor? I'm in desperate need of you and that incredible intellect of yours."

"Y-you know I'm always happy to help. Just ask me anything, and I will definitely do my beck—ack! My tongue!" Fayte almost smiled when the embarrassed Su became too enthusiastic and bit her tongue. Even though she could not see it happening, she could well picture it in her mind.

Su often did that when she became too animated.

"Thanks. You're the best." While Su began sputtering over the line, Fayte almost heaved a sigh of relief. With her friend's help, she could definitely do this. "Listen, I'm sending you a picture of someone's license plate. I want you to use it to locate the driver's residence. If possible, please let me know everything you can about this person. Their name. Their age. Whatever you can get your hands on."

"... You want me to track someone for you?"

"I know it sounds bad, but please don't say anything. I already feel guilty enough as it is. However, if the person I want you to locate is who I think he is, then he might be able to help me win the bet with Levon. Please, Su. Please help me."

Fayte hated how desperate she sounded, hated that she was guilting her kind and gentle friend into helping her with something like this, but she couldn't allow herself to wallow in these feelings. If that man was who she thought he was, he might be the only person who could help resolve the mess she was in.

"Okay. I'll do it. Please give me a minute. I'll call you back."

"Thanks, Su. I mean it. I really do."

"You're welcome."

The other line went dead, and Fayte pocketed her phone before heading over to a small coffee shop. It was practically empty. Most of their normal customers were probably standing in line at the new game store, waiting for their chance to get the newest game that hit the market just this morning. The fact that the barista was glaring daggers at the store might have clued her into this.

She got herself a coffee and ignored the barista as he tried to peer at her face. After sitting down in a seat at the furthest corner of the shop, she sipped her coffee without removing her veil. It required some trickery on her part, but she had no intention of letting someone see her face unless she had a good reason to.

Su called her around ten minutes after she sat down.

"Su? What did you find for me?"

"The owner of that license plate is called Adam Lancer. He's nineteen-years-old and lives with a seventeen-year-old girl. Aris Purety. She's listed as his younger sister, but they aren't blood-related. He was adopted into her family five years ago. Their parents died of Mortems Disease several years ago. They moved here about

three years ago. They live in an apartment in upscale New York. I can send you the address."

"As expected of you, Su. Not even fifteen minutes have passed, and you've already exceeded my expectations." Fayte could not see Su on the other end, but she could well imagine the girl's blush as she praised her. "Was there anything else?"

"T-there is," Susan took a shaky breath. *"Um... I've managed to find several medical documents for Aris. She.. she has... Mortems Disease."*

"So it's as I suspected," Fayte murmured. "I can use this…"

"W-what? Did you say something?"

"No. I didn't say anything. Anyway, thank you so much for helping me out, Su. I really appreciate it. Please send me his address. I need to speak with him as soon as possible."

"Y-you're welcome. I'm happy I was able to help you. I'll send his address now."

"Thanks again. I'll talk to you later."

With their conversation over, Fayte ended the call, placed her phone on the table, and leaned back. She stared at the ceiling for a moment. A struggle took place within her heart, but it only lasted for a moment. The moment soon ended. She stood up, pocketed her phone, and made her way out of the coffee shop.

✳✳✳

The elevator softly chimed and the doors slid open. Adam pushed the wheelchair with Aris on it into a brightly lit hallway. Not a soul was present, but that was to be expected since no one else lived here except them. No one else *wanted* to live here.

Before he reached their apartment, Adam pulled out his phone, accessed a security app, and unlocked the door. It slid open when he reached it.

Their apartment was a spacious three-bedroom, two-bathroom space that had been converted into a two-bedroom apartment thanks to some renovations he'd done. The renovations had been expensive but well worth it.

After the door closed shut with a soft click behind him, Adam slipped out of his shoes, put them on a rack, and moved in front of the wheelchair. He first turned off the life support system. A small cable was attached to Aris's right arm, helping her body function while outside, which he removed.

"And up we go," he said with a soft grunt as he slid one hand under Aris's thighs and the other around her shoulders. She weighed less than a feather. She was so light that Adam often worried about her blowing away if the wind became too strong. This lightness caused his heart to quiver in fear, because he knew it meant her muscles had atrophied to the point where they barely functioned. Her body barely had any muscles left.

"Hee-hee. I'm always happiest when I'm in your arms."

Despite their circumstances, Aris acted as if she was truly happy about their situation. This girl who seemed so weak and fragile had a will that was stronger than steel.

"I'm glad since I love having you in my arms," Adam said back with a smile that hid his pain.

He carried her into the master bedroom, which was large and featured an equally large bed. The king-sized bed was made from a type of foam that was said to provide the perfect sleep. It was covered in pure white sheets and a light blue blanket. The pillows were similarly white and light blue.

Adam laid Aris down on the white sheets, removed the blanket, then helped her remove her jacket, pants, and shirt. Now clad in nothing but a white bra and panties, Adam looked down at the young girl and struggled to control himself.

Despite the fact that her muscles had atrophied so completely she could barely move, Aris did not look at all like a cripple. Her white skin was flawless. While the proportions of her body were about average for a young woman her age, the tender swells of her breasts, barely hidden behind her bra, was enough to entice any man into wishing he could lay his hands on them. Her legs were long and supple. There was no indication that her body had degraded at all.

There was a reason for that.

"Are you ready for me to begin?" asked Adam.

Aris's already rosy cheeks lit up in a small blush as she nodded. "Yes, please."

"Okay. I'm starting."

"Mmm."

Adam sat on the bed near the end and lifted Aris's left foot, which he placed on his lap. Aris released a soft sigh as he began massaging her foot, starting from the soles and even massaging each individual toe. Her toes were tiny. They reminded him of small sakura petals. She had the cutest toes ever.

He soon worked his way up, massaging her calf and thigh, moving from the outside of her thigh to the inside at a slow and steady pace. Then he did the same thing with her other leg. As he worked, Adam bit his lip in concentration as he targeted acupressure points on her body. While Aris could not see it, small tendrils of colorless energy seeped into her skin through his hands, subtly strengthening her body and stimulating the nerves.

He didn't stop at her legs. Adam also massaged her hips, her stomach, her arms, and even her breasts and the area around her crotch. Her breasts and crotch were the hardest part for him. It was a struggle to touch those places and not lose himself. The only thing holding him back was the knowledge that if he had sex with her, there was a good chance her body would be unable to handle the strain and kill her.

"Mmm… Adam…" Aris moaned. "That feels… so good…"

Adam's breathing hitched as he began rubbing her breasts. He had already removed her bra and was in the process of slowly infusing his own energy into her body, allowing it to seep into her skin, reinforce her muscles, and enhance her internal organs so they would continue to function. Her light pink nipples were stiff and puffy. He wanted to take them into his mouth, swirl his tongue around them, and lightly tug on them with his teeth.

His lips became a thin line as he struggled against the roaring fire in his lower abdomen.

By the time he finished massaging every inch of her body, Adam's forehead and neck was covered in sweat and Aris was fast asleep. He stared at the girl for a moment, longing and heartache causing his heart to feel like it was being pierced, then leaned down and gently kissed her lips before standing up and walking out of the room.

"I need to make dinner, but first…"

Mumbling to himself, Adam wandered into the second bedroom, which looked more like a high-tech medical facility than it did a bedroom. All kinds of equipment resided inside. The biggest object was a machine in the very center that looked like a giant cylinder made of gleaming steel.

Adam wandered to the back. A cold storage shed spanned the entire back wall. He pressed the button that made the shed doors slide open with a hiss, then frowned when he saw the many empty test tubes resting on the seven shelves inside. After scratching his head for a moment, he released a weary sigh.

"I thought it was about time to restock."

Grabbing the test tubes one by one, Adam went over to the large device in the room's center and inserted each test tube into a small slot that opened on the side. The slot accepted each tube and took them into the device. Once all six thousand had been inserted, the slot closed and Adam wandered over to a large vat with a tube sticking out of it and traveling into the ceiling.

He quickly filled the tube with one hundred gallons of water. Then he grabbed a knife and raised his hand over the vat. Taking a deep breath, he concentrated all of his will power on his index finger as he cut it with the knife. The wound tried to heal almost immediately, but he fought against his own biological processes long enough for a single drop of blood to fall into the vat.

The vat and cylindrical device was referred to as a Diluter. Its purpose was to dilute the contents of powerful chemicals or ingredients used in medicine, then automatically fill the test tubes he had placed inside with said medicine.

After activating the Diluter, Adam watched as the liquid—just a simple combination of water and blood—mixed together before traveling up the tube and into the Diluter. The liquid's color was light pink. The blood had already long since been diluted to 100,000 micrograms. Once all of the contents in the vat was gone, the Diluter stopped thrumming with life and the slot on the side opened up. Adam took the tubes one by one and placed them inside of the racks in the cold storage shed.

He only kept one out.

Taking that one test tube, Adam wandered into the kitchen, placed the tube on a single holder rack, and got started on dinner. He made rotisserie chicken and coconut curry soup today. It was easy and healthy, with a balanced amount of protein, carbohydrates, fat, and it contained a variety of important vitamins and minerals. It wasn't long before the scent of his cooking began wafting through the room. Now all he needed to do was wake up Aris for dinner.

Just as he was about to head into the bedroom, a small beeping sound echoed in his ear. He paused, then reached into his pocket, pulled out his phone, and looked at the caller ID.

Astaroth.

A frown split his face as his eyes grew cold. He put a small bud in his ear, accepted the call, and said, "Astaroth. Is everything okay?"

"Everything is fine, Master. I just wanted to inform you that a young lady has entered the building and traveled up to your hallway. Seeing how you and the young miss are the only two people in this entire apartment, I can only assume she is here for you."

"Mm. I understand. I'm not surprised I was followed here. A young woman was following me and Aris in the city and took a picture of my license plate. Come to think of it, I should consider changing the address my license plate is listed on. Do you know who she is?"

"No. She just arrived and we haven't ID'd her yet. I will find out in just a moment. Would you like me to inform you of the results?"

"No, it's fine. I don't think this woman means any harm, and I'm sure she'll introduce herself anyway. Keep an eye on her just in case, though."

"Of course, Master."

As the call ended, Adam debated with himself over what he should do. Should he go about setting the table as if he wasn't going to have a guest, or should he not bother until he shooed the woman away?

Before he could come to a decision, the sound of his doorbell ringing echoed through the kitchen. He flinched at the noise. That sound might have woken up Aris.

He changed his debate from what he should do to whether or not he should invest in sound proofing the master bedroom even as he walked to the front door. He paused for a moment, hesitated, then hit the button.

The door slid open.

Adam's heart stilled.

The woman before him was the same one who'd been follow-ing him this afternoon. She wore the same clothes she had when she followed him with one minor difference.

She was no longer wearing her veil.

Adam felt like everything in the area except for this woman had become gray, a simple monotone. The woman before him had a face that defied description. Words like beautiful and gorgeous sim-ply couldn't adequately describe her appearance. She had gentle blue eyes, skin that appeared softer than the finest silk, a small nose, and ruby red lips that begged to be kissed. The long blonde hair sur-rounding her face traveled to the middle of her back. Her hair color reminded him of honey. He could tell from a glance that this woman was not wearing any makeup, but that only made her impossible to describe beauty all the more astounding.

If only she wasn't wearing such ugly clothes.

His astonishment only lasted for a moment before he settled his heart rate. The shocked expression on his face quickly disap-peared as he mastered his emotions.

"Can I help you?" he asked.

The woman looked shocked for a moment. Her eyes went wide and her mouth parted in a pretty O-shape. However, much like him, she seemed to calm down with admirable swiftness. The only thing she couldn't mask was the interest now shining in her eyes.

"Hello. I'm very sorry for intruding like this. Please allow me to introduce myself. My name is Fayte Dairing."

"Fayte… Dairing…" As he heard the name, a thought suddenly popped into his head. "You wouldn't happen to be related to Aaron Dairing, would you?"

Fayte stiffened, but she tried to hide it behind a strained smile. "Yes, I am. That person is… my father."

The way she said "my father" was as if she had swallowed a deadly poison. Was there bad blood between her and her father?

"Well, Fayte Dairing, is there something I can help you with? I don't mean to be rude, but I have to finish preparing dinner, so if there is nothing you need of me, I'd like to ask you to leave."

His dismissive words were meant to drive the woman off, but she didn't leave like he'd expected.

"Please wait! I would like to speak with you. I have a proposition for you that I believe can benefit us both."

"I'm not interested in propositions. If there's nothing else, then please leave."

Adam reached out to press the button that would close the door —

"I can cure your lover's Mortems Disease!"

The words stopped his hand cold. His entire arm trembled before, ever so slowly, he retracted it back to his side. Adam studied the woman standing in front of his door with a cold gaze.

"Do not toy with me," he said in a voice that made Fayte shudder. "Everyone knows that Mortems Disease is incurable. It attacks the body, breaking it down, destroying it from the inside out. First it attacks the muscles, then the nerves, and then it begins breaking down the organs, until it finally destroys the heart. No one has found a cure yet. If someone did have a cure, it would have been announced a long time ago."

The tone in his voice could have caused lesser people to die from a heart attack. It was cold and filled with a sense of danger, like a blade just about to be drawn. Despite this, Fayte did not back down.

"But what if there is a cure? What if I have that cure? Can you really afford to send me away if there's even the smallest chance that I can cure your lover?"

Fayte pressed on, determined, and while Adam wanted to turn her away because of how impossible her words sounded, he could not. His mind, body, heart, and even his soul trembled at her words.

He had moved with Aris to New York City because it was at the heart of the American Federation and had all the best technology, and it was also the best place for him to earn enough money to pay for all the medical equipment currently in his possession. He had been hoping to find a cure. However, in all the time he'd been living here, he had not once discovered anything that could cure Mortems Disease. The most he could do right now was slow down the degradation of Aris's body, but that was only a temporary solution. It only delayed the inevitable.

And now this woman was telling him she had a cure.

Could he really turn her away?

"Come in," Adam said at last, stepping aside.

"Thank you," Fayte murmured as she walked inside.

Adam watched her slip out of her black boots and set them by the shoe rack. She had very small feet, but he thought they suited her. This woman appeared delicate and otherworldly, like a goddess who had descended to the mortal world.

He glanced outside as the woman wandered further into his apartment, checking to see if anyone had followed her. There was no one present. Well, no one except for the shadow hiding in the corner of the hallway. Once he had confirmed that no one was around to spy on them, he shut the door, made sure it was locked, and turned to the woman called Fayte.

It was time to see what sort of proposition she had in mind.

THE PROPOSITION
HE COULDN'T REFUSE

"Whatever you are cooking smells delicious."

Fayte took several deep breaths as she smelled Adam's cooking. By this point, the scent had permeated every part of the kitchen and the connected living room. While the scent was strong, it had a very mild flavor since Aris couldn't handle bolder flavors and spices.

She used to love spicy foods...

"That's because I'm cooking dinner—*was* cooking dinner. I'm about finished now," Adam admitted.

"I'm sorry. It seems I interrupted you." Fayte's smile was truly apologetic, which helped Adam set aside his annoyance at someone he didn't know barging into his home.

"It's fine." He waved away her apology. "Why don't you sit on the couch over there? I'm going to grab some drinks. Is water fine?"

"Thank you. And yes, water is fine."

With a nod, Adam wandered into the kitchen, grabbed two glasses from a cabinet, and poured them both water from the tap. Every faucet in his apartment provided filtered water, so there was no worry about them getting sick or ingesting something toxic. This was another addition he'd installed after he and Aris began living here. While he got them water, Adam observed the woman now sitting on his couch.

She had taken off that ugly beige jacket of hers. Underneath it was a simple long-sleeved shirt, red and plain, but tight enough that it stretched across her well-endowed chest. Her breasts were a lot bigger than he first suspected. They were maybe three times larger than Aris's modest bosoms.

This was just something he noticed and not something he focused on for longer than a second; at the moment, Adam was not interested in her appearance but her reasons for seeking him out. After giving her a preliminary observation, he came back into the living room, set one of the glasses in front of her, and then sat just a few feet away on the same couch.

"Thank you." Fayte reached out with a slender hand to grab the glass and brought it to her lips. The action was delicate and refined, the kind of action that could only come from a woman of noble descent, as expected from the daughter of a wealthy family like the Dairing Family.

"You said you could cure Aris's Mortems Disease," Adam finally pressed, getting to the reason he had let this woman into his home.

"I did." Fayte set the glass down and placed her folded hands in her lap. She sat with her back straight, posture fully erect. Her eyes retained their gentle appearance, but there was a seriousness in them now that caused Adam to also sit straighter. "The method for curing Mortems Disease is something my grandfather hired someone to develop to cure his wife. He invested over one hundred billion dollars to come up with this cure... but his wife died before the method was complete. After that, he dismantled the project and hid it away. He died shortly after from grief and the project was forgotten."

"And I'm guessing you coincidentally discovered this miracle cure," Adam said.

Fayte nodded. "I did. When I was... leaving my family's house, I found a secret passage in my grandfather's study that led to the room where the equipment was stored. I decided to have it moved out before my father could discover it himself. The device used to cure Mortems Disease is complete. However. ."

"However, it's never been used before, right?" Adam finished when she trailed off, his eyes narrowing. He licked his lips. "This method you speak of is completely experimental. so there's no telling whether or not it will work. Does that sound about right?"

"Yes." Fayte's smile was a bit brittle as she answered him.

Adam leaned back on the couch and processed this information. She had a method to cure Mortems Disease, but since it had never been used, there was a high probability of failure. He'd give this device a one in one million chance of success... but perhaps he was being pessimistic. Countless doctors all over the world had been seeking a cure and none had discovered it. How could a cure like this suddenly just fall into his lap? It had to be fake.

But what if it wasn't?

Adam once more studied Fayte. He ignored her beauty, the softness of her face, the gentle red swell of her cupid's bow lips, and the graceful demeanor she possessed. All of his attention was on her eyes. She was staring back at him with an earnest expression. It was completely guileless, something he didn't expect from a woman of her stature.

"If you stare at me like that… I'm going to blush," Fayte murmured as she turned her head. Indeed, there was a small hint of pink on her cheeks.

"Sorry," Adam apologized. He at least had enough tact for that. "I was just wondering how certain you were of this cure working. If it has never been used before, then can you really say it will work?"

"Of course, there is a high chance of failure," Fayte admitted, and here her expression took on a determined quality. The fire in her eyes surprised him. "However, isn't it better to have even a small chance of success than a guaranteed failure? If you were given a one in a billion chance to save your lover, don't you think it would be worth it to at least try?"

And that was the crux of this situation right there. This woman was giving him that one in a billion chance. Could Adam really turn her away? One in a billion was better odds than the complete certainty of failure.

"Let's say I am willing to try. What do you want in exchange?" asked Adam.

Fayte's expression lightened just a little, as if a small burden had been lifted from her shoulders. She took another sip of water as if to wet her parched throat, coughed into her hand, and then spoke once more.

"Before I get into the bet I want your help with, I would like to confirm something. Are you the gamer who, three years ago, rocked the gaming world by consistently defeating the world's best international players? The one who was given the nickname the Untouchable Emperor because even the top ranked players in the International Power Rankings couldn't put a single scratch on him?"

While Adam's heart was thudding against his chest, he maintained his outward calm. He flexed his fingers a little and rolled his shoulders. He was primed like a detonation charge, ready to act on a moment's notice. The gesture was so slight he didn't think Fayte would spot it.

"Is that why you came to me? You are correct. I am the person you're thinking of. However, how did you discover who I was? I was certain I made sure to cover all my tracks. I even deleted every gaming account I owned."

"I'm so glad I was right." Fayte placed a hand against her chest, and this time, even Adam found he could not tear his eyes away from the way her bosoms heaved—he was still a man, after all. Fortunately, she didn't seem to notice and continued talking. "You did a great job at disappearing. No one would ever have been able to find you even if they realized Adam was your real name. Actually, if it wasn't for me seeing you while I was in line to get the new game system for *Age of Gods*, I would have never known it was you."

"And how did you know it was me? I always made sure to change my character's appearance when I played." Adam placed his elbows on his knees and leaned forward, piercing Fayte with a sharp look like pointed blades, though she did not seem bothered.

"It is true that your characters always looked different from game to game, but there are a few things you always kept the same like your height and body type. Your characters have the same physique you do. I suspect you did this because it's easier to move in a body that feels similar to your original body. Of course, that alone would never be enough to figure out who you are. The main reason I knew you are the person people called the Untouchable Emperor is because of how you walk." Fayte's answer surprised him, but before he could ask her to clarify, she continued. "Everyone has a certain way of walking, talking, and specific mannerisms that are unique to them. Your walk is like that of a natural born predator. It is deadly and makes me feel like I'm standing on the edge of a sword. The man known as the Untouchable Emperor walked the exact same way you do. I don't think I need to tell you this, but it is impossible for two people to walk in the exact same way—even identical twins cannot do it."

Her answer startled Adam, to the point where his eyes actually felt like they were bulging from his sockets. She recognized him because of the way he walked? What sort of joke was this? Even Adam, with his incredible skills of observation and perception, could not tell who someone was simply by looking at how they walked.

Fayte finally cracked a grin when she saw how shocked he was. "Of course, it's not as if that would be enough to figure out who you are. The truth is, I've been watching recordings of all your previous battles recently, studying them to see if there was anything that might help me solve my current problem. If it wasn't because I have a very acute memory and you—or rather, the Untouchable Emperor—have been on my mind this past month, I might not have recognized you."

Adam calmed down upon hearing her words, but he was still surprised. Even barring everything else, the fact that she was able to recognize him from the way he walked was incredible. Her perceptions must have been outstanding. Superhuman even.

An unconscious respect for this woman rose within his chest.

"So the reason you were studying videos of my competitions is related to the problem you want me to solve?" he asked.

"Yes." Now that they were getting to the crux of why she was here, Fayte became nervous. She began playing with her fingers and took several deep breaths. Adam waited patiently for her to begin talking again. "Do you know how powerful family's work in this day and age? How many of them are interconnected and become powerful conglomerates?"

"It's through marriage, right?" asked Adam.

"Yes. Marriage. Women born into a powerful family are groomed for marriage to the men of other powerful families. This is all done in order to secure a family's future prospects and increase the family's prestige among other wealthy and influential families." Fayte's eyes became bitter as she stared at her hands. "I come from the Dairing Family. We are a very powerful and very affluent family whose name is consistently near the top when it comes to wealth and finances. However, we are not the most powerful. In fact, while we are exceedingly wealthy, my family has never reached the top twenty in terms of rank, wealth, or influence."

Adam could already figure out where this was going. He could even vaguely figure out what she wanted from him, but he didn't say anything, instead letting this woman explain her circumstances.

Fayte continued when she saw Adam remained silent. "I'm sure you saw me when I was following you earlier. I was wearing a veil over my face. I usually travel with a veil on."

"I can see why," Adam said. "With your devastating beauty, it would cause any man who looked at you to lose their mind."

"You haven't," Fayte pointed out with a smile.

"I'm different from most men." Adam broke into a wry grin.

Her smile widening, Fayte continued. "My family and I ended up being invited to the party of a young master who was celebrating his twenty-sixth birthday. My… father… refused to let me wear my veil. He said it would be disrespectful to the young master. I don't think I need to tell you where this is going, do I?"

At Fayte's pointed look, Adam shook his head. "I'm guessing the young master saw you and became infatuated."

"He declared right in the middle of the party that he was going to take me as his bride," Fayte said with a humorless look in her eyes. "Of course, my father was ecstatic. This particular young master belongs to the current number one most influential family in the American Federation. He's the heir to a corporation worth fifty trillion dollars. If my father could marry me off to him, he would be able to raise his societal status far more than he ever could on his own."

"And what is the name of this young master?" asked Adam.

"Levon Pleonexia."

The moment Adam heard the name, his entire mind felt like it had shut down. Every cell in his body burned red hot. He clenched and unclenched his hand several times as he struggled with an intense loathing that caused his heart rate to skyrocket. It was as if he could actually feel his heart throb and thud against his ribcage.

"Are... are you okay?" asked Fayte.

The nervousness and genuine worry in her voice helped Adam calm down.

"I'm fine." He took a deep breath and focused back on their conversation. "So, Levon decided you were going to be his bride, and your father agreed to marry you off... but you did not agree with the idea. Is that about right?"

"You are completely right." Fayte still looked worried, but she nodded and pushed their conversation forward. "I did not agree at all. I publicly rejected Levon during the party. However, my father became angry at me and said I had no right to refuse. Fortunately, the law is still with me on this. I cannot be married against my will... but Father didn't care. After I refused to marry Levon, he disowned me. He told me I was no daughter of his. After I was disowned, Levon came and offered an out."

"The bet." Adam nodded. "What was it?"

"I must complete three separate goals within three years in order to win the bet." She held up a single finger. "One: I must accrue half the annual income of the Dairing Family." She held up a second finger. "Two: I must increase my standing and reputation to match or exceed the least powerful family among the top ten most powerful families in the American Federation." Finally, she held up a third finger. "And three: I must create a guild in *Age of Gods*, and that guild must be ranked among the top five guilds. If I can do all that, Levon will publicly announce that he has rescinded his marriage offer after giving it more consideration. He said he would even convince Father to repeal his decision to disown me."

Adam nodded once. "And I suppose if you lose, you'll have to marry Levon."

"Exactly," Fayte said.

"That third goal, is it national or international?" asked Adam.

Placing within the top five guilds would be difficult regardless, but there was a monumental difference between the national and international rankings. The American Federation only had two guilds that continuously placed within the top five. Those guilds also belonged to the two most powerful families in the country.

"National," Fayte answered.

Adam leaned back in his chair. He did not know how rich the Dairing Family was, nor did he particularly care. This right here was the reason she had come to him.

Now it was time to determine her character and get her to spell out what she wanted, even though he already had a hunch.

"So what is it you want from me? I do have a bit of money left over from when I was gaming, but it's not enough to help you."

"I would never ask someone I barely know for money." Fayte gave him a hard look like he had just insulted her integrity. "What I want is for you to get a copy of *Age of Gods* and join the guild I am forming in the game. I want you to raise your reputation, earn more acclaim than anyone else, and help me win the bet against Levon."

"I understand now," Adam said. "You want me to increase my reputation, and then work under you. Once *Age of Gods* opens its Money Exchange System, you can use my reputation to build up your own reputation, earn money in the game, and convert it into real world currency. Like that, it would be perfectly possible for you to earn millions or even billions of dollars in the virtual world. And with more money, you can achieve your goals that much more easily. You'd be killing two birds with one stone—no. I guess you'd be killing three birds with one stone."

Adam understood her plan extremely well since he had used that very method to buy this apartment, all the medical equipment, and everything else he owned. At the same time…

"You realize, of course, that it will still be next to impossible to make half the annual income of your family within three years even with my help, right? Disregarding the other two goals to your bet, this alone will be incredibly hard to achieve."

"I am aware." Fayte's determined smile did not leave her face, but the look in her eyes, the sense of resignation he saw present, caused him to understand that she knew exactly how impossible her task was. "However, even if the chance is one in a million… even if it is a one in ten trillion chance, I will not give up until I've failed. I suppose you could say this is my last act of defiance."

Ever since this woman told him about how she'd discovered who he was, Adam felt some respect for her. Now, as he listened to her talk about how she refused to give up even in the face of a hopeless situation, the respect he felt skyrocketed.

This woman was impossibly determined. She knew there was next to no chance of her succeeding, and yet she still refused to roll over and accept her marriage to Levon Pleonexia. That level of determination was something he'd never seen on anyone else except one person.

And that person was currently sitting in the room and talking to her.

"I understand your situation," Adam said at last. "And I am willing to help you on several conditions."

"Name them," Fayte said immediately.

"The first condition." Adam held out a hand and stuck his index finger out. "You cannot under any circumstances give out any information about myself or Aris. Our identities in the real world must remain completely confidential. The second condition." He held up his middle finger. "The doctor you get to cure Aris's Mortems Disease must be a woman and I must be present at all times. The third condition." He held out his ring finger. "In the event that your method doesn't work and Aris is not cured, I will not help you any further. That will be the end of our agreement. These three conditions are non-negotiable. You can take them or leave them."

The only reason Adam was willing to help this woman was on the off chance that she really could cure Aris of her disease. If she could do this, Adam would do everything within his power to ensure she not only met but exceeded her goals. He would give her everything. He would give her anything. However, if she failed and Aris was not cured, then the one reason Adam had to live would be gone.

He stared at Fayte, wondering whether or not she would accept such extreme conditions.

"I can agree to conditions one and three," she said at last. "The second condition isn't something you need to worry about. The device I have that can cure Mortems Disease doesn't require a doctor and is very simple to use. I know how it works, so I'll be the one activating it. That said, Aris will need to live with me while she's being cured. You can also move in with me since I can't imagine you'll want to be away from her."

Adam pondered her words for a few moments, then slowly nodded. "I can live with that arrangement."

"Then do we have a deal?" asked Fayte.

"I believe we do," Adam said.

Fayte held out her hand and Adam, realizing what she wanted, reached out and grabbed it. He could not help but marvel at how soft her hand was. Adam owned bed sheets made from the softest fibers in the entire world, and yet this woman's hand was a thousand times softer than anything he'd ever felt before. It was also warm, like the kindness in her heart had seeped into her skin.

"Thank you for agreeing to help me," Fayte said as he saw her out.

"You shouldn't thank me yet. There is still a chance I won't do it," Adam warned her.

"Be that as it may, I am still grateful to you," Fayte said, then paused. "I have to pick up the system for *Age of Gods*. It requires a DNA sample to synchronize with your mind. Do you want me to grab yours while I'm there? A lock of your hair should suffice for a DNA sample."

Adam didn't debate long before agreeing. He cut off a bit of his hair, sealed it inside of a container, and handed it to Fayte before she left.

He stood in front of the door for some time, reliving the events that just happened. He didn't know whether he was excited or scared. There was a chance that Aris could be cured. There was also a chance, however, that the disease would not be cured. If this could not cure her, then Aris would likely die within a few more months.

He sighed. "I guess it is true what they say. Nothing is more dangerous than hope."

"Adam?"

Dispelling those unpleasant thoughts at the sound of Aris's soft and sweet voice, Adam made his way into the master bedroom, where the young woman he'd dedicated his life to lay on the bed, wide awake.

"Hey. Have you been awake for long?" asked Adam.

"Mm. A little while. Were you talking to someone?" asked Aris.

"Just someone who wanted a favor," Adam said.

"A favor?"

"I'll tell you about it after dinner. Come on. I made rotisserie chicken and coconut curry soup today."

Because Aris's muscles had degraded to the point where she couldn't even walk and could barely lift her arms up, Adam was the one who helped her do everything. He carried her to the dinner table and sat her down, brought out the food, and fed her a little bit at a time. He also had her drink the "medicine" he made. Not only could she barely do anything, but she couldn't chew that well because the muscles in her jaw had also atrophied. That was the reason most of his food was a liquid like soup.

Seeing Aris like this made Adam's chest ache. He never got used to it. Only one incident in his life hurt as much as seeing her like this.

After dinner, Adam took Aris into the bathroom and washed her off. He filled the tub with hot water and used a washcloth to clean her. Since she couldn't stand on her own, he placed her on a stool and had her lean against his chest and he rubbed the cloth containing disinfectant over her body. When he reached her breasts, Aris's breathing hitched and a soft, beautiful sound emerged from her mouth.

Adam did his best to ignore it.

Immediately after cleaning her off, he lifted her up and stepped into the bath, then sat down in the warm water, positioning Aris so she was sitting between his legs, her back resting against his chest. From this position, he could see the swells of her modest breasts from over her shoulder. While they were not big, they were beautiful. The whiteness of her skin currently had a trace of pink thanks to the water's heat. Her enchanting little nipples had become stiff. He wanted to play with them, but he knew there was a chance he could lose control, so he refrained.

"You're poking me," Aris giggled.

"I'm not made of stone, you know." Adam rubbed his hands up and down her hips. "The most beautiful girl in the entire universe is naked and in the bath with me. I'd have to be gay to not react like this."

His words made her smile. "You can stick it in if you want. I don't mind. In fact, nothing would make me happier than if I lost my virginity to you."

"Please don't say that. I'm barely restraining myself as it is. If I had sex with you, there is a very good chance your body wouldn't be able to take it."

"I would rather die by your hands than from this illness," Aris said. Then she giggled. "Hee-hee, or would it be 'I would rather die by your dick'?"

Adam closed his eyes as a wave of pain shot through him. He adjusted his body and Aris's position in the tub so his fully erect dick was resting between her thighs instead of poking her. Then he wrapped his arms tightly around the girl and pressed his face against her neck.

"Do not ever say that, Aris. I am not going to let you die. In fact, there might be a way to save you."

"Mm. I know. It's in exchange for the favor that girl asked you for, right? The one who wants you to play the new video game that just came out?"

"You heard us talking? How much did you hear?"

"Hee-hee. I woke up when the doorbell rang, so I heard the entire conversation." Adam clicked his tongue and made a mental note to soundproof the master bedroom. Unaware of his thoughts, Aris continued. "Thank you for agreeing to help her. I know the only reason you did so was because you wanted to give me a chance to survive. I… to be honest, I don't think I have much longer to live. If this chance hadn't come up…"

Aris trailed off, but Adam knew what she wanted to say. Aris's doctor had told them that it was already a miracle for her to survive for as long as she had.

Mortems Disease was a powerful and deadly virus that attacked the body, eating into it and causing the muscles, bones, skin cells, and everything to degrade and atrophy. It was not only deadly but also relatively fast acting. Most people did not last more than six months before succumbing.

Aris had been infected with Mortems Disease three years ago.

"We have a chance to cure you now, so please do not give up," Adam whispered into her hair.

"I know. Don't worry. I promised you that I would never leave you, that we would eventually grow up, get married, and start a family. I could never forget. Since you're the one asking me to keep fighting, I will," Aris said with a determined gaze.

"Thank you," Adam said softly.

After staying in the tub for half an hour, Adam lifted Aris and got out. They could have stayed in longer. The bathtub was a state of the art device that regulated the water's temperature and kept it perfectly at whatever temperature he set it to. However, Aris was falling asleep, which meant it was time for bed.

After drying both her and himself off, Adam dressed Aris in pajamas and himself in a pair of boxers, and slid them underneath the covers of his bed.

He and Aris lay on their sides, facing each other. Adam was tenderly stroking Aris's cheek, brushing back her hair, and gazing into her soft eyes. His heart felt at ease. At this moment, at least, he did not worry about her Mortems Disease. He merely let himself fall into her eyes… the eyes that had saved his soul when he was on the brink of giving up.

"Adam, will you kiss me?"

"I thought kisses were something princes gave to princesses in order to wake them up."

"Hmph. They also give princesses a kiss to make them fall asleep."

"Is that how it works?"

"It is."

"There's no arguing with that kind of logic."

Adam scooted closer, until there was barely any space between their bodies. His hand was still on her face. He tilted her head up as he leaned down, sealing their lips with a soft kiss.

It was impossible not to feel Aris's gentle and soft breath against his lips as they shared several sweet kisses. Her breath, her lips, the glazed look in her eyes, all of it was enough to drive a man insane. Adam knew that if not for his strong will, he would have already succumbed and taken her virginity and, as a result, maybe even her life.

The kisses continued. Aris used what little strength she had left to thread her fingers through his hair. She kissed him as best she could with her weakened body. Her actions were enough to move him to tears. He wanted to cry, but that would have ruined the moment, so he refrained, just barely.

As the night wore on, Aris eventually fell asleep in Adam's arms. He held her close, his mind active, unable to sleep. Tenderly stroking her hair, he thought about Fayte's proposition. A cure. There might really be a cure for Aris. While Adam had searched high and low for even the slightest hint of a cure for Mortems Disease, he had never once found anything and was on the verge of giving up hope. Now a potential cure had fallen into his lap. He didn't know what to think.

He had never been a religious man. Adam could never bring himself to believe in religion or God after everything that happened to him.

But on that night, he prayed to whatever gods he could think of that Fayte hadn't been lying when she said she could cure Aris.

MOVING IN WITH FAYTE

Three days had passed since Adam met Fayte. He did not do a whole lot during that time. Like usual, he spent nearly all of his time with Aris when she was awake, and when she fell asleep, he spent most of his time cleaning the house, prepping their food, and ensuring everything was in order. There were only a few times during these three days where he did not take care of chores or spend time with Aris. Those times were spent gathering any and all relevant information he could find on Fayte, *Age of Gods*, and the Dairing Family.

Early in the morning on the third day since his meeting with Fayte, Adam found himself sitting on the couch as the news played on a screen in the background. The news was detailing the hype for the upcoming game, the same game he would be playing for Fayte: *Age of Gods*.

"I'm here at the newest Mystique Incorporated gaming center where, as you can see from the long line behind me, is still as busy as ever. There has been a constant stream of people lined up here all week from morning to dusk. This is despite the fact that the game won't become playable for another week. Everyone is eagerly waiting for their chance to grab the latest system to play what many are calling the hottest game to ever be released."

"It looks like that new game is going to be really popular," Aris said softly as she watched the news.

Aris was leaning on his shoulder. Her soft breathing echoed in his ear and made him constantly aware of her presence. He wished he could wrap an arm around her waist, but right now he was scrolling through a tablet and checking out the current networth of the Dairing Family.

"Yeah. It's been estimated that over five hundred million people have already bought the new system," he said.

"That many? There are only about five billion people alive now, right?"

"That's right."

About thirty years ago, World War III—the first and only nuclear war—decimated the Earth's population, killing about one billion people. Immediately after the war ended, Mortems Disease was born from a combination of nuclear radiation and pollution. It spread across the globe, killing another 1.5 billion people. At present, there were only an estimated 4.1 billion people alive—a good four billion less people than there had been before World War III.

"Ever since the armistice was signed by the world leaders, gaming has become the best way to settle disputes and turn a profit," Adam explained. "Even people from low-income families can earn tens of thousands of dollars through gaming if they're capable enough or join a guild run by a powerful family like the Pleonexia Family."

While he said that, it wasn't as if earning a profit through gaming was easy. It still required hours of time spent in-game. To really earn enough to make a living through gaming, it had to be something people focused on entirely. It meant leaving behind many real world endeavors and fully immersing themselves in the game world.

Some people were willing to do that. Others were not.

"When I get better, do you think I can also play *Age of Gods*?" asked Aris. He looked down at the girl, but she was not looking at him. Her eyes were still locked on the television screen. "I would like to play with you. I think it would be a lot of fun."

Adam was tempted to tell her no, that the gaming world was a lot more dangerous than people assumed, but he couldn't do it when he noticed the excited smile on her face. It was perhaps the one thing in this world that he possessed no defense against.

"Of course you can. In fact, I'll ask Fayte to get you a system when she picks us up today. By the time you're cured, you will be able to enter the game world with me."

"Hee-hee. I can't wait. I bet playing a virtual reality game will be even more fun than the console games we used to play."

Adam smiled as he leaned down to press his lips against Aris's hair. He then went back to checking over all the information he had compiled about the Dairing Family.

It looked like the Dairing Family had a networth of one trillion dollars and their annual income was 10.5 billion dollars, which meant that if Fayte wanted to win her bet, she would need to earn at least 5.25 billion dollars. He frowned. That was an impossibly large sum of money for a single person to earn in just three years, and it wasn't like the Dairing Family had been able to reach such lofty heights in a single generation. They had acquired this financial power after generations of hard work.

It was obvious to him that Levon had set her an impossible task. Nevermind gaining the fame to rival the top ten most powerful families of the American Federation. Forget creating a guild that reaches the top five most powerful guilds represented nationally. The money alone made this task next to impossible. Even if she entered *Age of Gods*, the most she could probably earn in three years was a hundred million.

Of course, this calculation was based on the idea that she was working alone.

He sighed.

It seemed he was going to have to work harder than usual this time.

Aris fell asleep against his shoulder at some point, and Adam stopped scrolling through his information to let the girl rest with her head on his lap. He set the tablet on the coffee table and watched the news while tenderly running his hands through her hair. The young woman was smiling as she slept. He liked to think her smile was be-cause she could feel his actions even in her sleep, but he knew that might be wishful thinking.

About an hour after she fell asleep, the doorbell rang. Aris was startled awake. She opened her eyes and blinked several times.

"Is… someone at the door?" she asked, yawning as Adam helped her sit up.

"It's probably Fayte. Hang one moment while I get that," Adam said.

"Kay," Aris said as Adam positioned her so she could watch the TV without falling over.

Adam walked up to the entrance, stopped in front of the door, and pushed the button to open it. As he expected, Fayte was on the other side. Of course, it was hard to tell who she was because she was wearing a veil that masked her entire face now. Her clothes to-day were also baggy and ugly just like the ones she had worn when they first met.

"Fayte."

"Adam, it is good to see you again. I hope you've been well."

What a polite way to greet someone. It was just the kind of greeting he expected from a woman of her stature and pedigree.

"I've been doing fine. Same as always, I suppose."

"That's good. I have the system for you." Fayte reached into a bag she'd been holding and brought out a small purple box that was about the size of his two fists put together. "The system is in here."

"Thank you." Adam took the box from her hands and studied it. It was just a plain box with no adornments, but he could sense a strange kind of energy coming from it. It made him feel like he was holding a sparking wire. Odd. This never happened with the other games he played. He looked back at Fayte. "So, about your end of the deal…"

"Don't worry. I haven't forgotten." While he could not see her mouth because of the veil, he was able to see the way her eyes crinkled in a smile. "The reason it took me three days to get this to you is because I was having some people I trust set up the device that will be used to cure Aris of her Mortems Disease. It's all ready for her. If you want, we can leave right now and travel to where I'm currently staying. That's where the device is set up."

"And you're certain it can cure her?"

"As certain as I can be without us having any test results."

Adam sighed, but he guessed that was the best he could hope for. Even a one in a billion chance was better than no chance at all.

Since the device was ready, there was no point in them remaining here. Adam went back into the living room and told Aris that everything needed to cure her was ready and they would be heading out. This was also the first time she and Fayte met.

"Hello, I'm Aris."

"It's a pleasure to meet you. You can call me Fayte." The woman who had come to request his help gazed at Aris with something resembling awe. "I can see why Adam loves you so much. You really are the cutest and most beautiful girl I have ever seen."

"I'm sure I have nothing on you." Aris smiled. "You're so pretty you even need to wear a veil so people can't see what you look like."

Fayte reached up and touched the veil hiding her face. Since he couldn't see her expression, Adam had no way to tell what the woman was thinking, but Fayte shook her head moments later as if dispelling her thoughts.

"Perhaps," she said mysteriously and left it at that.

They made their way out of the apartment complex. Because Aris could not walk on her own, Adam lifted her into a wheelchair and pushed her out. There were many automated wheelchairs that could move on their own, but he preferred this one because it let him be useful to her.

On the way to Fayte's car, the woman in question and Aris talked. Aris asked Fayte all kinds of questions, though none of them were about her background, the bet, or anything related to it. She asked about Fayte's hobbies, her friends, and what kind of boys she liked.

Adam learned that Fayte's hobbies consisted mostly of learning management, cooking, and gardening. She had a huge interest in knowing how to manage a business. She also owned a garden back at her family estate, though she could no longer maintain it since her family had all but kicked her out. The cooking surprised him. However, he knew not to judge a book by its cover.

"I'm not sure I like your family very much." Aris pouted. "They seem very mean."

They were currently in the elevator. Soft music played in the background.

Adam thought he sensed a sad smile through Fayte's veil as she responded. "They weren't always like that. My father used to be kind and benevolent, but once Mother passed away, he seemed to stop caring about me and focused entirely on elevating the Dairing Family's position in society."

"Hmph. Even if he wasn't mean before, he's mean now." Aris didn't look like she particularly cared for whether Fayte's father used to be kind or not and continued to pout, which caused Fayte to relax. Perhaps it was because she was so relaxed that Aris's next question caught her off guard. "And what kind of boys do you like?"

"Me? Well... I've never really thought about it," Fayte sounded uncertain. "I guess if I had to answer you... I would say I like boys who are capable and independent, but I would also like them to be kind and caring, and I want someone who would be willing to help shoulder my burdens but not take all of them onto himself. I guess... I like boys who would see me as an equal and not just an accessory to make them look good."

"I understand exactly what you mean," Aris said.

Fayte's eyes flickered to Adam before going back to Aris. "I'm certain you do."

After making their way outside, Fayte directed them over to a small and somewhat beat up convertible.

"Is... is this your car?" asked Adam, aghast.

He didn't think he could be blamed for the incredulity in his voice. The car she had was not only at least one decade old, but it looked like it had been rebuilt several times. The passenger and driver doors were different colors. The top was a different color from the hood. Several scratches and some oil stains covered the trunk. This car was the kind that not even a low-income family who barely earned enough to make ends meet would own, never mind the daughter of a trillion dollar net worth family who owned multiple businesses in both the real and virtual worlds.

"I know what you want to ask and why you're reacting this way," Fayte said in a soft but sardonic voice. He could sense the melancholy in her gaze. "My funds are extremely limited right now. In fact, the last bit of money I had was used to set up the device that can cure Aris's Mortems Disease."

"It sounds like you've had a difficult time of things, and yet you still aren't willing to give up," Adam said at last.

"Of course not. I refuse to give up until the very end," Fayte responded.

"Fayte, you are so cool." Aris cast her an admiring glance. Adam could practically see the stars in her eyes. "You're so strong and determined. I wish I could be like you."

"I'm not that strong," Fayte muttered in what sounded like bitter remorse. Adam was sure there was a story there, but now wasn't the time to dig up her past.

Since there were only two seats in this convertible, Adam and Aris shared the passenger's seat—not that either of them minded. He stowed the wheelchair in the trunk, then sat down with Aris on his lap. She leaned her back against his chest as he strapped them both in. Her warm body and the scent of her fragrant shampoo addled his mind, and the feeling of her soft butt resting against his crotch made him wonder if this was what people meant when they talked about being trapped between Heaven and Hell. Meanwhile, Fayte moved around to the other side, entered the driver's seat, and pressed the ig-nition button that turned on the car.

As the car sputtered to life, Fayte put the car on drive and left the apartment that he and Aris had spent the last three years of their lives in behind.

✳✳✳

Similar to the car she owned, the apartment complex that Fayte lived in did not impress. The apartment complex Adam and Aris were living in was actually a lot more impressive, being located in an expensive residential district just off Grand Central Parkway. Not only did this complex look a little rundown, but there was also a strange smell in the air, which caused Aris to cover her nose.

"I'm sorry about how terrible this place looks," Fayte mur-mured in a soft voice.

"It's fine," Adam said, not bothered by the stink. Rotting corpses smelled a lot worse than this. "I understand your situation better now, so I expected something like this. Don't worry. So long as you can cure Aris, nothing else matters. I'll help you win that bet against Levon, no matter the cost."

"Thank you. I feel a lot more confident with you onboard."

Adam nodded at Fayte's words as he lifted Aris into her wheel-chair and followed the elegant woman clad in ugly clothing into the apartment complex.

The inside was just as bad as the outside. While the floors, walls, and ceiling were all clean, it was clear from how old everything looked that this building was in sore need of maintenance. If Adam were a betting man, he'd say this building was something that had existed since before World War III. There were a lot of old and unused buildings that remained because the government simply didn't have the manpower required to renovate them.

Fayte's apartment was on the second floor in Room 254. While the apartment was clearly old, the doors were at least the same automatic ones that every other building used. It slid open after she ran a keycard through the lock. She stepped inside, and Adam followed her, pushing Aris along.

"It smells much better in here," Aris said with a smile as Fayte turned on the lights.

"That is because I prefer keeping it clean and used deodorizers when I first bought this place." Fayte slipped out of her boots, set them aside, removed her coat to reveal a simple turtleneck sweater underneath, and hung it on the rack. She also removed her veil. Walking forward for several feet, she stopped and turned toward them before making a grand gesture. "Welcome to my home. I actually just moved in about one week ago, but I've done my best to clean it up."

Adam followed Fayte's actions by removing his shoes and putting them by the rack. He detached her life support system, lifted Aris into his arms, and followed Fayte as she walked further inside.

"It's pretty nice. You've done a great job of cleaning the place up," he complimented.

Adam had been expecting to see, while not a messy apartment, at least one that looked as rundown as the rest of this complex. What he got instead was a neat and tidy three-bedroom apartment with a kitchen and a living space that had several brand new amenities. There was a sliding glass door on the other side of the room. He could see the balcony outside, but it looked like Fayte was using the balcony to generate solar energy. Several solar panels were situated outside along with a small hanging garden that only had a few tiny sprouts.

She's using solar power to save money on electricity? No, using solar power like this also means she's off the grid. No one can track her through energy companies. Very smart.

The more he saw of this woman, the more impressed he became by her determination, intelligence, and mental fortitude.

"Thank you," Fayte said, finally removing her veil and revealing a soft smile. "Anyway, the device for Aris is all set up, but perhaps we should wait at least until tomorrow before using it?" She focused on the girl in Adam's arms. "The device we'll be using is one that will put you to sleep until you're cured of Mortems Disease. According to the research notes Grandfather left, it will take anywhere from two to three months, so you two will be separated for a little while."

Adam glanced at Aris, wanting to hear her thoughts on the matter. This would affect her life even more than it affected his.

"I'd like to wait at least a day before doing this," Aris said.

"I feel the same way," Adam admitted.

"In that case, why don't I get started on dinner?" asked Fayte, clapping her hands together.

"Actually, how about you let me cook?" Adam suggested.

"Adam is a really good cook," Aris told Fayte. "He's the best."

"Is that so?" Fayte's amused smile at Aris's confidence in Adam's cooking told him that she probably wasn't as confident in his talents, or maybe she thought herself a better chef. It did feel a little like she was challenging him. "Well, I'm fairly confident in my cooking as well, but okay. After smelling what he made for dinner the day I met him, I am interested in seeing how well he can cook."

"You won't be disappointed," Aris said, pride lacing her voice. It was almost like she was talking about herself.

Since it was decided that Adam would do the cooking, he left Aris in the living room with Fayte so the two could get to know each other. He thought this was a good idea.

Aris did not have any friends. After she and her family contracted Mortems Disease, all of their friends and relatives avoided them. The only person who had stayed by their side that entire time was Adam. He had spent the better part of six months caring for Aris and her parents, and when her mom and dad died, they moved to New York City because Adam had become desperate to find a cure.

It must have been... roughly four or maybe three and a half years since her parents died. He wondered where the time had gone.

Fayte's fridge and cupboard was fortunately fully stocked with ingredients. He noticed she had a lot of pasta, so he decided to make spaghetti carbonara. It was easy to prepare, only taking about twenty minutes in total. He let the girls talk as he cooked dinner, set the coffee table, and brought out the food.

"Oh, wow. That really does smell delicious!" Fayte gasped in surprise.

"Hee-hee. I told you. Adam's cooking is the best!"

The three of them sat on Fayte's couch and used the coffee table as a dinner table. Fayte did not have a dinner table herself. She said there was no point in getting one since dinner tables were a place for family's to eat, and she did not have a family to eat with.

They began eating, and once more Fayte complimented Adam on his cooking.

"You were right, Aris. Adam's cooking really is incredible. I know how to cook myself, but I can't make anything that's this good."

While Aris could not move much, she still puffed up like a peacock. It was like the one who had been complimented was Aris herself and not Adam.

"I love Adam's cooking so much, though once I'm cured, I would like to begin making some of our meals," she confessed.

"You are a very talented chef," Adam admitted.

"Hee-hee. Of course I am. I was taught by the best."

The one who taught Aris to cook was Adam. This was before she and her parents developed Mortems Disease. She had always been a fast learner. Had she not contracted that deadly virus, she might have surpassed him eventually since, unlike Adam, Aris actually enjoyed cooking.

Adam only knew how to cook because it was a great skill for assassins. Even without lacing the food with poison, knowing how to cook a delicious meal worthy of a five-star restaurant helped him get close to many of his targets. Most of them never suspected their head chef was out to kill them.

Adam swirled some spaghetti onto his fork, not too much, and lifted the fork to Aris's mouth. The young woman's eyes glistened as she opened her mouth and let him insert the fork. She closed her mouth around the fork before he removed it and slowly chewed the food.

He normally didn't make solid foods. Aris's muscles were in such a state that it was hard for her to eat solids, but it wasn't like she couldn't. It just took more effort.

He used the same fork to get a bigger portion for himself and stuck it in his mouth.

"It's not hard to chew, is it?" he asked.

Aris swallowed and lightly shook her head. "It's not. Don't worry."

"Okay. Want another bite?"

"Yes, please."

Fayte watched as Adam fed Aris using his own fork and bit her lip. She seemed like she wanted to say something, but she was holding herself back for fear of seeming rude.

"Something on your mind?" asked Adam.

With a sigh at realizing she'd been caught, Fayte asked, "Are you sure that's safe?"

"Are you sure it's safe to have Aris live in the same apartment as you?" Adam asked back.

"I took the Mortems Vaccine last week."

"I'm immune to Mortems Disease."

"Immune?" Fayte's eyes went wide. "I didn't know that was possible. Even the vaccine isn't one hundred percent foolproof."

"Well, I'm kind of a freak of nature in that regard," Adam admitted.

He continued feeding both himself and Aris. Fayte quieted down a bit and ate her food, though she also continued to watch them from the corner of her eye. Adam thought he saw a hint of jealousy in her eyes, but he couldn't be sure, and even if there was, he didn't know what she could be jealous of.

Once they were done eating, Adam took their plates, cleaned them off, and came back with a small vial of pinkish liquid.

"I know we're here to cure you, but I would still like you to take this just in case."

Adam held out the vial to Aris, who nodded. She understood how important this was to him.

Just as he was about to tip her head back and help her drink the contents, Aris asked, "Can you feed it to me with your mouth?"

Fayte had just been taking a sip from a glass of soda when she spewed the contents all over the coffee table. She stared wide-eyed at Aris. Her cheeks were stained bright red.

"Aris," Adam said, a hint of warning in his tone.

"Hee-hee. I'm just kidding."

Adam shook his head and smiled before helping Aris drink the medicine he made for her. While he did that, Fayte sputtered a little before heading into the kitchen and coming back with a towel to clean up the mess she'd made. Not only were her cheeks red, but her ears also had a vibrant blush.

After dinner, the three of them continued to sit on the couch. Adam took out his tablet and began going through the news feeds that contained any relevant information about *Age of Gods*. The girls talked to each other. They seemed to be getting along well, which he believed was because they were both kind people with likable personalities. Either way, he was incredibly grateful that Aris and Fayte already seemed to have built a rapport. Maybe after Aris was cured, they could become friends.

"Do you mind if I ask how long ago you contracted Mortems Disease?" Fayte suddenly asked.

"It was about three years ago," Aris admitted. "I was fourteen at the time."

"S-so young?" Fayte looked shocked. "H-how did you survive until now? I mean…"

"Hee-hee. I know no one else has ever lived this long after contracting Mortems Disease, but I have a reason I can't die yet." Aris's soft smile was something no one could resist. Even Fayte found herself entranced by the girl's gentle expression, eyes glazing over like she was staring at something mystical. "Adam and I promised we would marry when we came of legal age, so I can't die until then."

"And that's the reason…?" Fayte didn't look convinced.

"Well, it might also have something to do with Adam's medicine," Aris reluctantly admitted.

"You mean that stuff you just drank?"

"Yep. I don't know what it is, but Adam began making it for me after we moved to New York City. It really helps. After I drink it, I feel like there's energy rushing through my body and healing me. It's hard to describe, but it's a very warm feeling."

Fayte didn't say anything about that. However, the glance she gave Adam immediately after Aris spoke told him that she was incredibly curious about what kind of medicine he had Aris take.

Evening eventually became night, and Aris began nodding off. Mortems Disease sapped a person's strength, making it so they had to sleep longer to maintain their body's primary functions. Staying awake for more than two or three hours at a time was exhausting. What's more, Aris had stayed up for a lot longer today than she normally did.

Adam helped Aris get ready for bed, which included brushing her teeth, washing her body, and changing her into a set of pajamas. Fayte had been surprised when she realized Adam bathed Aris. It was only after thinking about how they'd been living together for so long that she realized they had been doing this for years. After getting both himself and Aris ready for bed, Adam carried her into the bedroom that would be theirs for the foreseeable future.

The bedroom was not big, but it was not small either. A king-sized bed sat in the very center, looking brand new. Adam was certain Fayte had bought this immediately after he agreed to help her. There was very little in the way of decoration. The plain walls were unadorned, a simple dresser sat off to the side, and there was a window that granted them a view of New York City's skyline.

Adam tucked Aris into bed and then climbed in himself. As always, they lay on their side, facing each other. He liked falling asleep this way because he knew there was always a chance Aris would go to sleep and never wake up. This fear of her dying without his knowledge caused his heart to constrict and made him decide that, if nothing else, he would make sure the last thing he saw every night before going to bed was Aris. Just in case.

Yes, just in case.

"Hey, Adam?" Aris said as she cuddled with him. Her head was tucked neatly underneath his chin, and her modest breasts could be felt caressing him through her pajamas

"Hmmm?" Adam blinked his eyes open and gazed at the girl's head. All he could see was her beautiful brown hair.

"I have a request," Aris said.

"What is it?"

There was a pronounced pause.

"If this really works and I'm cured, I want you to take my virginity."

Adam took a deep breath, held it, and then released it.

There were very few things in this world that a man wanted to hear more than the woman he loved asking him to take her virginity. While Adam believed he had a stronger will than most men, even he could not deny that a pleasant hum ran through him when Aris asked this of him.

He held Aris tighter and said, "That's not something you need to ask of me. I was already planning on having sex with you after you're healed."

After. Not if. Adam was going to think positively. He wanted— no, he *needed* to believe that she would get better. If Aris died, then he would have nothing left to live for.

"Hee-hee. I thought so, but I wanted to make sure."

Once she finished speaking, Aris scooted a little closer to Adam, until her face was resting against his neck and collarbone, and slowly drifted to sleep. Adam remained awake for a few more minutes. He stroked Aris's hair before, with a gentle exhale, he shut his eyes and also drifted off.

GOING TO SLEEP

The next morning began the same as usual. After kissing Aris awake, Adam washed her body and hair, toweled her off, dressed her, and combed her hair before making breakfast. Since the process of curing Mortems Disease involved being put to sleep for a certain period of time, Adam made her favorite: red velvet cinnamon rolls with homemade frosting.

Fayte had also liked the cinnamon rolls.

In fact, Adam thought Fayte enjoyed the cinnamon rolls even more than Aris.

"Are you two ready?" Fayte asked after everyone was finished eating.

"Not really," Adam admitted.

"I would like more time with Adam," Aris confided.

"Then… do you want more time together?" asked Fayte in a cautious voice. "I can give you at least a week. *Age of Gods* doesn't become playable until next week."

Adam and Aris debated with each other the merits between going ahead now and waiting another week. If they went ahead and put Aris under now, and she was cured, then she would be cured that much faster. If they waited a week, she would be cured a week later. Both of them were eager to have the threat of her disease no longer hanging over their heads.

On the other hand, if they put her under and the process was not successful, then they would have wasted two or maybe even three months, and Aris would likely die shortly after. Another week of being together before she died was a small consolation, but it was still something.

"I think… we should begin now," Aris said.

"Right." Adam sighed. "No time like the present, right?"

"Hee-hee. Yes, that is exactly what I was thinking."

Fayte clapped her hands and stood up from the couch. "In that case, let me take you to the room with the equipment that's going to cure Aris."

With Adam pushing Aris's wheelchair, the group traveled into the third bedroom, which was not only sealed shut with an incredibly high-tech security lock that had obviously not been part of the original floor plan, but also required a passcode and retina scan to open.

"I'll install your retina map on the scanner so you can enter as you please. That way you can visit Aris while she's healing," Fayte said to Adam. "Anyway, let's go inside."

The room on the other side looked like a complex laboratory or a medical professional's office. Littered with all kinds of medical equipment—such as scanners that measured a person's vital functions, medical computers that displayed a variety of charts, and life support machines that were used to feed a person nutrients—this place looked like something he'd expect from an expensive private hospital for rich people.

In the very center of this room was a cryobed. It was a device that reclined on the ground, was about three yards long and three feet wide. Made from synthetic alloys and shaped like a pod, the device featured a clear glass dome that would allow people on the outside to look in and a computer system at the foot.

Adam felt like all the breath had left his lungs as he stared at the cryobed, at the equipment in this room, which was about ten or fifteen years ahead of the current most advanced medical practices. He was so shocked that he stumbled forward and almost dropped Aris on the floor.

"A-Adam!" Aris shouted in surprise. "What's wrong? Are you okay?"

With wide eyes, Adam glanced over at Fayte, who froze upon making eye contact.

"Adam, why are you looking at me like that? Your gaze is a little… disturbing right now."

"Fayte, do you know who your grandfather hired to make this device?" asked Adam, trying harder than he ever had to keep from shivering.

"I only know a little bit," Fayte confessed, giving him an odd look but answering nonetheless. "According to Grandfather's journal, he ran into a person calling himself Lucifer. The man claimed he could cure Mortems Disease but needed funds. Grandfather was skeptical, but after seeing Lucifer perform a miracle of some kind, he decided to trust him and invested hundreds of billions of dollars to have this cryobed created. Why do you ask?"

"No… no reason," Adam mumbled, closing his eyes.

No wonder this device could supposedly cure Mortems Disease. If it was made by *that* man, then it would undoubtedly be capable of curing any disease the world over.

This device looked a lot bigger than the one he remembered, which had been more compact and streamlined. It was clear that Lucifer had become more adept at building this machine later on in life. What sat before him now was clearly a prototype that had been created as a proof of concept machine. As he stared at the device, another and very similar but more streamlined cryobed overlapped with this one.

Adam closed his eyes and took a deep breath, trying to dismiss the images. It was hard. Even now, he could feel the phantom pain from when his body was strapped into that cryobed and injected with hundreds of thousands of different types of energy. His heart felt like it was shriveling.

"A-anyway, this cryobed will place Aris in a form of suspended animation," Fayte tried to get back on track and explained how the device was used. "Once her body's functions have been suspended, the chamber will release a substance called Leefa Drug. This substance is a poison that kills off any and all diseases and harmful bacteria, including Mortems Disease. The reason we need to place her in stasis like this is because the Leefa Drug is also a powerful poison. I don't know how it works, but the poison will be destroyed while the machines somehow keep her body from coming to harm. Once the drug has destroyed her Mortems Disease, the cryobed will begin a unique process that sucks out all the poison in her body. Only after the poison has been completely removed will the cryobed bring her out of suspended animation."

Everything Fayte said made sense to Adam. He also understood why there was a huge chance of failure.

Poison and medicine often went hand in hand. In fact, one could even say that poison was just a different form of medicine and visa versa. It made sense that a powerful poison could annihilate something like Mortems Disease, but using poison to cure a disease was like trading one death for another.

This was why Aris was going to be put in suspended animation. While her body and vital functions were all frozen, the poison would sweep through, eradicate her Mortems Disease, and then the cryobed's last function would activate and suck the poison back up, removing it from her body. It would be as if she'd never been poisoned or had Mortems Disease in the first place.

Adam felt a moment of fear as he realized how many things could go wrong with this process. The cryobed could break, the stasis effect that froze her body's functions could stop working, or the cryobed's last function that removed the poison could short circuit and release her with the poison still in her body.

Even knowing this device was created by the one man who could cure Mortems Disease did not help. He was plagued with all the things that could go wrong.

He looked at Aris again, took a deep breath, and did his best to calm down.

"Are you ready?" he asked.

Aris looked at him and smiled. "I am."

"While you can wear clothes in the cryobed if you want, I recommend taking them off. To put you under a state of suspended animation, the chamber will release a chemical called Arctic Gel. I'm not sure what that is, exactly, but it freezes your vital functions, putting you in a death-like state. It would be best if that stuff wasn't stuck to your clothes after the process is over," Fayte said.

"Right," Adam grunted a little as he lifted Aris off the wheelchair, placed her on his knee as he knelt, and began removing her clothes.

She was wearing a simple sundress, so peeling it off was easy. Underneath the sundress was pure white underwear. He took those off as well, sliding her panties down her hips, unhooking her bra, and setting them on the ground before carrying Aris over to the cryobed.

Standing there for a moment, Adam finally realized just how hard this moment truly was. What if this didn't work? What if it failed and she died? He couldn't bear the thought of something going wrong, and it caused him, someone who had unhesitatingly slaughtered hundreds of people without batting an eyelash, to freeze.

"Adam?" Aris called out to him.

He shook himself out of his stupor. "Sorry. I froze for a moment."

Aris's eyes softened as she gazed lovingly into his. "Don't worry. This cure will work, and once it does, we can spend the rest of our lives together."

"Right. You're right. Thank you, Aris."

They shared a smile before he gently set her on the cryobed. Fayte came over and grabbed a small cord attached to the cryobed. A needle was stuck to one end, which she gently inserted into Aris' arm. According to her, the poison was released through this needle, and it would be sucked back out through this needle, though Adam had no idea how that worked.

He leaned down further to give Aris a kiss. Out of a slight reluctance, Adam remained that way longer than a normal kiss would last. Aris didn't seem to mind.

"Have a good rest." Adam smiled and tenderly brushed some hair away from Aris' cheek. "I'll see you when you wake up."

"Yes. See you then."

Aris closed her eyes and Adam stepped back.

Fayte went over to the computer at the foot of the cryobed and typed in several buttons. The cryobed thrummed with life as the lid slowly slid closed and sealed shut. Adam pressed his hand against the glass, and Aris smiled as she also pressed her hand against it, though her hand soon fell back down as she lost strength.

Aris closed her eyes.

Fayte pressed another button. Green gel sprayed from vents near Aris's feet, head, and sides. It was not long before the entire interior was filled with that green gel. Aris, who was completely immersed in it, looked like she had been frozen in time.

Adam went over to Fayte, who was still typing away, and looked at the monitor. There was a silhouette of the human body. Almost every inch of it was bright red, but there were a few blue patches.

"I can't tell you exactly how this all works, but this shows where the Mortems Disease is most heavily located," Fayte explained. "It looks like almost her entire body has been infected with Mortems Disease. The only areas that haven't been infected are her heart and her brain, but everything else…" She shook her head. "I'm honestly shocked she's still alive and capable of moving so much."

"Will this affect her ability to be cured?" he asked.

"Not at all." Fayte tossed him a reassuring smile. "The Leefa Drug is an incredibly toxic poison that completely eradicates Mortems Disease. It doesn't matter how infected a person is. This will destroy it in its entirety." She paused long enough to grimace. "Well, that is what Grandfather's notes say."

Adam nodded and said no more as he watched Fayte finish the process of activating the second phase. A soft hissing sound soon erupted from the coffin. He couldn't see any changes coming over Aris through the viewing glass, but he knew the poison that could destroy Mortems Disease had just been injected into her body.

"There." Fayte took a step back and clapped her hands. "It's done. The only thing we can do now is monitor her every few days. We'll check to see when the Mortems Disease has been eradicated from her body, then commence the third phase, which will remove the poison before unsealing her."

"I understand," Adam said softly. "Do you think I can remain here for a little while longer?"

Fayte's understanding smile was filled with sympathy as she gazed at him. "Of course you can. There's a chair right over there near the desk if you'd like to sit down. Also, you can monitor how much of the disease is left in her body with the monitor. I have a few phone calls to make, but after that, I will make us some lunch. Does that sound good?"

"It does. Thank you."

Fayte cast him and Aris one last glance before she traveled out of the room. As the door slid shut behind her, isolating him from the outside world, Adam grabbed the chair she pointed to, pulled it up to the cryobed, and sat down. He gazed into the glass that allowed him to see her face, studying Aris's frozen features.

And there he remained for several hours until it was time for lunch.

***

Adam found himself with an unusual amount of free time that he didn't know what to do with.

For the past several years, Adam had dedicated his entire life to Aris. Few were the moments where he and Aris were separated, and even when they were apart, it was, at most, a single door that stood between them. He had never been without her for longer than an hour. Now she was gone, stuck in suspended animation, and he found himself with almost nothing to do.

He spent most of his time checking up information on *Age of Gods*, but sadly, all the articles he read never contained anything concrete. It was all just speculation and rumors from those so-called game critics.

There were rumors floating around about how this was going to be the most realistic virtual reality game of all time, how the battle system utilized a classic RPG leveling system, how combat was based on realism and people who could fight in real life would be better off than those who couldn't, and so on. Dozens of rumors containing all sorts of information could be found all over the internet. Problem was that no one actually knew anything. The creator of the game was keeping very tight lipped.

Outside of reading whatever rumors he could regarding *Age of Gods*, Adam spent at least one hour sitting with Aris, and the rest of his time was spent with Fayte.

Fayte…

Adam would never admit this out loud because he felt like it was a betrayal of his feelings for Aris, but he was incredibly grateful for Fayte's presence. She was often busy making phone calls and talking to someone she called "Su," but she always made sure to spend time with him as well. Her presence was encouraging and supportive.

They would often keep each other company and ask questions. None of them were too invasive and they never tried to pry into each other's personal lives, but they did learn a little more about the other person.

For example, Adam learned that Fayte had a hardcore sweet tooth. She often abstained from sweets entirely because having even a single bite of something sweet activated this desire. A day after she'd eaten one of his red velvet cinnamon rolls, he'd caught her eating cookie dough ice cream straight from a container. He would never forget the blush that had been on her face for the rest of his life.

They also learned that both of them were passionate about old-school video games—namely, the fighting games that used consoles and controllers instead of virtual reality.

"You have really good hand-to-eye coordination."

"Of course. I've trained both my mind and body to handle a lot of information and work at high speeds. Very few people have better hand-eye coordination and reflexes than me."

"Ugh… is that why you keep beating me? I haven't won once."

"Not my problem."

Adam and Fayte were currently playing a game called *Street King VII*. It was an older fighting game from the early twenty-first century. The graphics were nothing compared to new VR graphics, which were so realistic it was enough to make people think they weren't in a game at all. The avatars they were controlling in this game looked fairly cartoonish in comparison.

"Ha… I lost again." Fayte slumped in her seat and set the controller down. "Guess that means I'm making dinner again tonight." She cast him a sideways glance that contained both amusement and exasperation. "And here I was hoping I could finally eat some of your cooking again."

About three days ago, after her third consecutive loss to him, Fayte had made a bet with him. Whoever won that day's "fighting tournament" would be the person who cooked dinner. She said it was to help motivate her into doing better, that she worked harder when she was under pressure. Adam agreed to her bet. It wasn't like he had anything better to do.

She hadn't won once even after three days had passed.

"If you really want to try my cooking, I'm willing to cook today," Adam offered.

"Thank you, but no. When a person makes a deal, whether it's a simple bet or something that can affect their entire life. it is important for that person to uphold their end of the deal. I'll be cooking dinner tonight."

Fayte tossed him a grateful smile before moving into the kitchen. Adam turned his head to watch her as she grabbed a cute apron with floral prints decorating the front, put it on, and tied her long hair into a ponytail. This act exposed her slender neck and made her look even more elegant and feminine than usual.

A hard feat considering her already enchanting appearance.

Even though he had lived with Fayte for several days now, the effect she had on him hadn't diminished. Adam had already decided that she was dangerous. If it was just her appearance, he was certain she wouldn't be able to affect him like this, but on top of being gorgeous, Fayte had a gentle personality. She was kind and understanding, but she was also determined and unyielding when she had a goal. Her unwillingness to let him cook because she'd lost a game were good examples of the latter half of her personality.

He never said anything, and she could never replace Aris in his heart, but he found himself liking that personality of hers more and more as the days passed.

That was what made her so dangerous.

Fayte made beef with broccoli and white rice that evening. It was a simple dish made with whisked soy sauce, chicken stock, honey, vinegar, brown sugar, garlic, and several other ingredients. The beef was sliced into thin pieces that were cooked on a skillet until browned and the broccoli was stirred into the soy sauce mixture. The appetizing smell was wafting through the living room before she even finished.

"I really am impressed to see that someone raised in such a wealthy family can cook so well," Adam said as he ate side by side with Fayte. His fork moved quite fast as he devoured his portion quickly.

"I've never liked relying on others," Fayte admitted softly. Her cheeks suddenly reddened. "Also, I've always had a slight interest in cooking as a hobby ever since I was young. That garden you see on my balcony is filled with herbs and spices I'm growing so I can use them in my cooking. When I was still in grade school, I asked the servants if they could teach me, so I was able to learn a few things like how to make simple pasta and bake bread. These days, I just follow recipes to make something edible."

"Either way, you have my respect," Adam said.

Adam felt odd talking to Fayte. She was not Aris. She and Aris were so completely different they were like night and day from each other, and yet he did not feel uncomfortable just casually chatting with her like they were old friends. He didn't fall in love with her at first sight like he had with Aris, whose very smile had saved his soul from destruction. Adam didn't even love Fayte at all. At most, he would say what he felt for her was respect, but even so, he'd never expected to become so comfortable with someone whose name wasn't Aris so quickly.

It made him feel awkward.

Fayte smiled at him, her cheeks and ears a little red as she changed the subject. "*Age of Gods* will become playable at midnight tonight. Are you ready?"

"I am," Adam said, shifting gears. "I plan to log in the moment the game becomes playable."

Tucking a strand of hair behind her ears, Fayte said, "Me as well. I wonder what we can expect?"

"No idea." Adam grimaced. "There are so many rumors floating around right now that it's hard to tell if any of them are even remotely true. I think it's better to go in without expectations."

"You might be right," Fayte agreed.

"Anyway, since you cooked dinner again, I will be doing the dishes."

Adam stood up, grabbed his and Fayte's bowls and utensils, and then headed for the kitchen.

"Thank you," Fayte said.

"You're welcome."

After Adam washed the dishes, the skillet and pans, and put everything away after drying them, he spent another hour sitting by Aris' side as he waited for the fateful moment when *Age of Gods* would become playable. At 11:50 pm, he went back into his bedroom and opened the box containing the VR gaming system for *Age of Gods*.

It looked like a high-tech choker. There was a clasp on one side that locked it in place. The clasp went on the front, while the system itself sat against the base of the spine. According to the basic information found in a pamphlet that was also inside the box, the device used the nerve endings along the spine to connect the brain to the game system, allowing someone's "spirit" to enter the gaming world.

His choker was dark red.

Adam attached the system to his neck. He was about to lay down, but then a thought occurred to him.

He grabbed his phone off the charging station, scrolled through his contacts, and selected the one called Lilith.

"Master?" a smoky and seductive voice said from the line.

"How many times have I told you not to call me that?" asked Adam with a sigh.

"I have lost count. What do you need of me?"

"I'm about to enter *Age of Gods*. Fayte is too. I want you to get the system for *Age of Gods* and enter this world as well. Find Fayte and help her out for me."

"Yes, Master."

Lilith did not even question Adam and just agreed to do as he wished, which made him sigh as he hung up and climbed into bed, not bothering to climb under the covers as he laid down with his head on the pillow and shut his eyes. He took a deep breath, slowly exhaled, and let his body fully relax.

12am. It was time.

"Activate," he called out, and the entire world went black.

***

Within a dark room, a man sat behind a desk, his elbows planted firmly on the surface, fingers clasped together as he leaned forward and gazed through the window into an isolated room. The room was empty, save for a single item in the very center. It was a gold-covered wooden chest with a lid that had two angels on either side, their wings stretched forward as if to touch their tips together in union.

"Sir," a voice said behind him. He turned to find a young man with a blank look in his eyes. "It's time."

"So it's finally begun," he said, lips peeling back in a grin. "I've been through many trials, dealt with numerous problems, and nearly died, but at long last, the next stage of my plan is beginning. What a momentous occasion."

He walked away from the isolation chamber and toward a large screen that currently displayed a number. 1,544,236. It was quite the number, and it continued to rise even as he stood there, causing him to chuckle.

"Look at how many people have decided to join me. So many individuals, brimming with life... ripe for the plucking."

Another chuckle.

"Go ahead and play. Enjoy yourselves to your hearts' content, right until the very end."

The young man behind him remained there, his expression as dead as his eyes.

Entering the virtual reality world for *Age of Gods* felt... strange. Different. Adam had no better way to describe it. It was like... like something had been pulled from his mind. He felt a slight tug inside of his head as if someone had grabbed a hold of his brain and was yanking it out of his skull through his ear—except it wasn't actually painful. It didn't hurt. It was just a feeling, an ephemeral sensation.

It was something he had never experienced before while gaming.

When he opened his eyes again, Adam found himself standing in... a library? He looked at the bookshelves surrounding him on all sides. The room he had been transported to was circular and possessed a domed roof with a painting of four beautiful women bathed in light fighting against a devil-shaped woman cast in shadows. This was different from the standard white space world he often found himself in during the character creation process, but he took it in stride.

Within this room was a winged figure. She was an ethereal beauty with silver hair, blue eyes, and pale skin. Semi-translucent wings fluttered on her back. The outfit she wore was a long robe that trailed down to her bare feet. She smiled at him, and then opened her mouth to speak.

"Welcome to Age of Gods. *My name is Lim, a virtual fairy who will be your guide during the character creation process. I am also in charge of announcing rankings and notifying people of important breakthroughs such as when the first person leaves the Village of Beginnings, when someone breaks a new record, when the first guild is created, and so on."*

Adam said nothing. The fairy named Lim continued.

"The world you are about to enter is vast and filled with many wonders and mysteries. Before you can get started on your journey, you must first build your character. Now, please enter your name."

As she finished speaking, a small screen appeared in front of him:

Your Name:	?

Adam debated with himself for a moment. Should he use his real name like he did when he was earning money for Aris's medical equipment and expenses? It might help his reputation if people discovered he was the Untouchable Emperor, but he didn't think anyone would remember him since it had been about two and a half years since he last played.

Another moment passed before he decided.

Your Name:	Adam

It was just his name, sans his last name. He honestly didn't think anyone would figure out who he was based on just that. There were hundreds of thousands of people named Adam, after all, and most people never used their real name when playing. Figuring out his identity would be easier if someone didn't rely on his in-game name.

"You have chosen to call yourself 'Adam.' Is that okay?" Lim asked.

"Yes," Adam said.

"You are in luck. No one else has used the name 'Adam' yet. The name 'Adam' has been confirmed as your name."

At that moment, the screen in front of him disappeared and another one took its place. This one contained a table:

Choose your class:
Assassin
Archer
Mage
Summoner
Priest
Warrior

Choosing a class that suited your particular style of combat was imperative in virtual reality games. Some people were better at fighting close-range, while others were great at long-range. Some people didn't like fighting, so they chose the priest class, which focused primarily on healing and buffs. Of course, this was just the beginning stages of the game. Adam assumed that, like most online role playing games, this one would allow people to upgrade or change classes later on.

Adam chose the Warrior class. This was a close combat class that was well-balanced between attack and defense, and was often best for fighting on the frontlines, which was something he would need if he wanted to shock the world and increase his reputation.

"You have chosen the Warrior class. Is this okay?" asked Lim.

"Yes," he said.

"All right. I've confirmed your class. You are a Warrior. Now that you have chosen your class, please select which stats to allocate your status points to. Please note, you only have 25 status points available. You will gain more points as your level increases. Please note that allocating status points is permanent. You cannot change what statistics they go into once you have finalized your choice."

Another screen replaced the one with the classes:

Amount of status points currently available:	25
Strength:	0
Constitution:	0
Dexterity:	0
Intelligence:	0
Speed:	0

These looked like pretty basic stats. If this followed standard RPG settings, then Strength determined the attack power a person had, Constitution determined the amount of health a person possessed and their defense, Dexterity was their ability to hit something and dodge attacks, Intelligence determined their magic points and magic attack power, and Speed was how fast they could move ingame.

Adam didn't hesitate to allocate his stats:

Amount of status points current available:	0
Strength:	5
Constitution:	5
Dexterity:	5
Intelligence:	5
Speed:	5

Since Adam's class was a purely attack class with no magic involved, he wanted to disregard the Intelligence stat, which would only be useful to magic classes, but he thought better of it for now. Having at least +5 on all of his stats across the board sounded logical. He could focus on the Strength stat after leveling up.

"I see you've allocated your status points. Please check again and confirm if they are acceptable."

"They are," Adam said.

"Very well. Your status points have been allocated. It looks like you are just about ready to begin. However, before you enter Age of Gods, *there are a few things you must know. First and foremost, because your "spirit" is what's being sent into this world, it is possible to feel pain. However, it will not be as harsh as when you feel pain in your own world. Your ability to experience pain in* Age of Gods *is only 15% of what it is in your world. This is not only to help make the* Age of Gods *world feel more real, but also to alert you to when your 'spirit' has been damaged and requires rest."*

"Oh?"

Adam crossed his arms. He'd never heard of something like this before. Most games were painless no matter what happened.

Adam had once lost an arm in a game and didn't feel a thing. A virtual world where a person could experience pain was new to him.

But this still wasn't a problem.

He was well-versed in pain.

He would even call pain an old friend.

"Finally, while those stats you currently have are the main stats available, there are such things as hidden stats. In order to acquire hidden stats, you must earn them in the game through your actions. The two hidden stats 'Comprehension' and 'Luck' can only be acquired if you accomplish something extraordinary."

So there were extra stats he could gain by doing something amazing in the game? If he had to guess, Comprehension likely had something to do with his ability to learn more techniques and maybe understand the *Age of Gods* world better, while Luck probably involved matters such as item drops. For example, if he had a high Luck stat, an enemy he killed might drop rarer items than someone without the Luck stat who killed the same enemy.

"Do you have any questions? If so, please ask them now. If not, I will send you to the Village of Beginnings. Oh. Before I forget, the Village of Beginnings is where all players start off. In this village, you will learn the basics of gameplay and the leveling system. You may think of this as the tutorial stage, but it is not like most tutorials as you know them. Your ability to learn will depend largely on how quickly you can adapt."

"I do have one question," Adam said.

Lim tilted her head. It was a curiously human gesture that looked off on her too-perfect features.

"What is your question?"

"What about my character's appearance? Do I not get to choose what my character looks like?"

Adam always made sure his character looked different from his real world appearance. He kept some things the same like his height, physique, and body weight because it made integrating himself into his character easier, but his face, hair, and skin was always changed to be as different from his own appearance as possible.

Lim blinked once as if a light had gone on. *"Oh! I guess I forgot to mention this, but you cannot change your appearance in this game. This game uses an incredibly advanced synchronization program that transports your 'spirit' into the game world. In other words—"*

"In other words, my appearance is based on how I perceive myself in the real world," Adam finished for her.

"Yes, that is correct. Do you have any more questions?"

Adam shook his head. Not being able to change his appearance was going to cause problems later on. It would be annoying, but he would have to see if he could get a mask or something that he could use to at least hide his face. The last thing he wanted was someone using his appearance in the game to locate him in the real world.

"In that case, I will send you to the Age of Gods *world now. Good luck, Adam."*

With those final words, Adam's vision went completely dark as he left the library.

THE VILLAGE OF BEGINNINGS

When Adam's vision returned, he realized he was no longer inside of the library but standing in a cathedral. He didn't know how much time had passed. It felt like only a second had gone by, but really, he couldn't be sure of that. His sense of time had become skewed by the sudden shift of his location.

Observing his surroundings revealed that he was standing on what appeared to be a slightly elevated platform. There were steps leading off the platform. On either side of a red carpet that traveled down the center of the cathedral were unoccupied benches, the kind he expected to find people filling as they listened to sermons on weekends—if this game world had weekends. Light filtered in through a stained glass window near the front and the scent of dust and aged wood filled his nose.

Wait a second. The smell of dust and aged wood?

Adam took another deep breath of air and realized that, indeed, he could smell. In fact, his sense of smell in this game was just as strong as it was in the real world. That was odd. Very odd. He hadn't played a lot of virtual reality games in the last few years, but from what he could remember, the world's technology had not advanced far enough that anything but vision and touch could be affected—and even one's sense of touch was dampened because the connection between a person's brain and the system was incomplete.

Barely a second after he appeared, several balls of light floated down from above. He glanced at one and nearly jumped back when the ball flashed and a person appeared. It was a young man. Looking at where the other light balls had landed, Adam saw that people had replaced each ball.

"So this is *Age of Gods*! Awesome! Hahaha! I'm finally in the game!"

"It's time to begin! For the glory of the mighty Black Beard Alliance, I will begin my adventure here! Arg!"

"Black Beard Alliance?! Ha! You're a part of that weak-ass guild?! My Rising Phoenix Alliance is the number 1 guild in the entire world!"

"Number 1? Ah ha ha ha ha ha! Don't make me laugh! Your guild is just a branch guild! You guys are nothing but dogs wagging their tails for their master!"

"What was that?! You wanna die?!"

"You're the one who's gonna die!"

"Grrr! Who cares?! We all start this game with the same stats! Just wait! I'll show you!"

Adam grimaced as the people around him kept talking, but everyone fortunately had no desire to remain inside and rushed toward the exit. No one paid him an ounce of attention.

With slow and careful steps, Adam walked down the stairs, and he marveled at how realistic it felt. He raised his hand to stare at it. This was his hand. It looked exactly like his hand in the real world right down to the scar running across his palm. It even felt like his hand did in the real world.

When he was playing virtual reality games to earn enough money for Aris's medical treatments, the games had always felt slightly awkward. It had felt like he was controlling somebody else. This game felt like he was inside of his own body.

He pushed the aged double doors open and stepped outside. Warm sunlight rained onto his body as a small village appeared before his eyes. As he walked down the steps of the cathedral, he looked around the village that appeared reminiscent to villages found in medieval Europe. Most of the buildings were made of wood or stone, with thatched roofs composed of straw. A few had signs up, but they didn't have words written on them, instead using images to denote what they were.

Those must have been shops.

Several people were going about their business, walking, gossiping, and greeting each other. Most of them were dressed in what he assumed were commoners' clothing. They wore baggy pants and overalls, shirts, and dresses. Most of them were an off-white color, though a few were dressed in muted reds and blues. A man standing by the cathedral and staring at him wore slightly better clothing than the rest. He also had a hat.

As Adam stared at these people, a small bar and lettering appeared above the people's heads. He gazed at one person in particular and focused on the letters.

Name: Earnest Hemmingway	Description: Villager	Lvl: 1	Health: 50/50

He blinked and walked the rest of the way down the cathedral steps.

"Welcome, young otherworlder," the man waiting for him said. Adam focused on the letters over this man's head and read them.

Name: Cyrus Stevens	Description: He is the Town Mayor of the Village of Beginnings.	Lvl: 6	Health 120/120

So this person was the town mayor. That explained why he was dressed a little better than everyone else.

"Hello," Adam greeted in a polite tone.

"Quite a few otherworlders have been showing up today. You are the one thousandth otherworlder to appear within the last hour," Cyrus said with a wry smile. "Would you permit an old man to take a bit of your time? I know you are in a rush to get started on your new adventure. People wishing to leave this Village of Beginnings must reach level 10, so I'm sure all of you are in a hurry. The Sun Goddess knows the other otherworlders could not wait to disappear and ran off without even listening to me. However, should you permit this old man to ramble, I believe you might find the information I can provide worth your time."

Adam debated listening to this man versus leaving and decided to listen. The other players who had arrived ahead of him were probably rushing to level up so they could leave the village. However, while leveling up was indeed imperative, listening to this man might provide him with an extra quest or even give him some experience points.

"I don't mind. Can you tell me about this world?" asked Adam.

The old mayor's eyes lit up as he began speaking. "The world you currently find yourself in is called the Forgotten Realm. This world of ours is made up of five continents and many islands. The Village of Beginnings is located on one of those islands. We call islands like ours Beginner Islands because it is here that otherworlders first appear when they wish to begin their adventure."

While all this was pretty standard information, Adam listened to the man anyway. He believed this was important. And even though this was a game, showing respect towards your elders was still something he believed in.

Unless he was trying to assassinate his elders.

"How many Beginner Islands are there?" asked Adam.

"Hmm… that is a very good question. I don't rightly know." Cyrus crossed his arms and scrunched up his face. The gesture was so realistic that Adam almost believed this was not a virtual image created via technology but an actual person. "There are so many villages like ours that it is impossible to keep track of them all. Last I heard, there were over one hundred thousand Beginner Islands. Each island has a village called the Village of Beginnings."

One hundred thousand, huh? That was quite the number, but he was not surprised. More than half the world's population had become gamers since the WWIII Armistice. That was 2.5 billion people worldwide, and he'd read that over 10.9 million people had already gone out to buy this game. There had to be a lot of these villages to fit that many people.

"In any case, the continent this Village of Beginnings is closest to is called the Sun Continent. It is controlled by the Sun Goddess and her parthenon. Oh! I should mention, the Sun Goddess's name is Stella. She is the entity our continent worships. Anyway, the other four continents are the Moon Continent, the Earth Continent, the Sea Continent, and the Forgotten Continent, which is what our world is named after. Each continent is controlled by a god or goddess and their parthenon—except the Forgotten Continent. That place is a dark land in which numerous devils and monsters reside. No one who has gone there has ever returned."

All of this was basic information about the world, but since it was still something he didn't know, Adam kept listening. Who knew when this kind of information would become useful. In some of the other virtual reality MMOs he had played, there were dungeons with quizzes and puzzles that required a person to know that game's lore.

"You don't need to know too much about the other continents right now. I'm sure you'll find out more about them as you continue your adventure. What I really want to talk about is the ancient history of our world." Cyrus paused as he looked at the sun, eyes glazed over as if remembering the past. "Ten thousand years ago, a Great Calamity struck the Forgotten Realm. We have long forgotten what this calamity was, but we do know that it was the calamity which caused the original continent to be split into five. If you ever manage to find a [world map], you will be able to see that the five continents look like they have been sliced apart by sword or some kind of bladed weapon. In either event, this Great Calamity was eventually stopped by the four goddesses, and the world became peaceful once again."

Adam waited patiently as the man sighed. It seemed whatever happened ten thousand years ago was no longer common knowledge and had been lost to the annals of history. That was unsurprising. Games like this often left their lore open to interpretation because it made playing more interesting—or so some critics claimed. Others just got upset by what they deemed laziness.

"Anyway, thank you for listening to my story, young man. Here, take this as a symbol of our meeting."

Cyrus held out his hand, which had a ring resting on the palm. There was also a scroll. The ring was just a simple brass ring with no adornments, but when Adam looked at it, he saw some information appear above it.

Name: Brass Ring	Item Type: Ring	Grade: Low	Equipment Requirements: No requirements	Description: A simple ring made of brass. There is nothing special	Attributes: Speed+1

			about it.	

So it was just a simple item that could enhance his current stats, though the ring was so low-class it only upgraded his Speed stat by +1. That wasn't much.

He took the ring and scroll and slipped the ring on his index finger. The ring was too large, but then it shrank to fit his finger. Nifty. Once the ring was on, he thought about how to find out what his stats were, and as if just thinking about it was all he needed to do, a window popped up in his field of view and showed him his stats.

Name: Adam	Class: War-rior	Lvl: 1	SP: 0 AP: 0	Ex-perience: 0/150
Strength: +5	Constitu-tion: +5	Dexterity: +5	Intelli-gence: +5	Spee d: +6
Physical Attack: +10	Health: 50/50	Hit Rate: 5%	MP: 10/10	Mov ement: +6
	Physical Defense: +10 Magic De-fense: +5	Dodge-Rate: ???	Magic At-tack: +5	

For a moment, Adam could only stare at his Dodge-Rate, which contained not numbers but question marks. What the heck did that mean? He furrowed his brow, but he couldn't think of a reason for why that particular statistic would be so odd.

After memorizing his stats, Adam looked away from the window, which disappeared, and glanced at the scroll in his hand next.

Item Name: Scan Scroll	Item Type: Spell Scroll	Grade: Low	Use requirements: None	Description: A low-level scan scroll	Abilities: Allows the person who activates the scroll to scan the level of an enemy 20 levels higher than their own.

Oh? Now this scroll was something he could see being useful. It also told him a lot about this world. Namely, it told him that he couldn't scan an enemy without something like this scroll or a spell. That meant any battle he went into, he would be going in blind unless he could acquire more of these scrolls.

"Now how do I put this away…" Adam mumbled.

"You can just store the scroll in your item pouch," Cyrus said.

"Huh?"

It was only after the old mayor mentioned his pouch that Adam realized he was wearing clothes completely different from anything he'd ever worn before. The coarse fabric of his short-sleeved shirt felt irritating on his skin, and the pants he wore were a little tight against his legs. Black boots protected his feet. He also had a belt around his waist, and attached to the belt was a small pouch made of leather. It was a very standard item with a flap that could be opened and closed.

It did not look large enough to fit this scroll.

He tried to put the scroll inside anyway.

He was shocked when it worked.

"That pouch you have is something all otherworlders have at the beginning of their journey. It allows you to carry up to ten items. Doesn't matter what size the item is. You can also upgrade your item pouch, but I hear you need to find special materials and someone who is capable of upgrading it. I've also heard there are some items people can acquire that can increase your pouch's storage space," the mayor helpfully informed him.

"Useful," Adam said with a nod.

"Indeed it is. I sometimes find myself jealous of you other-worlders," Cyrus said, sighing wistfully. "I'm sure you are ready to get started on your adventure, but might I suggest you first head over to the barracks? You should talk to Sterk. He's an old soldier from the Sun Continent who washed up on our shore several years ago. He's been helping us keep the peace. He is very talented with a sword and can definitely teach you how to protect yourself."

The moment the man finished speaking, a soft "ding" like the chiming of a bell echoed around Adam, though the Mayor didn't seem to notice. Immediately after that, a small window appeared in front of him. Again, the Mayor didn't appear to notice even though it was right in front of him. Wearing a small frown, Adam looked at the display.

[Congratulations on completing your first quest! For speaking with the Village of Beginnings' Mayor, Cyrus Stevens, you have earned +50 experience points and +5 status points. Status points are generally referred to as SP, and they are used to upgrade your

five primary stats of Strength, Constitution, Dexterity, Intelligence, and Speed. Please take note: You can only earn SP by either leveling up, completing quests, or breaking a record like being the first person to defeat a dungeon. You also have been given your second quest: [Talk to Sterk!] Will you accept? Yes? No?]

Adam stared at the two options on the screen, then reached out and pressed "yes."

[The quest: [Talk to Sterk!] has been accepted!]

Now that it looked like he'd done everything he could here, Adam began walking around the village, searching for the barracks. This village wasn't very big. He counted only thirty buildings in total. The most extraordinary building was the cathedral he had come from, but there was also the mayor's house—the only two-story building in the village—several shops with signs hanging above the door to signify what they sold, and a square building with a courtyard surrounded by a wooden fence.

He assumed the square building was the barracks.

Standing within the courtyard was an old man with a muscular body, slightly rusty steel armor, and a broadsword in a sheath dangling from his left hip. He had graying hair and was standing next to a wooden training dummy. Like everyone else, when Adam stared hard enough at the man, a window appeared above his head and displayed some basic information.

Name: Sterk	Description: A retired soldier who washed up on shore.	Class: Warrior	Lvl: 40	Health 30,000/30,000

	He has made it his personal duty to keep the peace in this Village of Beginnings.			

There was another person standing beside Sterk. He was young and dressed in the same clothes Adam was wearing. Because Adam could not get even the most basic information on this man—no window appeared above his head—he assumed the person currently swinging the sword at the training dummy was another player.

After the player left, Adam walked up to Sterk. His feet crunched against the grass. He twitched only a little as the scent of fresh grass filled his nose.

"Excuse me. Are you Sterk?"

"I am." Sterk crossed his arms. "Who are you? Another one of those otherworlders?"

"I am," Adam confirmed.

Sterk snorted. "Hmph. So I've got another otherworlder coming here to acquire my skills. I've seen quite a few of your kind in the last few hours." The man looked Adam up and down, then nodded approvingly. "At least you've got a pretty sturdy body—much more athletic than the last several dozen otherworlders. Do you have experience wielding a sword?"

Adam shook his head. "I can wield knives, and I'm trained to wield a spear, but I've never used a sword before."

"A spear, eh? That's a pretty difficult weapon to wield, but it's powerful if you can master it. Sadly, I don't have a spear for you to wield. Would you like to learn the basics of swordsmanship?" asked Sterk.

"Yes, please."

"Then take this sword and attack this training dummy. Stand with your feet shoulder width apart, hold the sword in front of you —and for the love of Lady Stella, don't try to get fancy! The last idiot who tried to use some weird stance nearly chopped his own hand off! Now, I want you to cut that training dummy in half with one swing."

Sterk removed the sword from his belt and handed it to Adam, who studied the weapon with a critical eye. The sword was pretty basic. It wasn't embellished with any intricate craftsmanship. Even the hilt, pommel, and guard were made from simple steel and wrapped in black leather.

Name: Sterk's Broadsword	Item Type: Sword	Grade: Low	Use requirements: Warrior class	Description: A low-grade steel sword.	Abilities: Attack+5; 1% chance of causing bleed status effect

The stats looked pretty basic, but he equipped the weapon anyway. Not like he had another weapon to use. Now with the sheath hanging from his waist, Adam turned to the wooden training dummy, which was just a log that had been stuck into the ground.

While Adam had never wielded a sword before, he at least understood the basics of swordsmanship. He slid his feet across the ground until they were shoulder-width apart, placed his dominant foot forward, and held the broadsword in a simple two-handed grip. He took a deep breath. Holding it, he counted down to three, two, one…

Exploding into action, Adam swung the sword horizontally from his left to his right. He felt a moment of resistance as his sword bit into the wooden log. Then the log was severed, the top half flying off while the bottom half remained embedded in the ground.

"Impressive," Sterk said with a raised eyebrow. "You sure you've never wielded a sword before?"

"I'm positive," Adam said as he sheathed the blade.

Sterk shrugged. "Either way, you've already proven that you know the basics of swordsmanship. Just remember that enemies aren't going to stand still and give you time to attack like this training dummy. You might understand the basics, but knowing how to swing a sword and knowing how to kill your enemies are two completely different things. I should also let you know that just swinging your sword around won't do anything to your enemies. To injure an enemy, you need to use specific skills like [slash] and [thrust]. I know. Why don't I give you a quest? Go slay ten [wolves]. Your current level isn't high enough to kill [wolves] yet, so I recommend killing weaker enemies like the [wild rabbits] roaming around outside the Village of Beginnings until you reach a suitable level."

Ding!

[You have completed your second quest! +50 experience points! +5 SP! For completing the quest [Talk to Sterk!], you have acquired your first two skills! [Slash] and [Thrust]! These two skills are something you can only acquire by possessing the Warrior class. You have also been offered a new quest: [Slay 10 Wolves!] Do you accept? Yes? No?]

Adam reached out and pressed the "yes" button.

Ding!

[The quest: [Slay 10 Wolves!] has been accepted!]

Since it looked like he now had two new skills, Adam thought about the skills and how he wanted to see them, which caused a window to open in front of his eyes.

Skill Name: Slash	Description: A basic skill where the player swings his or her sword and attacks the enemy!	Current lvl: 1 AP needed to reach next lvl: 10	Ability: Causes 100% damage to enemy if it hits	MP consumption: 1	Cooldown time: 0 seconds
Skill Name: Thrust	Description: A basic skill where the player thrusts his or her sword at the en-	Current lvl: 1 AP needed to reach next lvl: 10	Ability: Causes 110% damage with a 1% chance at landing a critical hit	MP Consumption: 2	Cooldown time: 1 second

	emy!				

They were very basic skills, but this was only the beginning of the game, so that was natural. These skills would work fine anyway. He might not know much about swordplay, but he was confident in his reflexes and ability to swing a sword.

Since it looked like he had a weapon, basic skills, and a quest, Adam decided it was time to leave the village and accomplish his goal.

As he walked out of the village, Adam saw many players rushing outside aside from himself. It was easy to tell who was a villager and who was a player not only by their basic equipment, but also because every player was traveling into the plains surrounding the village.

When he got outside, Adam spotted large groups of players racing across the grassy plains and killing the [wild rabbits] to level up. There must have been at least a hundred players in just this plain alone. Of course, because there were so many players, a number of disputes started when one player accused another of stealing their kill.

While there were quite a few fights, Adam noticed several groups that were not fighting and seemed to be working together. These groups likely belonged to the so-called guilds. While there were currently no guilds formed in *Age of Gods* because the process to establish one likely required a token or something similar, that did not mean there weren't any guilds around. Many of these guilds were ones that had been established for many years in the virtual world. They took part in almost every virtual reality game since the first game was conceived. Some of them like the Ploenexia Alliance had been around for almost a decade and were world renowned amongst players.

Adam snorted and traveled past the plains where all the level 1 monsters were located, heading toward the forest. That was likely where the wolves would be found.

After reaching the forest, Adam paused at the entrance, reached out, and placed his hand against the tree. He could feel the bark scrape against his palm. Not only could he feel it, but the bark felt real just like everything else.

He removed his hand.

Adam walked into the forest in search of his prey. He found everything from level 2 [deer] to level 2 [wild rabbits], but there didn't appear to be any [wolves] near the forest entrance.

There were several players grouped together inside of this forest and grinding for experience. Most of them were killing the [deer] and [wild rabbits], but he found a few fighting against level 4 [grass snakes], which were several feet long snakes that attacked when you stepped into their territory. They were the first aggressive monster he had come across. It looked like the players, which were still at level 1 and only had a single level 2 among them, were struggling.

Adam ignored all the people and monsters in this area to go even further in. Within the next area he found the [wild boar] monster, which had a level of 5. It was not a [wolf], but since its level was pretty decent, he decided to start leveling up with that.

The current [wild boar] that was his target didn't appear to be doing anything. It was just roaming around aimlessly. Adam thought for a moment before kneeling to pick up a rock—and marveling at how the in-game mechanics allowed him to pick up a random rock —took aim, and threw it at the [wild boar].

-1

A small number appeared over the head of the [wild boar] as the rock struck it. The [wild boar] unleashed an enraged squeal as it turned toward him, its eyes red with anger. It stomped its hooves against the ground, squealed again, and charged at Adam, who re-mained calm as he unsheathed his sword and waited for the creature to reach him.

[Slash]

-15!

Just before it looked like the [wild boar] would ram him, Adam dodged to the left, swung his sword, and felt the resistance of the en-emy's flesh as he cleaved through it. A pained squeal echoed behind him, followed by a thump. When Adam turned, it was to find the [wild boar] picking itself back up and shaking its head. He couldn't see any blood. However, it looked like there was an odd gash on its side to signify the damage Adam had done.

Adam wondered how much HP this [wild boar] had, but he didn't want to waste a scan scroll on it. He also noticed that unlike the villagers, who he could see the basic status of, he could not see the status for this enemy, meaning the only way to discover its stats was to either use the scroll or acquire the [Scan] skill.

Since he didn't know how much HP it had, Adam went on the attack while it was still recovering. He used another [Slash] followed by a [Thrust]. The creature squealed in anger and tried to attack him, but he would swiftly dodge its charge each time and attack after it moved past him.

-15; -17; MISS; MISS; -15; MISS; -15; MISS; MISS; MISS!

One thing Adam noticed as he attacked was that he didn't always hit the [wild boar]. He would sometimes miss even when it seemed like he had hit it. That was probably due to his Hit-Rate stat, which was only at 5%. He was probably lucky to hit the [wild boar] as many times as he did.

Out of curiosity, Adam swung his sword but did not use a skill.

-1!

"Oh?" Adam perked up.

He swung his sword, again without using a skill.

-1!

"So attacking something without using a skill results in only -1 point of damage being dealt," Adam murmured.

-1; -1; -1; -1; -1!

"What's more, it seems I have a 100% Hit-Rate while attacking without activating a skill. That's interesting."

Done playing around, Adam struck the [wild boar] exactly ten times with [slash] before it died. He quickly calculated its HP in his head. He hit it ten times and did about -15 damage with each attack, plus the -6 he'd done with his attacks that didn't use skills, which meant it had somewhere around +150-160 HP.

Ding!

[You have defeated the monster [wild boar]! Items dropped: [wild boar's ear] and 30 gold coins. +50 experience points!]

Ding!

[You have leveled up! You are now at level 2! HP+10, MP+10, +5 SP!]

"Oh?"

Adam had not expected to level up so soon, but that was only until he realized he had just solo'd an enemy four levels higher than his current level. It made sense that he would gain more experience than someone who killed a monster at the same level or when a group of players killed a higher level monster.

Since he was a little curious, Adam decided to check out his new stats:

Name: Adam	Class: Warrior	Lvl: 2	SP: 15 AP: 0	Experience: 0/300
Strength: +5	Constitution: +5	Dexterity: +5	Intelligence: +5	Speed: +6
Attack: +15	Health: 60/60	Hit-rate: 5%	MP: 20/20	Movement: +6
	Physical Defense: +10 Magic Defense: +5	Dodge-Rate: ???	Magic Attack: +5	

It looked like the way his stats increased was Strength+1 = +2 Physical Attack, Constitution+1 = +2 Health, +2 Defense, and +1 Magic Defense, Dexterity+1 = 1% Hit Rate (it probably also affected Dodge-Rate, but he didn't know how since his was full of question marks), Speed+1 = +1 Movement, and Intelligence+1 = +2 MP and +1 Magic Attack.

Adam didn't really understand what the Speed attribute was for. What was Movement? Did that mean the higher his Speed was, the faster he could move? That was what it sounded like to him. He could not see a use for it right now, but maybe it would let him travel more quickly over long distances.

It looked like he also had +15 status points available, so he invested them all into his Strength stat, which caused his Physical Attack to increase.

It looked like whenever he leveled up, whatever his current stats were added to his overall abilities. When he was at level 1, his Strength had been +5 and his Physical Attack was at +15. That was because Strength+1 added +2 to his Physical Attack. At +5 Strength, his Physical Attack was +10 plus the additional +5 from his sword. With his Strength now at +20, his Physical Attack was +40 plus the additional +5 he gained from the sword.

Since these [wild boars] were at a fairly high level compared to him, Adam decided to grind his level here—at least, until he found a [wolf] to slay.

THE MISSING SON

Ding!

[You have leveled up! You are now at level 6! +10 HP, +10 MP, +5 SP!]

Adam wiped the imaginary sweat from his forehead. He'd been grinding for several hours now… well, he thought several hours had passed. In truth, he didn't even know what time it was or how much time had passed since he began playing. For whatever reason, there was no in-game window with a clock, leaving him to guess the time himself.

After leveling up the first time, Adam had noticed that the [wild boars] did not give the same amount of experience. It looked like the further the level gap was between him and his enemies, the more experience he gained per kill, meaning he needed to consistently fight stronger foes if he wanted to keep gaining a lot of experience points.

To that end, Adam had traveled deeper into the forest and eventually came across the level 6 [wild dog] and the level 7 [wolf].

Since his current quest [Slay 10 Wolves!] was to kill this type of monster, Adam decided to stay in this area and kill all the [wolves] therein.

He had killed the first 10 [wolves] required by his quest easily enough, but since they gave such good experience points, he decided to stick around and keep killing them until he reached level 6. Now that he had, he could allocate the new status points he had acquired, which he put into his Strength.

Now his stats looked like this:

Name: Adam	Class: Warrior	Lvl: 6	SP: 0 AP: 0	Experience: 162/4,800
Strength: +50	Constitution: +5	Dexterity: +5	Intelligence: +5	Speed: +6
Physical Attack: +100	Health: 100/100	Hit-rate: 5%	MP: 50/50	Movement: +6
	Physical Defense: +10 Magic Defense: +5	Dodge-Rate: ???	Magic Attack: +5	

He looked over at his stats. While his stats were skewed toward Strength, he didn't see this as a problem. The best defense was to not be there when an attack struck. So long as he was able to accurately evade his enemy's attacks, how much health he had didn't matter. The only thing he really needed to worry about was his Hit-Rate, which was horrendous.

At least these monsters weren't very strong right now. Even if his Hit-Rate was awful, he could still kill them with ease.

Since he was finally at level 5, Adam decided it was just about time to log off. Several hours must have passed by now. However, before he could log off, there was something he needed to do first.

Adam traveled through the forest. As he came upon the forested areas with weaker enemies, he noticed there were a lot more groups gathering together and grinding. He observed them but didn't stop moving.

"Quickly surround it and attack! Archer and mages, provide cover fire! Priests, heal the injured!"

"Take that! Ha!"

"It's so fast!"

"Come here, you stupid snake!"

All the players close by belonged to the same guild, though he didn't know which since they had no identifying clothing yet. That would change once the game really started. If this was like any other game, then once they left the Village of Beginnings, players would be able to change from a combat class to a non-combat class like Tailor, which would allow players to create customized clothing. In the last game, large guilds had created unique uniforms based on things like family colors and coat of arms.

"For the Rising Phoenix Alliance!"

Ah. So they belonged to the Rising Phoenix Alliance. That was a relatively large guild in the gaming world. He couldn't remember which family had created that guild, but it wasn't like he actually cared. The only guild he had an interest in right now was the Pleonexia Alliance.

After leaving the forest, he traveled back to Sterk at the barracks and presented him with ten [wolf pelts]. The man looked quite shocked by his arrival. His eyes went wide and his mouth dropped, but he still took the pelts.

"Well, I'll be damned. You actually managed to kill 10 [wolves] so quickly. You know, you might not be the first otherworlder to talk with me, but you are the first one to complete my quest. You can have that sword as a keepsake. Also, you can have this cuirass. It's the best piece of armor I have and should provide you with decent defensive capabilities until you leave the Village of Beginnings."

Ding!

[Congratulations! You have completed the quest [Slay 10 Wolves]! Experience +500! Items received for quest completion: [Iron Cuirass] and 100 gold coins!]

The Iron Cuirass that Sterk gave him looked like something from a fantasy VRMMORPG. It was a classic metal cuirass with a dull gray coloration. There were no decorations, so it didn't have anything special about it. One thing he did notice, however, was its weight. It was heavy. Other VRMMOs never added weight to their clothing, armor, weapons, or other equipment. It always felt like he was wearing feathers.

Item Name: Iron Cuirass	Item Type: Armor	Grade: Low	Use requirements: Warrior class	Description: A low-grade iron cuirass given to you by	Abilities: Defense +10

				Sterk.	

It didn't look like this chest plate was all that good, but if he compared it to the equipment he was currently wearing, which couldn't even be called equipment, then it was amazing.

He put the iron cuirass on, which just required pressing it against his body to equip. The iron cuirass in his hands disappeared and reappeared on his body. This method of equipping items was unrealistic, but he wasn't going to complain about that.

"You look like an actual warrior now!" Sterk laughed.

Adam smiled politely before asking a question he'd been wondering about. "Do you know if any of the other villagers might have quests for me?"

"Course they do," Sterk said, crossing his arms and looking at Adam like the answer should have been obvious. "I know for a fact that Trader Wilkins is currently having issues. You can find him in the potion shop. He's the store owner. Just look for a building with the sign of a potion hanging over the door. I'm told that his son has gone missing. Hasn't been seen for several days. Could be that his son was attacked and killed by wolves, but he might also just be lost in the forest. In any case, you can ask him if he needs help finding his lost son... or at least finding his son's corpse."

"Thank you for the information," Adam said with a polite bow.

Sterk laughed at how polite he was, which caused Adam to once more feel a little astonished. He had noticed it before, but these NPCs had very un-NPC-like personalities. No one would have been able to tell this person was not a real person if they didn't know *Age of Gods* was a game. Even knowing it was a game, he found himself subconsciously thinking of Sterk and the Mayor as real people.

Since Adam had gained everything he wanted for now, and several hours had likely passed since he logged in at 12am this morning, he decided to log out.

The world around Adam suddenly went black. Then a ceiling appeared above him. He took a deep breath and sat up, stretching his muscles out. He didn't feel too bad considering his mind had been sent into a virtual world. He was a little tired because his mind had still been active all this time, but his body felt oddly rested. Did that mean if he slept in the game world, it would be as if he was sleeping in the real world? That was probably a question for those philosophical people who cared about such things.

A glance at the clock revealed the time to be 8:30am, which meant he'd spent over eight hours in the game world. He felt like one of those shut-ins who spent all their time playing video games and never leaving their rooms.

Chuckling at the thought, Adam grabbed an outfit from his dresser, left his room, and traveled into the bathroom. This apartment had two of them. One of the bathrooms was for Fayte's personal use, but the other belonged to him and Aris whenever she woke up. He relieved himself, took a quick rinse underneath scorching hot water, and dried himself off.

He put on his underwear, slid the black jeans up his legs, then donned a simple white T-shirt with an atom on the front. Since he wasn't planning on leaving today, Adam didn't bother putting on socks and left the bathroom.

Because it was a habit, Adam went straight to the kitchen and began preparing breakfast. His first thoughts were about Aris and what she would like, but Aris was currently in suspended animation and would be for at least a month and a half if not longer, so he shifted gears and thought about Fayte. She wasn't a fan of savory foods and preferred lighter fare. At the same time, she didn't want to eat anything too sweet for fear that her sweet tooth would act up.

"A parfait then," Adam mumbled to himself.

He looked in the fridge and pantry to see if they had the necessary ingredients, which they did, fortunately. It would have sucked if he needed to travel to a grocery store just to make breakfast.

Parfaits were pretty easy. It was yogurt combined with sliced strawberries, blueberries, and crumbled granola. He could have also added blackberries and raspberries, but Fayte didn't have either of those in her fridge. He combined all the necessary ingredients into a 10 ounce cup. After making the simple meal for Fayte, he cooked four sunny-side up eggs for himself and lightly seasoned them with salt and pepper. They sadly did not have any bacon, but he did add a slice of toast with some butter.

He also made a pot of coffee.

He had just set his and Fayte's food down at the coffee table and was getting ready to turn on the television when Fayte appeared before him. She was a vision of loveliness as she walked into the room, dressed in simple pink pajama bottoms and a white T-shirt that was several sizes too large. One side had slid down, baring her left shoulder. That look would have caused most men's mouths to go dry and their hearts to throb with desire.

Adam only appreciated the view for a moment.

"Good morning," he greeted. "I've made breakfast."

Adam gestured to the yogurt parfait and coffee mug with the depiction of a grinning fox on it. Fayte smiled as she walked over, sat down next to him, and first grabbed the coffee.

The moment she came over, a gentle and aromatic scent entered Adam's nose. He could tell Fayte had just taken a shower, not only because her hair was still damp, but also because he could smell her shampoo. Mixed in with the shampoo was the slightly bitter aroma of coffee.

"Good morning. Thank you for making breakfast," Fayte said in a voice so soft and delicate that Adam was reminded of the lilting melodies of a professional singer. She took a slow sip of coffee, sighed as it warmed her insides, and then set the mug back on the coffee table. "I'm guessing you played *Age of Gods* the moment it went live?"

"I did." Adam confirmed his words with a nod, then glanced curiously at the woman next to him. "You?"

"I did, though I didn't play for more than four hours. It was already late, so I was tired." She tucked a strand of hair behind her ear. It was a smooth and fluid action that drew Adam's eyes to her slender neck and beautiful collarbone. "The only reason I went on last night anyway was to connect with the other member of our guild."

"And who is the other member of our guild?" asked Adam.

"Her name is Susan Forebear, but I usually call her Su. She's currently sixteen years old and is one of my best friends. I met her during a social function several years ago. She's a very kind and timid young woman who has trouble saying 'no' to people, but she's also incredibly intelligent and a talented hacker. She's the reason I was able to track down your location."

Fayte grinned at him as she nudged his shoulder, then took a spoonful of the parfait and brought it to her mouth. Her eyes closed as if she was experiencing bliss. After that first bite, she ignored the coffee in favor of finishing the parfait. Meanwhile, Adam watched her with an amused smile.

"So this Susan is the one I have to thank for our meeting," he murmured. "I'll have to treat her kindly. If it wasn't for her, you and I wouldn't have met, and I would have never been given the hope I have now."

The blissful expression Fayte wore turned into a kind and charming smile that could have invoked the flames of passion and desire within any man. Adam found himself momentarily breathless, though he was getting used to her beauty. It helped that Aris was every bit the gorgeous young woman this missus was, albeit, beautiful in a different way.

He sometimes likened Fayte to the moon and Aris the sun. Fayte had a mysterious and enchanting beauty about her, while Aris was innocent and pure. Both were stunning. However, their beauty took entirely different forms.

"You will definitely have to treat her well." Fayte teased him. "I won't tolerate you bullying her."

"Good thing I'm not a bully then," Adam said with a smile.

Fayte became slightly dazed when she saw that smile on his face. It wasn't until he began waving his hand in front of her that she snapped out of her stupor and turned her head. The tips of her ears had become a light pink.

They spoke a little more, but the talk shifted from subtle teasing to what they had planned for the day. Adam was going to spend a bit of time with Aris, but then he planned on traveling back into the game. Fayte was also going to play as well, but she wanted to get some more sleep first.

Adam was a bit unusual in that he only needed a total of two hours of sleep to continue performing at optimum efficiency. It was enough time to completely recharge him, and since playing Age of Gods was still resting his body, he determined he would only need one hour to recharge. Since his goal was to raise his strength and reputation to help Fayte win her bet, he decided that he was going to make the most of the period Aris was asleep to get his level up as high as possible.

He and Fayte parted ways not long after breakfast. She thanked him again for the meal and headed back into her bedroom. Adam, meanwhile, traveled into the third bedroom where Aris was currently sleeping inside of the cryobed sitting in the room's very center.

Nothing had changed about the young woman since she had first been put to sleep. Her skin was pale white and her eyes were tightly shut. It looked like she was just resting, except there was no rise and fall of her chest to signify she was breathing. She was a sleeping beauty who'd been frozen in time. The diagram that revealed how much of the Mortems Disease had been cured showed that only about a fourth of the disease was gone.

I think she's healing faster than Fayte predicted...

Despite knowing Aris couldn't hear him while stuck inside the cryobed, Adam still talked with her about everything he could think of. He mentioned the game, how much he missed her, and how he hoped she would get better after this so they could spend the rest of their lives together. He also talked about Fayte.

"You only saw Fayte for a bit, so you aren't aware of how amazing she is. It's hard to find anyone with that level of determination, intelligence, and grit. I think you will like her once you get out of there," he said with a smile.

Little did he know that someone was listening into his conversation from the other side of the door.

***

Despite having told Adam she planned on heading to bed, Fayte did not travel to bed right away. She was not quite able to sleep just yet. A part of it, she theorized, was because she had too much nervous energy. *Age of Gods* had just realized, and while she was playing because of the bet she made with Levon, she was also very interested in the game itself. She really wanted to keep playing.

The other reason was because she was still curious about Adam.

She and Adam had been living together for a week now. They had spoken a lot during this time. She had learned quite a bit about him, but she also felt like everything he told her was just touching the tip of a very large iceberg. There was so much more hidden beneath the depths. Fayte wanted to uncover those hidden facets of him.

This was the first time Fayte had ever felt so curious about a man before. She believed it was partly thanks to the close proximity they were living in. Anyone would be curious about the person they lived with, but she felt like the greater reason for her curiosity was because Adam was just that interesting.

He recognized her beauty but wasn't enamored by it.

He spoke to her with ease and hadn't tried to make a move on her even once since they met.

He was completely and utterly dedicated to Aris, or at least, that was how it seemed to her.

It was because of these three reasons that she decided to talk to him before he went into *Age of Gods*. He was not in his room, which meant he could only be in Aris's room. She wandered up to the door and raised her hand to knock.

"You only saw Fayte for a bit, so you aren't aware of how amazing she is. It's hard to find anyone with that level of determination, intelligence, and grit. I think you will like her once you get out of there."

She paused when she heard Adam's voice. He was obviously talking to Aris. He did that quite often. It never failed to make Fayte's heart ache, though she was certain her feelings were sympathetic over Adam's situation. He normally told Aris about his day or his plans for that day.

However, this time, he was talking about her.

Fayte bit her lip and hesitated for a moment, a war taking place within her conscience, but curiosity eventually won out and she leaned against the door to listen in as Adam continued to talk about her. She wanted to know what he thought of her.

"I know there's a lot about her that I don't know yet, and she's probably keeping some secrets from me, but I don't think that really matters. It's easy to tell she's a good person in a bad situation. I know I'm not... the best person in the world. I don't do things out of the kindness of my heart, and I would have never considered accepting her request if she didn't have this cure, but I think I might have helped her out regardless of whether she could cure you or not now that I know her a little better. She deserves so much more than being forced to marry a douchebag like Levon Pleonexia."

While his "douchebag" comment made her cover her mouth to stifle a giggle, the rest of what he said caused her face to feel like a furnace. Was that really what he thought of her? It was so embarrassing, but at the same time, it made her chest feel simultaneously tight and warm. Adam might not think he was a good person, but she could definitely say he was underestimating his own kindness.

Because Fayte didn't think she could face him after hearing all that, she left the room and went back into her bedroom. She laid down on her bed, but she was now even more awake than before. A sigh escaped her parted lips as she realized she wouldn't be getting any sleep right now. Since that was the case, she sent Susan a quick message and logged onto *Age of Gods*.

Her avatar appeared inside of the Village of Beginnings—one of many. Like everyone else, she was wearing the simple clothing the game had first given her. It was a white collared shirt, a brown bodice, and a white skirt of about ankle length. Brown boots adorned her feet.

The only difference between her appearance and everyone else's was the veil she had that covered her face. There was nothing special about it. It was just a simple accessory she had bought at the trader's shop after earning enough money from her kills. She was also carrying a staff, which marked her as a mage.

Several other players were present when she appeared. Most of them were men. They stopped and turned to stare at her like they had just caught a glimpse of heaven.

"Whoa! Babe alert!"

"Who is that? She's gorgeous!"

"Why is she wearing a veil?"

"Who cares?! Think she'll give me her gamer tag if I ask her?"

"In your dreams maybe. Women like that aren't interested in losers like you."

"Why you!!! You picking a fight?!"

"Bring it on, bruh!"

Because of her experience when it came to members of the opposite sex, Fayte was able to easily ignore the conversations taking place around her. She began walking to the edge of the village. As she did, a voice called out to her.

"Fayte!"

A genuine smile, hidden by her veil, appeared on Fayte's face as she turned around. A young girl was running toward her.

Susan Forebear was a lot shorter than Fayte. The sixteen-year-old girl only came up to about her chest. She had doe-like brown eyes that made her seem more innocent and pure than any human had a right to be. A cute button nose sat above a small pink mouth. While her figure was a little childish, Fayte believed that Susan would become a stunning young woman in the future. Her mother had, after all, been known as the most enchanting beauty in the American Federation when she was still alive.

While Fayte was wielding a staff, Susan had a bow in her hands.

"Su," Fayte greeted the girl, who was not wearing a veil like her. "I did not realize you had come back into the game. I'm sorry. I should have checked my friends list. Oh, shoot!"

"W-what is wrong?" asked Susan, tilting her head.

"I forgot to ask Adam what his gamer tag was so I could add him to my friends list," Fayte said with an irritated sigh. She shook her head. "Well, no use worrying about that right now. Would you care to join me?"

"Of course." Susan bobbed her head several times.

"Thank you."

"Speaking of Adam, can I… I mean, would you mind if I asked about what kind of person he is?" asked Susan, looking down at the dirt road.

"Not at all."

Fayte smiled and began telling her friend what she knew about Adam so far as they left the Village of Beginnings and traveled into the open field. She and Susan were only at level 2 right now, which was about the average for most people at present, but they needed to level up quickly. Her fate was dependent on it.

***

Adam once again entered *Age of Gods* and found himself standing in the same place he had before logging off: Right in front of Sterk. The old warrior leapt back in shock when Adam suddenly appeared, but then he placed a hand against his chest plate, sighed, and glared at him.

"I know you otherworlders can come and go as you please, but could you not suddenly appear in front of me like that?"

"Sorry." Adam apologized and scratched the back of his head. The old man just released an irritable sigh.

He left Sterk and traveled away from the barracks.

Doing as he'd been told to before he logged off last time, Adam sought the building with a sign that contained a potion hanging above the door. It was easy to find. There weren't that many buildings to begin with.

The inside of the potions shop smelled of what he at first thought was mildew, but he soon realized that it was just the combination of odd ingredients used for potions. His nose, which had never smelled these scents before, was unable to categorize them.

He looked around as he walked in. This store didn't have much. There were bottles sitting on shelves stacked against the walls, and at the back of the room was a counter, behind which a nervous man paced back and forth. He had graying hair and a bald spot near the back of his head. Unlike Sterk, who was all muscle, this guy was all flab and had a gut hanging over his pants.

"Excuse me," Adam said as he walked up to the counter. "Are you Mr. Wilkins?"

As if he was a frightened rabbit, the man jumped and spun around to face him, nearly tripping over his own two feet in the process. Adam shifted a little. Such an exaggerated reaction made him wonder what kind of programmer made this NPC.

"Huh? Oh. You must an otherworlder. Welcome to my potion shop. My name is Trader Wilkins. I apologize for not noticing you sooner. I am currently distracted with a small issue…"

"I know. Your son is missing, right?"

"You know?" Trader Wilkin's eyes went wide.

Adam nodded. "That is actually the reason I am here. I thought I would offer my services to you. Would you like me to help you find him?"

"Y-you would do that?" A moment after he asked that question, Trader Wilkin's eyes misted over and he grabbed Adam's hands before the young man could pull away. "Bless you, otherworlder! If you can find my son, I will gladly give you a suitable reward. He is my only son. Please find him!"

Ding!

*[You have been offered a new quest: [Find Trader Wilkins'
Missing Son!] Will you accept? Yes? No?]*

Adam pressed the "yes" button as he spoke to Trader Wilkin's.
"Do not worry. I will find your son. Can I ask where he was last
seen?"

Ding!

*[The quest: [Find Trader Wilkins' Missing Son!] has been ac-
cepted!]*

"My son often travels into the forest to search for potion ingredients," Trader Wilkins said. "Most of the ingredients we need can
be found in the forest to the west. However, I have always warned
him to never travel in too deep. The monsters near the entrance are
not very aggressive, but they become more powerful and more aggressive the further in you go. I am afraid he might have traveled
deeper into the forest and encountered a powerful monster. Please
find him and bring him back, and if... if he is already dead, then
please bring back proof of his death."

"Don't worry. I will," Adam said before a thought occurred to
him. "By the way, do you sell masks?"

Back when Adam was acquiring money to pay for his apartment and Aris's medical equipment, he would change the appearance of his in-game characters. This was because he didn't want
anyone discovering his identity and bothering him and Aris. He
didn't want anyone to destroy the life he had with the girl he loved.

Fat lot of good that did. Fayte had discovered him somehow
anyway, but he believed she was an anomaly. In either event, since

he could not change his character's physical appearance, he needed to wear a mask that would hide his face from others.

"I don't sell masks. This is a potion shop, so I'm not allowed to. If you'd like a mask, I recommend going to Madam Milly's Clothier. Her shop is the one with a shirt on it."

"I'll do that then. Thank you."

Adam left Trader Wilkin's shop and traveled to Madam Milly's Clothier, which had a sign with a shirt on it, just like Trader Wilkin's said. The inside of the store looked like a traditional clothing shop but slightly different. As he walked over creaking wooden floorboards, he looked at the variety of clothes folded on tables. There were only a few different styles. Most of the shirts were like the one he was currently wearing.

"Can I help you?" asked a woman standing near the back. She was a middle-aged woman with graying hair and some wrinkles lining her face.

Adam turned to her "Do you sell masks?"

"Not usually, but I do have a few that I got during the Goddess Fair. Would you like one?"

"I would. How much?"

"This mask is very simple and doesn't have any enchantments. All it can do is disguise your face. 10 gold coins is fine."

"I'll take it."

Adam paid Madam Milly ten gold coins in exchange for a mask, which the woman handed over. He read the information on the screen that appeared over it.

Item Name: Plain Mask	Item Type: Mask	Grade: Low	Use requirements: Can be equipped by any class.	Description: A low-grade mask.	Abilities: It can hide your face from view.

Once he had the mask, which was just a plain white mask, Adam put it over his face to equip it. Then he left the store. He had a quest to complete.

THE MYSTERIOUS CAVE

Adam journeyed back into the forest. He ran into many groups who were all grinding their levels without any regard for the potential of hidden quests. There must certainly have been some people who understood that merely grinding would only avail them a higher level but not give them any other benefits, but it appeared as if the vast majority of people only cared about getting to a high enough level to leave the Village of Beginnings.

Perhaps they did not think any of the quests they could take in the Village of Beginnings would be worth it? He couldn't say for sure.

"Hey! Look! Look at that! It's a 1-star enemy!"

"Oh, wow! I never thought we'd run into a 1-star enemy so soon!"

"Stop jabbering and surround it! Hurry up!"

While Adam was wandering through the forest in search of Trader Wilkins' missing son, he ran into an unusual scene. A group of players was surrounding a [wild boar] that was about three times larger than the [wild boars] he'd been fighting before. It stood about five or six feet taller than the average adult male, had bloodshot eyes seeping with rage, and large tusks that looked like they could easily impale a person regardless of what sort of protective armor they were wearing. Its fur coat was also covered in strange glyphs that gave it an ominous appearance.

Its name when he looked at it was still [wild boar], but attached to the name was also a class: 1-star.

It was at level 10.

Sadly, that was all the info he could get because he didn't have the [scan] skill.

The players were all dressed in the regular garb everyone had arrived in *Age of Gods* with, but they were all carrying weapons. There were five in total. All of them were men. It looked like they had a fairly well-rounded group, with one Mage, one Priest, two Warriors, and an Archer. The two Warriors were closing in on the [wild boar] from either side.

Adam stopped walking and stuck around to observe the fight. This could prove useful to him, after all. He didn't know what the difference between a [wild boar] and a 1-star [wild boar] was besides their level and appearance.

The two Warriors were both at level 3, while the Archer, Mage, and Priest were at levels 2, 2, and 3 respectively. Since Adam had never joined a party before, he didn't know how leveling up worked in this game. Were their levels skewed because the higher level players had done solo grinding as well, or was there another reason? Perhaps the person who killed the enemy received most of the experience?

He would need to find out.

Eventually.

The two Warriors quickly attacked from the side with a basic [slash], but as he expected, it didn't do any damage. A large -1 appeared above the [wild boar] and that was it. Their level and Attack Power stat was too low to actually injure such a high level monster.

"Shit! Did my attack really do nothing?!"

"This 1-star enemy is too strong!"

"M-maybe we should retreat…"

That last suggestion from the Priest sounded reasonable, but the [wild boar] had already been attacked and was enraged. Its eyes became madder red as it snorted and ground a heel into the ground.

The two Warriors had pulled most of its agro. This meant they were the unfortunate victims of its rage. It attacked them first, slamming into them with its tusks and sending them flying.

-160; -160!

Adam shook his head as the two Warriors' corpses hit the ground, bounced, and remained there. The large black numbers that flashed above their heads when they were hit let him know the attack had dealt them fatal damage. It was a one-hit kill.

The remaining players panicked.

"It's way too strong!"

"Dammit! I knew we shouldn't have attacked this 1-star monster when it appeared! What were we thinking?!"

"Retreat! Run away!"

The Archer, Priest, and Mage tried to flee, but now that the Warriors were dead, the [wild boar] locked onto them. An enraged squeal escaped its mouth as it flew forward like it had wings on its feet. It speared its tusk through the Mage. The tusk went through the Mage's back and out of his chest. It was weird for Adam to see someone get impaled and no blood to spurt out.

-300!

The Mage was dead before the [wild boar] even shook him off its tusk. Then it went after the Archer, who tried to fire his arrows at it, though they only did -1 point of damage. Idiot. He was speared through the chest when the 1-star [wild boar] charged at him in a murderous rage, doing another -300 points of damage and insta-killing him.

Because the others had all died and the Priest had not stopped running even to look back, he at least managed to get away. Now Adam was alone with the [wild boar].

He licked his lips. His blood was rising, beginning to boil.

He'd finally found a challenge!

Adam rushed forward while the [wild boar] was stomping its front hooves in frustration and used [thrust] to attack its flank.

-104!

A large number that was in the triple digits appeared above the head of the 1-star [wild boar]. Adam wasn't sure how much health this thing had, but that number seemed pretty good.

The [wild boar] squealed in rage and pain as it turned around and tried to attack him, but Adam was already moving, darting left as he spun on the balls of his feet and ran away. This angered his enemy. With another enraged squeal, it charged Adam as he ran straight for a tree. Two yards. One yard. One foot. When he was barely half a foot from the tree, Adam rolled away and allowed the [wild boar] to slam headfirst into the tree.

-1

STUN!

The tree snapped like a twig. It fell with a crash.

While the [wild boar] didn't receive much damage from hitting the tree, it did get stunned. The [stun] affect, from what he understood, should keep it from moving for several seconds. Because those several seconds were crucial and precious, Adam attacked the enemy with a series of [thrust] and [slash] attacks.

-104; -95; MISS; MISS; MISS; MISS; MISS; MISS; -104; -95; MISS!

While a lot of his attacks missed, he managed to land four strikes before the [wild boar] recovered. The creature soon shook its head as if ridding it of cobwebs, then turned and glared at him. It stomped its left hoof against the ground, roared like an angry sumo wrestler, and charged.

Adam dodged, turned on his heel, and ran toward another tree.

-1!

-STUN!

Once again, running into a tree caused the [wild boar] to become stunned. Sword in hand, Adam once more attacked it.

-95; -95; MISS; MISS; MISS; MISS; MISS; MISS!

He only managed to hit it twice this time before it recovered, but Adam didn't let that discourage him. When the [wild boar] recovered, he simply repeated the process, running toward a tree, dodging, letting the enemy slam into the tree and stun itself, and then attacking with everything he had. Sometimes he hit every time. Sometimes he missed every time. However, Adam kept attacking over and over, until, at last, the [wild boar] released a pained squeal and fell to the ground.

It was dead.

Ding!

[You have defeated the monster 1-star [wild boar]! Items dropped: [wild boar's tusk], [Ring of Accuracy], and 200 gold coins. +1,000 experience points! +50 ability points!]

With the additional experience points, Adam's experience gauge was now at 1,162/4,800, which meant he could potentially level up if he killed at least four more of these 1-star enemies. However, beyond the experience gained, what he really found himself interested in was the ability points he had gained. This was the first time he'd acquired AP in the game. It looked like, in order to gain AP, he had to kill these 1-star monsters. They must have been like the equivalent of a dungeon boss or something similar.

Before allocating his AP into his skills, he looked at the [Ring of Accuracy] he had acquired from the 1-star [wild boar].

Item Name: Ring of Accuracy	Item Type: Ring	Grade: Low	Use requirements: Can be used by any class.	Description: A low-grade ring made from steel. It has been enchanted to increase a player's Hit-Rate.	Abilities: Hit-Rate–10%

It wasn't much, but even increasing his Hit-Rate by a small amount would help right now. He hated how more than half of his attacks kept missing. It was annoying. He slipped the ring on his left index finger. It looked like he could only equip two rings at a time, so now he had the [Ring of Accuracy] on his left hand and the [Brass Ring] on his right.

With the ring now increasing his Hit-Rate, Adam looked at his skills.

Right now he had two skills: [slash] and [thrust]. Both of them were basic skills and they only required 10 AP each to level up. Since he now had 50 AP, he spent 20 AP and brought them both to level 2.

Skill Name: Slash	Description: A basic skill where the player swings his or her sword and attacks the enemy!	Current lvl: 2 AP needed to reach next lvl: 20	Ability: Causes 110% damage to enemy if it hits	MP consumption: 1	Cooldown time: 0 seconds
Skill Name: Thrust	Description: A basic skill where the player thrusts his or her sword at the enemy!	Current lvl: 2 AP needed to reach next lvl: 20	Ability: Causes 120% damage with a 1.5% chance at getting a critical hit	MP Consumption: 2	Cooldown time: 1 second

Now his skills had both been upgraded to level 2, but he still had 30 AP left, so he invested 20 more points on the [thrust] skill since he, as a spearman, deemed it more useful than [slash].

Skill Name: Thrust	Description: A basic skill where the player thrusts his or her sword at the enemy!	Current lvl: 3 AP needed to reach next lvl: 40	Ability: Causes 140% damage with a 2% chance at getting a critical hit	MP Consumption: 2	Cooldown time: 1 second

Adam grimaced when he saw how little the attack power was raised. Right now he had +95 Physical Strength, which meant if his [thrust] hit, it would do about -133 points of damage. That wasn't a huge difference. He sighed and ran a hand through his hair. It seemed these beginner class skills just couldn't be improved by much. He hoped there would be a chance to change classes after leaving the Village of Beginnings.

✳✳✳

The group that had been slaughtered by the 1-star [wild boar] that Adam killed belonged to a powerful guild called the Rising Phoenix Alliance. While the other members of the party died and reincarnated back inside of the cathedral, the Priest who managed to escape ran toward where the guild master, who had coincidentally been brought to the same Village of Beginnings as him, was located.

His guild master had been really excited when he learned a 1-star enemy had been sighted.

"Are you sure there is a 1-star enemy here?" asked the Rising Phoenix Alliance guild master.

"I'm positive, Guild Master Daniel. Me and my group were all attacked by it! It was a level 10 1-star [wild boar]!"

"Attacked? You mean you six saw an opportunity to take all the experience points and ability points for yourselves, but you ended up biting off more than you could chew, right?" the guild master said with a cold snort.

"…"

The Priest could say nothing as the man hit the nail right on the head.

"Forget it. Show me where this level 10 1-star [wild boar] is."

It wasn't just the guild master who was traveling with the Priest as he took them to where the [wild boar] was located. All of the guild members who had been with Daniel were also following along. After all, a level 10 1-star enemy was not something they, with their level 3 powers, could hope to defeat on their own. Even the guild master was only at level 4 right now.

The fourteen guild members plus the guild master entered a clearing alongside the Priest.

"This is where we found the 1-star [wild boar]," the Priest said, gesturing with his left hand toward the clearing.

Daniel raised an eyebrow as he looked around the clearing. He looked left, right, straight ahead, and even behind him, but no matter where he looked, no level 10 1-star [wild boar] appeared before his eyes. There wasn't even a regular [wild boar] in sight.

"Are you sure you saw a real 1-star enemy here?" he asked.

"Of course I'm sure! It was right here! I swear it was! You can even ask my party members when you go into the Village of Beginnings!"

The Priest seemed to be panicking as he realized the [wild boar] was gone, but he was adamant that what he saw was real. Daniel looked at the Priest, then turned around and looked at the clearing, which was currently empty of even a single enemy. He pondered this for a moment.

"If what you say is true, then the only thing I can think of is that after your party was killed and you escaped, someone came and killed it," he said at last.

"Killed it? But no… that can't be. Only a large group of at least ten or fifteen people would be able to deal with such a strong enemy! Wh-what's more, I wasn't gone for that long! Even if they were really able to kill it, I don't believe they would be able to leave before we arrived!"

"That is true…"

Daniel stroked his chin and tried to think about what could have happened. He decided to give this guild member of his the benefit of the doubt, but really, it was hard when all evidence of a 1-star enemy being present was now gone. There wasn't even a corpse.

He sighed. "Well, whether a level 10 1-star [wild boar] was here or not doesn't matter anymore. It's gone now. That's too bad. If what you say is true, then that would make this the first time a 1-star enemy has appeared in a Village of Beginnings."

"Been checking the forums again, Boss?" asked one of his men.

"Always. Information is half the battle, after all."

Since it looked like there was no 1-star enemy present anymore, Daniel turned around and gestured for his men to follow him. They couldn't afford to stick around in a place with no enemies.

***

-133; -104; MISS; -104; MISS; MISS; MISS; MISS; MISS; -104!

Ding!

[You have defeated a [wolf]! Items dropped: [wolf's pelt] and 50 gold coins! +150 experience points!]

Adam frowned as he cut down another level 5 [wolf]. He'd been walking through the forest for what felt like hours now, and he had yet to find a single sign of Trader Wilkins' missing son. Well, he supposed that was why he was called "missing." At the same time, he was really beginning to wonder if this quest of his could even be completed.

He shook his head. It had to be something a player could complete. There was absolutely no way the developer for *Age of Gods* would create a quest that could not be completed.

Since it looked like sticking around in the level 5 area of the forest was not yielding any results, Adam began traveling deeper into the forest. The scent of wood and the feel of grass and gravel underfoot accompanied him as the lights from the canopy above disappeared. He looked up. The canopy was getting thicker, blocking out the sunlight, to the point where it was becoming harder to see where he was going.

Adam frowned as he wondered what he should do. Go back? No. He couldn't go back when he hadn't completed the quest.

Thinking for a moment, Adam decided to try something. He furrowed his brow and concentrated, searching for the energy present within every person. He was looking for a stream of power inside of himself, a well-spring of energy that emanated from his chest.

This was not his real body. It was something that had been created by the game, but his "soul" had been implanted into this body according to Lim, the fairy who'd helped him create his character. He had a theory that if his soul was present in this game, then it should be possible to use his esper powers, which were also a part of his soul.

It took several minutes, but his expression eventually cleared as he discovered the stream of energy flowing through his body. A smile lit up his face as he channeled that energy to his eyes. This caused his green eyes to become so bright they began glowing in the dark like a predator with night vision. Aside from the cosmetic change, his vision also became much brighter.

Which allowed him to see the giant mouth lunging for his face!

Adam's reflexes kicked in. He ducked and swung the sword above his head. There was a strong feeling of resistance as the blade cut through something. The sword was nearly knocked from his hand due to the power of whatever knocked into him, which caused his fingers, palm, and wrist to go partially numb. This shocked Adam. He knew this game boasted an almost impossibly realistic setting and physical sensations, but how could anything feel this real?!

-104!

Scrambling to his feet and turning around, Adam found himself face to face with a jungle cat of some kind. It didn't look like a panther or any of the rainforest predators found on Earth. It actually looked like a normal house cat, but it was three times bigger, covered in bristling black fur, had vicious yellow eyes, and fangs so sharp they could probably rend flesh from bone with ease.

The words above its head identified it as a level 8 [feral cat].

Goodie.

Adam didn't wait for this overgrown house cat to take the initiative. He rushed forward and attacked it with a [thrust].

MISS!

The [feral cat] dodged his attack by leaping to the side, but Adam was not deterred and attacked several times with the [slash] skill before the one second cooldown time for [thrust] ended and re-initiated another [thrust].

-133!

Adam had learned through trial and error that combat skills gained in real life could be applied to combat within the game. A person would not do the same amount of damage if they simply swung their weapon without activating a skill, but basic skills like [slash] could be continuously activated no matter which angle a person swung their weapon from. This meant every time Adam swung the sword in his hand, [slash] was activated, which allowed him to release a constant stream of attacks.

MISS; MISS; MISS; -104!

Of course, Adam was not a swordsman. He was proficient in wielding a dagger and a spear. Even so, his physical prowess allowed him to easily swing the sword in his hand without worrying about tiring.

-104; -133; -104; MISS; MISS; MISS; MISS!

His battle against the [feral cat] continued as the two traded blows. This enemy was particularly agile and didn't just rely on simple one-dimensional attacks like the 1-star [wild boar] had done. It took to the trees, leapt from the branches, and attacked Adam with a powerful pounce. Had he been someone less experienced with real combat, he would have been hit. As things stood, he was able to leap away from the [feral cat] before it could reach him and attacked it with another [thrust].

-266!

Ah! He got a critical hit! A fierce grin appeared on Adam's face as he continued to dodge and attack the [feral cat], until its HP at last ran out and it died.

Ding!

[You have defeated a [feral cat]! Items dropped: [durable cat fur] and 150 gold coins. +300 experience points!]

The amount of experience points wasn't that much and Adam didn't even know what to do with the item it dropped. Only the money seemed useful right now.

He continued traveling after killing the level 8 [feral cat], heading deeper and deeper into the forest. Several other [feral cats] attacked him, but they were all dealt with the same way he killed the first one. Even when they ganged up on him, Adam didn't flinch. He mowed them down and increased the experience points he had, until his experience gauge was at 2,930/4,800.

Adam had lost track of the time. It was easy to do when roaming through a dark forest. However, after traveling deeper and deeper, until the enemies became level 9 instead of level 7, he finally found something that he thought might be a clue as to the whereabouts of Trader Wilkins' missing son.

He knelt and picked up the object he accidentally kicked while walking. It was a leather boot, the kind he'd seen the villagers wearing. Adam could not imagine many villagers were willing to travel this deep into the forest. He was positive this boot belonged to Trader Wilkins' missing son. Perhaps whatever algorithm this game ran on had decided he'd walked enough and was now giving him a clue?

There was one way to find out.

Placing the boot inside of his item pouch, Adam stood back up and looked at the cave mouth in front of him. It was a gloomy entrance. The cave mouth opened wide like the gaping jaw of a monster. Even Adam would admit that it was spooky, though he was not in the least bit afraid.

"Is Trader Wilkins' son in this cave?" he wondered out loud.

No one answered him. There was no one around *to* answer him. And since he wasn't going to get any answers by standing around like an idiot, Adam tightened his grip on the sword in his hand and walked into the cave.

The first thing he noticed upon entering the cave was the steep decline, which would have caused most people to pitch forward in surprise and take a tumble down. He bent his knees to steady his walk. As he slowly moved deeper into the cave, he strained his ears and listened for signs of a potential enemy lurking within the darkness, but all he heard was the dull *plank, plank* of water droplets falling to the ground.

The cave eventually leveled out into what he thought of as a naturally formed hallway. The walls were uneven and curved. As he traveled further, a light appeared in the distance, which he soon realized came from a pair of torches set against a wall at the far end.

A wall with a door.

Adam studied the rickety old door with a contemplative gaze. A door signified that someone was present behind it, meaning there was likely a person or perhaps an enemy on the other side of this door. Was it Trader Wilkins' missing son, or was it the person who had kidnapped him? Adam reached out and felt the old grains of wood before, with a slight push, he opened the door and stepped inside.

The first thing that happened after he walked inside was the door behind him swinging shut. He spun around and tried to open the door, but no matter what he did, it was no use. The door refused to budge. Even attacking it with his sword availed him nothing. His sword just sprang off like a magical barrier was protecting it.

After the door sealed shut, the area around him began growing brighter. Several torches along the walls lit up, revealing a simple circular room. This room was definitely not naturally formed. The floor was smooth and several motifs of unknown origin had been carved into it, seeming to depict a woman being attacked by skeletons. There were also a number of bones lying on the ground.

Adam felt his breathing grow a little heavy as he stepped forward. The moment he did, the bones lying scattered across the ground rattled. He stopped walking and watched in shock as they combined together, creating several different skeletons. Each skeleton stood to its feet, grabbed a sword lying on the ground, and turned to him, their glowing red eyes burning with a malevolent aura.

Level 10 [undead skeleton].

Jaws clacked. Arms raised. Like that, the skeletons—twenty in total—attacked.

Adam leapt back as the skeletons came at him en masse, swinging their swords, jaws clacking and bones clattering together. The chilling sight of [undead skeletons] attacking made even Adam feel shocked. It didn't help that these skeletons were so realistic it was impossible to think they were just constructs created for the sake of a game.

None of the attacks hit Adam. He calmed down when they missed and gripped the weapon in his hand tighter before adopting a two-handed sword stance. Like that, he waded into the [undead skeleton] horde and attacked with the [slash] skill, which allowed him to ceaselessly chain the skill together. His sword struck bones. The [undead skeletons] also attacked him, but he was keeping his body primed and wove around all the attacks sent his way. Theirs were honestly clumsy. Avoiding them was a simple matter of predicting where the attacks would come from and weaving out of the way before they struck.

-104; -104; -104; MISS; MISS; MISS; MISS; MISS; -104!

After attacking, Adam retreated before he could become surrounded, ran to the other side of the room, and waited until the [undead skeleton] horde was just a yard away. Then he charged forward and attacked again.

-104; MISS; MISS; MISS; -104; MISS; MISS; -104!

Because these [undead skeletons] were nothing but bones, Adam did not use [thrust]. It had a higher chance at missing than [slash]. This was, at least, what he assumed. Even if he used [thrust], there was a good chance his attack would go through their ribcage and not hit anything.

-104; -104; -104; MISS; MISS; MISS; MISS; MISS!

Adam attacked, dodged, retreated, attacked, dodged, retreated, repeating this simple process over and over again. He didn't know how long he kept this up. One [undead skeleton] eventually died. A second [undead skeleton] followed soon after. One by one, the skeletons fell until there were none left.

Ding!

[You have defeated 20 [undead skeletons]! Items dropped: [steel sword], [steel shield], [adventurer boots], and 400 gold coins. +3,000 experience points!]

Ding!

[You have leveled up! You are now at level 7! +10 HP! +10 MP! +5 SP!]

Adam looked at the SP he had gained and thought about where to put it. He frowned. His HP and MP were pretty weak, but [slash] and [thrust] didn't require much MP to use anyway, so he didn't think he needed more. HP was… useless. It looked like anything he encountered here would be at level 10 and therefore able to insta-kill him if they hit him even once. He put the +5 SP into his Strength stat once more.

He looked at his stats and, upon deciding they were good, observed the room he had found himself in. The [undead skeleton] remains were gone, and there were two doors on opposite sides of the room. One of them was sealed shut. The other was open. It was obvious to Adam that he only had one choice.

"It looks like the only way to get out of this is to continue moving forward," Adam muttered before walking to the door, through which he could see nothing but an inky blackness. He took a deep breath. "Into the abyss we go."

With a smile on his face, Adam walked through the door, which immediately sealed shut behind him.

THE NECROMANCER

Just like what happened with the first door, the one behind him was locked, and no amount of door bashing or sword swinging would break it down. He wondered if these objects were unbreakable. That was fairly typical for games back in the latter half of the twenty-first century, but most games went for realism these days and made everything breakable—including buildings and even mountains. Could these doors be enchanted with protection magic?

Shaking his head, Adam dispelled all those thoughts and turned around to face his new surroundings. It looked like he was in an ancient corridor. The stone walls were covered in cracks and mildew. A strong, rotting scent filled his nose. He glanced at the wall on his left, then the one on his right, judging the distance between the two to be about four yards. That was quite a bit of space. If nothing else, he would not have an issue swinging his sword.

"What I wouldn't give for a spear or at least a dagger," he grumbled.

Before he began walking, Adam checked the equipment he got from the [undead skeletons] he fought in the previous room. There was the [steel sword], [steel shield], and [adventurer boots].

Item Name: Steel Sword	Item Type: Weapon	Grade: Low	Use requirements: Can be equipped by any level of the Warrior class.	Description: A low-grade sword made of steel.	Abilities: Attack+20
Item Name: Steel Shield	Item Type: Shield	Grade: Low	Use requirements: can be equipped by any level of the Warrior class.	Description: A low-grade shield made of steel.	Abilities: Defense+10
Item Name: Adventurer Boots	Item Type: Clothing	Grade: Low	Use requirements: can be equipped by any level of any class.	Description: leather boots for adventurers. They are very comfortable.	Abilities: Speed+5

It looked like all of these increased his stats to some degree. The [steel sword] also had a higher attack power than [Sterk's broadsword], but it didn't deal slashing damage. He had no use for the shield. That said, he did put on the boots and equip the sword since it would let him deal more damage. With the [steel sword] equipped, his Physical Attack was now +125.

With his new equipment now equipped, he began moving.

There didn't seem to be anything in this corridor. All he could see was the cracked and mildew covered walls. All he could hear was the sound of his own boots thumping against the floor. As he walked forward, torches along the walls began lighting up as though guiding his path. He finally reached the end of this corridor, but it led to a T-junction.

He groaned. "If my guess is correct, one of these is the correct path, while the other leads to a trap…"

Adam had never been an indecisive person, so when presented with a choice, he randomly chose the left path. There was no particular reason for this.

He walked along the corridor, which eventually led to a single wooden door. It was unlocked. He opened it, stepped inside, and shut the door behind him.

Click.

Adam heard the sound of the door locking and clicked his tongue. In that same moment, the room he found himself in, a square room with nothing but the skeletal remains of people, lit up with a bright glow. A chandelier hung overhead, rusted and dull, but glowing with an eerie luminescence. The skeletons rattled. Their bodies shook. Just like in the previous room, the bones in this room came together and formed numerous [undead skeletons].

"Well…" Adam sighed. "I guess I was getting a little bored."

With nary a thought for his own safety, Adam allowed instincts to take over and charged toward the first [undead skeleton]. He activated [slash] and sliced into the enemy one, two, four, eight times.

-137; MISS; -137; -137; MISS; -275; MISS; -137!

He grinned when he saw that one of his [slash] attacks was a critical hit. Skipping back, he avoided the return swing from the [undead skeleton] and struck again with [slash] several more times. Every time he struck the enemy, its body would rattle and chips of bone would fly off. He could feel the way his sword resisted cutting into the enemy. His hands actually grew a little numb from the attacks. If he was a normal human, attacking these level 10 enemies at his level might have actually hurt him!

-137; -137; MISS; MISS; -137; MISS; -137; -137!

Like the last time Adam fought against [undead skeletons], he used blitzkrieg tactics, hitting the enemy hard and fast before retreating to avoid being surrounded. He continued this until, one by one, the skeletons were all destroyed.

Ding!

[You have defeated 20 [undead skeletons]! Items dropped: [unknown key] and 2,000 gold coins. +2,500 experience points!]

With the additional +2,500 experience points, Adam needed +6,560 more to reach level 8. He wanted to complain to whoever made this game. No other game he played required such a ridiculous amount of experience points to reach the next level at the beginning of the game.

Before he could begin really grumbling, he noticed something at the back wall of the room. It was a chest. There was nothing particularly special about this chest. He could tell from the way it was rusted over that it was old. Who knew how long it had been here for.

He took out the [unknown key] that one of the skeletons had dropped. Could this key unlock this chest? There was only one way to find out.

He walked up to the chest, knelt before it, and shoved the key into the lock, turning it once and smiling when he heard a soft clicking sound. The chest opened with ease. Glancing inside, Adam was surprised to find what seemed like fairly decent armor and leggings inside. The armor was a lot brighter than the somewhat dull armor he was wearing right now. Likewise, the leggings were made of black leather instead of simple wool.

Item Name: Enchanted Steel Armor	Item Type: Armor	Grade: Medium	Use requirements: Can be equipped by Warriors level 5 and above.	Description: An enchanted steel chest plate. Grants increased defense.	Abilities: Defense+25; +5% resistance to slashing, blunt, and piercing damage
Item Name: Enchanted Leggings	Item Type: Armor	Grade: Medium	Use requirements: can be equipped by players of any class level 5 and above.	Description: Leggings that were enchanted by an unknown mage. Grants increased defense and speed.	Abilities: Physical Defense+10; Movement+5

These items were a lot better than his previous equipment, so Adam had no issue discarding his leggings and chest plate in exchange for this new stuff. He quickly equipped them, which increased both his Physical Defense and Movement a little bit. The most significant boost was, of course, from the chest plate. Not only did it give him a +25 on defense, but it also gave him an increased resistance to various types of physical damage.

Curious to know how this affected his stats now, he pulled up his stat screen.

Name: Adam	Class: Warrior	Lvl: 7	SP: 0 AP: 5	Experience: 3,080/9,600
Strength: +55	Constitution: +5	Dexterity: +5	Intelligence: +5	Speed: +6
Physical Attack: +110	Health: 110/110	Hit-rate: 15%	MP: 60/60	Movement: +11
	Physical Defense: +35 Magic Defense:+5	Dodge-rate: ???	Magic Attack: +5	

Resistance:	Blunt: 5% Slashing: 5% Piercing: 5%

Adam immediately noticed the new addition to his status screen, which displayed what he was resistant to. It looked like this was only something that would appear if he had resistance to something. Interesting.

The door behind him had unlocked after Adam defeated the [undead skeletons]. He walked back down the corridor and took the passage he had ignored the last time. This corridor was even longer than the previous one, and when he finally reached the end, what he discovered was not a door but a staircase.

"I guess there's no choice but to travel down," he said.

The stairs did not seem at all stable, but Adam walked carefully to avoid falling or potentially breaking the stairs. Actually, he wondered if these stairs even *could* break. He didn't want to test out whether they were breakable or not, so he decided not to do anything potentially dangerous.

Reaching the bottom of the stairs revealed nothing out of the ordinary. A stone floor and walls greeted him. There was only one door leading out, and since that was the case, he went over, opened the door, and walked through. He didn't know what he expected to find, but another corridor was… probably very close.

He sighed and began walking.

Adam did not get far before a terrified male shriek filled the air. His instincts kicked in and Adam bolted down the corridor, reaching the end in record time. There was no doorway this time. All he found was a large archway that looked like it had been made from the skeletal remains of people unfortunate enough to be killed here.

The shriek came again. It was followed by sobs.

"Please… please don't… don't kill me… I promise not to come this way again. Never again. Let me go… please…"

Adam did not know who was talking or who the person was talking to. It sounded like someone had been captured and was pleading with his captor. Could it be Trader Wilkins' missing son?

As he peered around the corner of the archway, he found an odd scene like something from a fantasy story. The room on the other side looked like an ancient magician's laboratory, a place where they concocted potions and performed various magical experiments. That aesthetic was ruined by all the old-school torture devices. There was a stone table with straps, numerous bloody tools sitting on it, and an iron maiden situated against one corner of the room. He even saw a wooden horse, another torture device used to inflict pain using the subject's own weight by keeping their legs open, tied with ropes from above, and lowering them onto the wedge-shaped object. It was a pretty brutal method of torture.

There were also two bookshelves, but they seemed to have items other than books. Adam wrinkled his nose when he noticed an eyeball floating in a jar filled with green liquid sitting on the second to last shelf.

In the very center of this room were two objects that caused a thrill to run down his spine.

The first and most intimidating object in the room was not an object at all, but a large figure dressed in a ragged black cloak. Adam could not see that many defining features about this creature. The only thing he saw beyond the cloak was its hands. It did not possess any flesh, blood, or muscles. Its hands were entirely white bone. This cloaked figure was not a human, but a skeleton at least two feet taller than him.

It was a level 15 2-star [necromancer].

Beside the [necromancer] was a small cage hanging from the ceiling, and inside of the cage was a plain-looking young man with brown hair, brown eyes, and the clothes of a villager. When Adam looked up the information on him, he saw that this was Trader Wilkins' missing son.

The son had been kidnapped by a [necromancer].

A 2-star enemy.

He wondered if a 2-star was more powerful than a 1-star.

Adam froze for a moment as he realized how vast the level difference between him and this creature was, but then he snapped out of his daze and took the [scan scroll] from his pouch. He ignored the terrified wails of Trader Wilkins' son and unfurled the scroll while still hidden behind the archway. Once it was unfurled, the scroll began glowing with a soft white light. Then it broke apart. In that moment, all the information on the [necromancer] was revealed by a window.

Name: Necro-mancer	Descrip-tion: A creature born from darkness and resent-ment. Necro-mancers are undead skeletons who have existed for at least one thousand years and gained a form of sentience. Every necro-	Class: 2-star	Lvl: 15	Health: 30,000/30,000 MP: 5,000/5,000

	mancer was a powerful mage in their previous life as a human. Now in death, they wish to continue their experiments and defile the world's natural order.			
Physical Attack: +90	Constitution: +100	Dexterity: +50	Intelligence: +500	Speed: +20
Turn Undead: Turns a corpse into an Undead MP cost: 10 MP Cooldown time: 10 seconds.	Black Miasma: The Necromancer releases a powerful miasma that deals +10 damage every 5 seconds and has a 10% chance of causing the poison status effect to anybody who inhales it. MP cost: 25 MP Cooldown time: 5 seconds	Deathly Stare: The necromancer's stare is deadly. When it uses Deathly Stare, any player who looks it in the eyes has a 25% chance of dying instantly. MP cost: 1,000 MP Limits: Only activates when necromancer is at	Rend: This is the necromancer's most frequent attack. It uses its sharp nails to rend flesh from the body. MP cost: 15 MP Cooldown time: 0 seconds.	

		30% HP. Can only use once per battle.		

It looked to Adam like this monster was bad news. He was only at level 7 right now, so this creature was 14 levels above him. What's more, its HP was ridiculous. +30,000? Supposing Adam hit this creature every time without a single miss, he would still deal at most -137 points of damage. How many times would he need to attack this thing before it died?

At the same time, Adam hated admitting defeat before a battle even began. He could already feel his blood boiling as he realized what an overwhelming challenge this fight would be. He wanted to fight this creature. It had been so long since Adam had faced such a powerful challenger that he'd almost forgotten what this feeling was like.

A grin appeared on his face.

Bursting into the room, Adam leapt onto the nearby table and launched himself off it and toward the [necromancer]. It must have sensed him. The [necromancer] turned around just as Adam activated the [thrust] skill, shoving his sword forward and striking the necromancer in the face!

-500!

Ah?

Adam was a little shocked when he saw the number, but he realized he must have gotten a lucky critical hit. Maybe it's face was also a weak point? If that was the case, then striking its face constantly would yield better results than if he just attacked its body.

The [necromancer] did not make any sound outside of clattering bones when it turned to face Adam completely. It raised a hand. Adam leapt back and began moving away as black mist sprayed from the voluminous sleeve of its cloak. That must be the miasma. He ran around the creature, avoiding the miasma, waited for the black fog to disperse, and attacked it from behind with [slash] several times.

-137; -137; -137; MISS!

Adam backed off once again. This time, the [necromancer] spun around and swung its hand out to attack him. This must have been the [rend] skill he read about from the information revealed by the [scan scroll]. He jumped back and landed several feet away from the monster, which was no longer paying attention to the man in the cage after Adam pulled its agro.

Sadly, the man in the cage had noticed Adam.

"Hey! You! Are you here to save me?! Please help! I don't want to die!"

"Can't you see that's what I'm trying to do right now! Don't talk! It's distracting!"

"Don't worry, bro! I'll be quiet! I won't say a word! You won't even hear a peep from me! Just get me out of here!"

"Didn't you just say I wouldn't hear a peep out of you?! Shut up!"

Adam hopped back several more feet as miasma billowed from the [necromancer]. This [black miasma] skill it used seemed to have a range of about five feet, which wasn't far, but it made up for that by spreading out in all directions to surround the [necromancer]. It was an area of effect, or AOE, skill. That meant for as long as it was active, Adam couldn't get close. All he could do was wait for the miasma to disperse before attacking again.

Once the miasma dispersed, Adam darted forward, avoided his enemy's [rend] skill by lowering his body to dodge, and then coming up with a [thrust] that impaled the [necromancer] through the ribcage.

-175!

He backed away and ducked to avoid another [rend], then moved behind the [necromancer] and attacked several times with [slash].

-137; -137; MISS; MISS; MISS; -137; MISS; MISS; -137; MISS!

The [black miasma] came out of the [necromancer] again. Adam backed away quickly to avoid being hit by that insipid poison, then repeated his previous attacks. He continued this process, slowly whittling away at the [necromancer's] health, but while his tactics were doing their job, Adam himself began to feel the mental strain of attacking this thing for so long.

Virtual reality video games had become increasingly popular ever since the armistice was signed after World War III, but there were also many advocates against gaming. Their concerns were that playing VR games for too long caused a serious strain on the mind. There were many studies that showed people who played for too long without logging off suffered from severe mental stress, which was stress caused by staying in an alert state of mind for too long.

While this theory of theirs was disproven, it was true that focusing for long periods of time on a single activity could indeed cause undue stress of the mind.

Adam could no longer tell how long he had spent playing this session, nor how long he'd been fighting the [necromancer], but it felt to him like days had passed. What's more, he had only dealt -10,000 points worth of damage. This damn monster still had +20,000 HP left!

Gritting his teeth, Adam closed in again, avoided the monster's [rend], and attacked it from behind. If it followed its normal pattern, then it would launch [black miasma] at him.

It did not follow its normal pattern. Adam stared wide-eyed when he saw a bony hand coming for him! He raised his sword out of instinct to block, but the attack struck him anyway, lifting him off his feet and sending him flying.

-45!

"Gaah!"

This was the first time Adam had been struck in *Age of Gods*, and while the pain he felt now was nothing compared to the pain he'd been through while being trained as an assassin, that did not mean it didn't hurt. He was shocked by how much it hurt. It felt so real! And the surprise at feeling actual pain while inside of a video game was enough to send a jolt racing through his body.

As Adam lay there on the ground, the [necromancer] looming over him, he wondered if he could really defeat this thing. He had the utmost confidence in his own abilities, but he also knew his limits. This [necromancer] was at level 15. That was 8 levels higher than him. What's more, his mind was beginning to fritz like an overheating computer. His brain felt like it was melting out his ears. He could feel his mind shutting down to protect him from the accumulated stress.

However, just as he thought about giving up, something warm and damp appeared on his forehead.

Fayte said goodbye to Susan and logged off *Age of Gods*. She blinked several times upon seeing the familiar sight of her bedroom ceiling, then sat up in bed and stretched her hands into the air. Her muscles felt a little tight, like she'd been sleeping for several hours, but they didn't feel bad.

"It looks like it's time for dinner," Fayte murmured as she glanced at a clock hanging on her wall. It read 6:00pm. Her stomach was letting her know it needed sustenance. She was very glad no one else was present in the room. While she might not care about what people thought of her, even she did not want others hearing the incredibly un-feminine sound of her stomach gurgling.

After straightening her wrinkled clothes, Fayte headed into the kitchen and thought about what to make. She didn't have much in the fridge. There was some leftover chicken, a variety of fruits and vegetables, and that was about it. She would need to do some grocery shopping soon.

Fortunately, there was boxed pasta in the cupboard, so she decided to make some pasta. She boiled water, added the noodles, and put in a pinch of salt. She didn't have any sauce, but she made do with olive oil, butter, and shredded Parmesan cheese.

Since she had used the entire box and figured Adam must also be hungry, she made an extra plate for him. She set both plates on the coffee table and traveled to his bedroom.

"Adam, are you up? I have dinner ready," she said, knocking on the door. There was no answer. She knocked again. "Adam? Are you in there?"

Her lips slipped into a frown when he didn't answer a second time. Feeling concerned, she debated whether it was worth invading his privacy to satisfy her concern before ultimately unlocking the door and stepping inside. If he was fine, she could always apologize, but she would never forgive herself if something happened to him while he and his lover were living with her.

"Adam?" she asked, coming up to the bed.

The person she'd come to see was still lying on the bed, on his back. His eyes were closed like he was sleeping, but the expression on his face, the furrowed brows and pained grimace, told her that he was not having a pleasant time. If she didn't know better, she would have said he was experiencing a nightmare. She assumed he was in the game and doing something that required all of his concentration.

A soft glow brought her attention to his neck. The *Age of Gods* system was lit up with symbols that she didn't recognize traversing the entire device. She wondered if those symbols were for aesthetic reasons, though she couldn't see much point in them.

"Just how long has he been playing?" she asked before noticing the sweat drenching his face, neck, and shirt.

Adam suddenly released a pained groan. Panic raced through her, but she calmed down and quickly decided on what to do. She went into the nearest bathroom—the one used by Adam and Aris—grabbed a washcloth, dampened it with water, and came back into the bedroom. She sat on the bed and used the cloth to wipe away the sweat from his face and neck. She hesitated for another moment before lifting the shirt to wipe the sweat from his chest and stomach as well.

Fayte felt her breath hitch when she saw the chiseled six-pack abdominals and well-defined pectorals. She wasn't the kind of girl who went crazy over boys with muscles. She wouldn't even call herself particularly boy-crazy. At the same time, while it wasn't something she drooled over, that did not mean she didn't appreciate a man who kept himself in great shape. Adam had the most defined torso she'd ever seen. Even underwear models lacked his exquisite physique.

Feeling the heat rising to her cheeks, she wiped away the sweat from his chest and stomach; she only felt a little guilty for secretly enjoying the feeling of his muscles against her hands. Once she was done, she noticed there was more sweat on his face. She wiped that away too.

"I don't know what you are doing in there, but do not give up," Fayte said softly, though she knew he couldn't hear her. "Whatever you are doing, please do not give up. I believe in you."

***

Adam could not figure out what this feeling was, but it was pleasant and cool. It felt like… like that time he'd been taking a bath and Aris had come in offering to wash his back. When had that been again? Back then, he'd been treating her like a little sister instead of a lover. She couldn't have been older than twelve or thirteen-years-old at the time, which would have made him… fourteen or fifteen. He didn't know for sure since Adam had no idea how old he was.

"Don't give up…"

Adam blinked when a voice reached him, telling him not to give up, encouraging him. The voice sounded familiar, but he could not place it. He shook his head. The voice, whoever it was, whether it was an illusion or something else, inspired him to keep fighting.

The [necromancer] was above him and using [rend] once more, but Adam rolled away before the attack could hit. The hand struck the ground. Sparks flew as bone struck stone. The [necromancer] jerked back, recoiling and off balance. Adam used that chance, leaping onto the table and launching himself at his foe.

[Thrust]!

-500!

Once more he struck the creature in the face. His attack dealt plenty of damage and even knocked the [necromancer] off balance, which Adam took advantage of upon landing on the ground. He activated [slash] once more and began attacking with renewed zeal.

-137; -137; MISS; -137; MISS; MISS; -137; MISS!

Before the [necromancer] could recover, Adam retreated just in time to avoid the [black miasma] attack. He watched as the black, mist-like gas covered the area around the [necromancer], his eyes narrowed. He only had +55 HP left and no potions that could heal him, but so what? That wasn't going to stop him!

Adam continued to fiercely battle against the [necromancer]. Even though this was just a game, he thought he could feel his skin becoming slick with sweat and his breathing growing heavy. The exhaustion of his mind was also still an ever present problem. He might be determined to win, but he was still running on nothing but pure determination and grit. Regardless of whether he wanted to or not, his mind would eventually shut down.

But he was determined to kill this blasted thing before that happened!

-500; -137; -137; -137; MISS; -137!

His teeth were peeled back as he snarled at the [necromancer] like it was his most hated enemy. Indeed, at this moment, he had never wanted to defeat a video game enemy more than he did right now. He was going to win and reap whatever rewards were to be had for killing this monster!

-137; -137; -137; MISS; MISS; -137!

Adam licked his lips as he retreated from the [black miasma] attack. His shoulders heaved as he struggled to breathe. He blinked several times to keep his vision from fading, but dammit, there were black spots appearing in front of his eyes now! He knew that was a bad sign.

The [necromancer's] health was now down to +10,000. Once it reached 9,000 HP, it would use [deathly stare], which had a 25% chance of instantly killing him. If possible, he would prefer not to let this creature use that, but he didn't have any attacks that could cause more than -500 damage to this thing.

What should he do?

In desperation, Adam cast his glance around the room. There were tables, bookshelves, the cage which Trader Wilkins' son was trapped in, the iron maiden sitting in the corner, and that was about it. Would any of these assist him?

A sudden thought ran through his mind as he stared at the bookshelves. His idea would never work if this was a normal game, but *Age of Gods* seemed abnormally real so far. Surely these bookshelves were not fixed in place, right? It was worth a shot!

Adam didn't attack when [black miasma] dispersed and instead raced over to the nearest bookshelf. He channeled energy into his legs and leapt over twenty feet into the air, landed on top of the bookshelf, and crouched down, glaring at the [necromancer]. His enemy's red eyes flashed with malevolence as it stalked toward him. The sound of its skeletal feet striking the floor created a staccato rhythm that was mismatched to his rapidly beating heart. He tried to slow his heart rate down as he waited, and waited, and waited, until the [necromancer] was just a foot away from him and reaching out with its bony hand.

Now!

His actions swift and decisive, Adam pressed his feet against the bookshelf, his back against the wall, and pushed. A loud creak echoed from the bookshelf. Then, to his immense pleasure, the bookshelf tipped over. He leapt off it as the bookshelf fell and landed square on the [necromancer].

-1,500!

A grin appeared on his face as his outrageous idea worked. Not only did it work, but it had dealt -1,500 damage, and it had knocked the [necromancer] onto its back!

Adam landed on the floor and viciously attacked the [necromancer] with [slash] and [thrust] continuously. Whenever the cooldown time on [thrust] wore off, he would use it, and then he would go back to using [slash]. Not only did he not stop attacking, but he attacked the [necromancer]'s head instead of its body.

-500; -500; -600; -500; -500!

The monster's health had been at +9,500 after he smashed the bookshelf on it, but now it was steadily decreasing. +9,000. +8,500. +7,900. +7,400. +6,900. +6,300. Adam didn't stop attacking the [necromancer] even after it pushed the bookshelf off its body and began climbing back onto its feet. By the time it stood up, his enemy's HP had been reduced to +400!

Gritting his teeth, Adam raced toward the wall, ran up it, and kicked off it in order to launch into the air. The [necromancer] turned to face him, its eyes flashing red as it prepared to use [deathly stare], but then Adam swung his sword and activated [slash] just before it could use its ultimate attack.

-500!

Adam landed on the ground with a harsh thud, his body finally giving out. He tumbled across the floor and landed on his side. Behind him, the [necromancer] remained standing in place for several seconds before its skeletal body broke into dozens of pieces and scattered across the floor.

Ding!

[You have defeated the 2-star enemy [necromancer]! Items dropped: [rusty key], [Staff of Darkness], and [Cloak of Despair]. +10,000 experience points! +1,000 ability points!]

Ding!

[You have leveled up! You are now at level 8! +10 HP! +10 MP! +5 SP!]

Ding!

[Thanks to your efforts and determination, you have acquired a new skill! [Blood Sacrifice] is a skill born from your determination and unwillingness to give up in the face of an overwhelmingly powerful enemy. This skill is unique to you and allows you to increase the amount of damage you do for 10 seconds in exchange for half of your HP. This is a self-sacrificial skill gained after fighting against a hopeless situation and succeeding! Congratulations!]

Ding!

[Warning: We have detected abnormal fluctuations in your mental state that coincide with extreme stress caused by overusing the mind. You will now be logged out of Age of Gods. Furthermore, you will not be able to log in for at least 24 hours. Please remember to play safely.]

A series of announcements and warnings appeared on a screen in front of Adam, but he was far too tired to do more than cast them a cursory glance. He shut his eyes and released an exhausted sigh. What he wouldn't give for a few hours of sleep right now...

BLOOD SACRIFICE

When Adam opened his eyes, he was no longer in *Age of Gods*. He stared at the white ceiling above his head. His mind felt like it was wading through sludge, and he needed a moment to regain a sense of clarity. It had been a long time since Adam had stressed his mind to the point where it shut down like that.

As he lay there on the bed, something on his right shifted, causing him to turn his head and stare in surprise at the beautiful and gentle face resting on the mattress not a foot from him. It was Fayte. He did not know what she was doing in his bedroom, but she was sitting on the floor with her feet tucked underneath her bottom and her head resting on the mattress. Only after he got over his shock did he feel the towel that had been placed on his forehead.

He removed the towel and stared at it. Now that he was thinking about it, while he'd been fighting against the [necromancer], he had felt something wet and cool on his face and chest. Could it be that she had been wiping the sweat off his body? Also, there had been that voice he'd heard during the battle. Had the one speaking those encouraging words to him been her?

Adam closed his eyes as a small space inside of his heart seemed to swell with powerful emotions.

Because he didn't think Fayte would be comfortable lying with half her body on the ground like that, Adam carried the woman into the living room and laid her down on the couch. He glanced at the clock and discovered that it was well after midnight. He started playing *Age of Gods* early the previous morning, which meant he had been playing for at least twelve or fourteen hours straight.

That was pretty insane even for him.

His stomach rumbled and reminded him that he had not eaten anything since breakfast. He went into the kitchen and searched through the fridge. There was a plate of pasta wrapped in saran wrap. The pasta didn't have any sauce, but he noticed the cheese and spices giving it some extra color. It looked like Fayte had cooked him dinner, but he'd never woken up, so she must have left it in the fridge.

Adam grabbed the plate and a fork, walked into the living room, and sat down on the empty side of the couch. The couch was shaped like a large L. Fayte took up one side as she lay there, soundly sleeping, while he took the other. He quietly ate his meal, occasionally glancing at Fayte. When he finished, he placed both the plate and fork in the dishwasher before heading back into the living room and looking at Fayte.

"What am I going to do with you?" he asked himself.

He'd brought her with him because he figured she'd wake up and would panic if she noticed he was missing, but now it seemed like she was deep asleep. She must have worried herself into exhaustion. After scratching the back of his head and thinking about it, Adam lifted the woman like a princess and carried her into her own bedroom.

Fayte's bedroom was fairly barren. There were no pictures, no posters, or anything to denote the resident's personality. That made sense. She did not have the money to spend on niceties because her father had disowned her, but even if she did have money, he thought a more spartan appearance suited this woman. Fayte was not the kind of person who frugally spent money on things she didn't need.

Only her bed was nice. It was a king-sized bed shaped like a circle, with a canopy over head, soft curtains that were semi-translucent descending around it, and a mattress so soft it felt like sitting on a cloud. He thought the bed was made from some type of hyperelastic polymer. The light blue sheets looked basic, but they were made from an incredible fabric that was light but absorbed heat. It would keep someone hot during the winter and cool during the summer.

Once he tucked Fayte into bed, Adam wandered into the room where Aris was currently sleeping. He glanced at the monitor showing how much of the Mortems Disease had been destroyed and was pleasantly surprised to see nearly a third of it was gone. That was much faster than he expected. This gave him hope that she would be cured sooner than later.

"Hey, Aris," Adam said as he sat down on the chair next to her cryobed. "You seem to be doing a lot better. I have high hopes that it won't be long before you're completely healed. Once that happens, you can join me in *Age of Gods*. I'm sure you'll have a great time. You always enjoyed it when we played console games together."

Adam spoke with Aris about everything that happened in the game, from getting the quest to find Trader Wilkins' missing son to fighting against a 2-star [necromancer]. He also talked about the skewed game mechanics.

"The level up system is ridiculous," he complained. "Every time you level up, the amount of experience points you need to reach the next level is double what it was before. By the time players reach level ten, they will have to gain hundreds of thousands of experience points to reach the next level. It's like the creator was trying his hardest to make things as difficult for us as possible."

Adam couldn't even begin to fathom what sort of maniac had created *Age of Gods*. The game was the most realistic virtual reality world he had ever seen. He even still had all five of his senses, which should have been impossible to affect with the world's current level of technology. Sight and sound were one thing. Touch, taste, and smell were another thing entirely.

"Honestly, the only person I believe who has technology advanced enough to do something like this is Lucifer, but he disappeared years ago... and you don't even know who that is anyway."

As he was talking to Aris, the door to the room opened and Fayte walked in. He turned his head to look at her as she stepped forward with a gentle smile.

"When I woke up in my bed, I thought it might be because you put me there," she said as she pulled up an extra chair and sat down beside him.

"I didn't think you would be very comfortable sleeping on the floor like that." He shrugged. "You might have woken up with a bad crick in your neck."

Fayte did not say anything in response to his words. She glanced at the monitor that showed how much of Aris's body was infected by Mortems Disease. Her eyes widened a little.

"It seems Aris is healing a lot faster than I thought she would."

"You think so too? I remember you telling me it would take two or three months for her to heal, but it's only been a little over one week and her Mortems Disease is a third gone."

Fayte once again went silent, but this time, it seemed like she was thinking about something heavy. Her brows were furrowed, and there was a glimmer in her eyes as she stared at the sleeping Aris. Adam found himself loathe to interrupt her.

"I actually... have a question regarding Aris's Mortems Disease. I hope you won't mind answering me."

She looked at him as though asking whether or not it was okay to ask what she wanted. Adam ran a hand through his hair, thought about it, then smiled.

"You have given me hope where before I had nothing. Ask whatever you want. So long as it isn't something I'm uncomfortable talking about, I will do my best to answer you."

His words seemed to make her happy. At least, that was the sense he got from her smile.

"I've studied a lot about Mortems Disease after finding my grandfather's device. It is common knowledge that this disease is not only considered incurable by many, but that anyone who contracts this disease dies around six months afterward. The longest a person has ever lived while having Mortems Disease is seven months, according to the medical records I've read." Fayte bit her lower lip, glanced at Aris, and spoke in a soft voice. "And yet, from what you have told me, Aris contracted Mortems Disease around three years ago. I have to ask… how did she survive for so long? Is it because of that medicine you gave her?"

Adam didn't say anything for the longest time. This was a secret he'd possessed and never shared with anyone, so he was hesitant to tell even this woman, who had given him the light of hope when he was lost in the darkness.

"I'm sorry," she said with a smile. "Maybe that was too personal a question. You can forget I ever asked…"

"The drink I had Aris take isn't really medicine," Adam finally said with a sigh, interrupting her.

"It… it's not?" Fayte blinked.

"Well, I suppose you could call it medicine, but it's not your typical medicine, that's for sure."

"Then… what is it?"

In response to her question, Adam went over to the counter where several pieces of medical equipment rested, grabbed a scalpel, and came back. He sat down, lifted his hand, and pressed the scalpel to his palm.

Fayte shrieked as he sliced his hand open from one side of his palm to the other. Blood welled up over the cut. Droplets flowed down his hand and splashed against the tiled floor. Seeing this made the woman go pale. She shot to her feet in a panic.

"W-what are you doing?!"

"Watch," Adam said calmly.

"How can I watch this?! You're… you… you… what?"

Adam's hand had a lot of blood welling up on his palm, but it wasn't as much as Fayte would have expected it. Using a small napkin, Adam wiped the blood away, further revealing an astonishing sight to Fayte. The woman could not help but gasp in shock as she stared at the cut, which was slowly closing up.

"It… it's healing!" Fayte realized what this meant and her eyes widened further. "You're an esper!"

Espers were people who had psychic abilities. In the past, people used to think espers were witches and would burn them at the stake, but in the late 1700s, the United States had created the first ever Esper Corps during the war for independence against Britain. That was when espers became widely acknowledged. Of course, they didn't gain true acceptance until recently. Now espers were not only a part of society, but powerful families like the Plecnexia Family employed them as bodyguards.

"It normally heals faster than this," Adam admitted. "I'm slowing the process down so you can see it more clearly." Fayte did not say anything, nor did she look away from his palm, now completely healed without even a scar to show for what happened. "I have an incredibly powerful healing factor. It's not even healing so much as a form of high-speed regeneration. Not only am I able to heal from physical wounds like cuts, stabs, and even regenerate missing limbs, but whenever my body contracts a disease, the cells will automatically kill the diseased cells and new ones will be regenerated using my body's internal energy. It will be as if I never got sick in the first place. I'm immune to all forms of injury and disease. Of course, this includes an immunity to Mortems Disease."

Fayte was an intelligent woman. Adam knew she had figured out what the "medicine" Aris took was the moment he told her about his regeneration.

"So… that medicine… it's…"

Adam nodded. "My blood is incredibly potent, so it's impossible to inject it or give it to her as is. Her body would break down even faster than someone with Mortems Disease. I dilute a single drop of my blood several tens of thousand of times with water and have her drink it. Thanks to that, I have been able to keep her alive for these three years… though I couldn't cure her. Perhaps if I used a stronger dose, but that would kill her more readily than the disease."

He studied the woman with sharp eyes that were like a hawk's. There was no way Fayte couldn't know about what she could do if she obtained his blood. The first part of the bet she made with Levon could easily be solved if she got even a liter of his blood, diluted it hundreds of thousands of times, and sold it to a large-scale pharmaceutical company. While his blood wasn't a cure, letting someone with Mortems Disease live for another three years was already a huge achievement.

Never mind earning 10.5 billion dollars. If Fayte sold his diluted blood, she could make several trillion dollars.

He expected her to ask if he'd be willing to part with some blood. If she asked it of him, even though it was technically not part of their agreement, he would do it.

However, contrary to his expectations, Fayte did not ask him to share his blood.

"You really do love Aris so much. She was very lucky to have met you."

Adam was once again stunned when the woman sent him that wonderful and gentle smile. It was like the thought of using his blood for her own purpose hadn't even occurred to her. Did she not realize what she could accomplish if she sold his blood on the market? She'd be a trillionaire!

"I think I'm going to head back to bed." Fayte stood up. "Do you mind if I have your in-game name? I can add you to my friend's list and call you whenever I need to."

"My in-game name is Adam," he said.

Fayte looked like she wasn't sure what to make of that. "Adam? Just Adam?"

"Yes." Adam gave Fayte an amused smile. "Is that a problem?"

"Well… no. I guess not." Fayte blushed. "I just thought you would use a different name, an alias or something… but I guess you did use your real name back then too. A-anyway, have a good night."

"You too. Sleep well."

Fayte soon left the room, and Adam spent a few more minutes with Aris before he headed back to his room. He was unable to log onto *Age of Gods* because the system had restricted his access after forcefully logging him off. He would spend an entire twenty-four hours lounging around like a couch potato. Fayte teased him about it when she saw him in the kitchen early the next morning.

✷✷✷

Adam did not expect to find himself lying on the ground when he logged into *Age of Gods*. He also didn't expect the floor to be wet. A grimace twisted his face as he felt the wetness from the floor seeping into his pants, making it feel like he'd pissed himself. Damn it. Whoever created this game was seriously twisted! There was no need to make it this realistic!

"Ah! You're back!" a voice suddenly shouted. "Hey! Hey! Can you get me out of here?! I would really like to go home!"

Adam sat up and looked at the cage. The young man who had been about to become that [necromancer's] latest experiment was still inside of the cage that was dangling from the ceiling. He was grasping the bars and staring at Adam with a pleading expression.

Adam ignored him for a moment and instead looked at the items he'd acquired from the [necromancer].

Item Name: Staff of Darkness	Item Type: Magic Staff	Grade: High	Use require-ments: Can be equipped by a	Descrip-tion: The Staff of Darkness is an old staff	Abilities: MP+200; Intelli-gence+2 0; has a 10%

			Mage level 10 and above	made from a weathered branch of the Life Tree that has been soaked in blood. It is very good for mages who use dark magic and necromancy.	chance of casting blindness; has a 1% chance of instantly killing enemy Innate Skill: Raise Undead - allows user to make a corpse rise from the grave with all of its previous level and skills. Can work on player and non-player characters
Item Name: Cloak of Despair	Item Type: Clothing	Grade: High	Use requirements: can be equipped by a Mage level 10 and above.	Description: A cloak worn by a powerful necromancer. Grants any	Abilities: Defense+ 20; Magic Defense+ 40; 10% resistance to dark magic

				Mage who wears it a powerful defense against dark magic.	and the status effects poison, blindness, and silence
Item Name: Rusty Key	Item Type: Key	Grade: None	Use requirements: Anyone can use it.	Description: A rusty key you picked up from the body of the [necromancer].	Abilities: Unlocks cage

Both the [Staff of Darkness] and [Cloak of Despair] were great items, but it was too bad he couldn't use them. He could at least save them in case Fayte or Susan were of the Mage class.

Adam stored the equipment into his item pouch, which was almost at full capacity now, and only then did he turn to look at the man who was locked in the cage.

The man who was now screaming at him.

"Hey! Are you listening?! Hey! I want to get out of here!"

"Shut up! I can hear you just fine!" Adam snarled at the man who didn't know how to keep his fat trap shut. What was with these NPCs? Why were they so realistically annoying?!

"Ah… sorry," the man stammered. "You weren't paying attention, so I thought…"

"It doesn't matter what you thought. Are you Trader Wilkins' son?"

"Y-yes, that's right." The man perked up. "Did my father send you?"

"He did ask me to find you." Adam walked up to the cage and unlocked it with the [rusty key]. He opened the door and allowed the man to step out. "Do you think you can find your own way out? I'm going to continue exploring this dungeon, and I don't know what sort of dangerous situations I will run into. There might be monsters even more powerful than that [necromancer]."

"Yeah. Don't worry about me," Trader Wilkins' son said. Now that Adam wasn't focused on the [necromancer], he could see that the man's name was Josh Wilkins. His class was listed as "Trader Wilkins' son," which Adam thought was a dumb class name. "Anyway, thank you for rescuing me. I will be sure to let my father know about how you saved me from that [necromancer]. He's sure to give you a great reward."

Josh Wilkins left, not through either of the two doors, but through a secret passage that had appeared where the old bookshelf was. The bookshelf was still toppled over, and the [necromancer] corpse was still there. Adam wondered how he had missed that secret passage. Could it also take him to the surface?

It probably could, but Adam wasn't interested in traveling up to the surface just yet.

The first thing Adam did was allocate all of his new status points and ability points into his stats and skills. He maxed out [slash] and [thrust], both of which had a max level of 5. He also upgraded his new skill [Blood Sacrifice] to level 2.

Name:	Class: War-	Lvl: 8	SP: 0	Experience:

Adam	rior		AP: 200	3,480/19,200
Strength: +55	Constitution: +10	Dexterity: +5	Intelligence: +5	Speed: +6
Physical Attack: +150	Health: 120/120	Hit-rate: 6%	MP: 60/60	Movement: +11
	Physical Defense: +45 Magic Defense: +10	Dodge-Rate: ???	Magic Attack: +5	

Resistance:	Blunt: 5% Slashing: 5% Piercing: 5%

Skill Name: Slash	Description: A basic skill where the player swings his or her weapon and attacks the enemy!	Current lvl: 5 MAXED	Ability: Causes 150% damage to enemy if it hits	MP consumption: 1	Cooldown time: 0 seconds
Skill Name: Thrust	Description: A basic skill where the player thrusts his or her weapon at the enemy!	Current lvl: 5 MAXED	Ability: Causes 200% damage with a 5% chance at getting a critical hit.	MP Consumption: 5	Cooldown time: 1 second

Skill Name: Blood Sacrifice	Description: By sacrificing 50% of your blood (HP), you gain the ability to increase your physical attack power for a limited period of time! This skill is unique to the player Adam.	Current lvl: 2 AP needed to reach next lvl: 1,000	Ability: Raises Attack Power by 200% for 30 seconds. Disregards skill cooldown times, allowing the user to attack with every skill without limit	MP consumption: 20 Special limit: Drops HP by half	Cooldown time: 30 seconds

Once he finished upgrading his stats and skills, Adam went over to the door at the far end. It was unlocked now. He stepped through and found himself in another hallway. Unlike the previous one, this one didn't branch out at all and led to a room that looked remarkably similar to the first one at the beginning of this cave. It was practically empty, save for the single figure standing in the center of the room.

The figure standing in the very center of the room was another undead, but this one was listed as a level 12 1-star [skeleton knight]. It was decked out in ancient armor, held a broadsword in one hand and a shield in the other, and possessed the same glowing red eyes as other undead monsters. It was three levels below the [necromancer], but that was still four levels higher than him.

The moment he appeared and the door locked behind him, the knight removed its sword from its sheath and attacked. Adam did not hesitate to leap out of the way. He dodged the first downward swing, which struck the ground and caused sparks to fly, and then attacked with a combination of [thrust] and [slash]. Sparks flew off the [skeleton knight] when his sword struck its armor.

-200; -160; -160; MISS; MISS; MISS; MISS; -160!

Adam backed away and tried to shake the numbness from his arm. It seemed the armor this [skeleton knight] was wearing gave it a powerful defense. He didn't know what was going on, but he could feel the sturdiness of this enemy, which had a solid enough defense that it felt like he had been smacking his arm against a rock wall. The amount of damage he inflicted was also less than he normally did.

Fortunately, fighting against this enemy was easier than fighting the [necromancer]. Adam might not be a swordsman by nature, but he had a lot of experience with close quarters combat.

Dodging the [skeleton knight] was very easy. Its swings were predictable. Adam was able to determine how it would attack based on how its shoulder joints twitched. The only thing he needed to watch out for was that shield. It occasionally used the shield to bash him, but he was still able to determine when it was coming and move out of the way.

-160; -160; -160; -160!

Adam saw the small numbers constantly appearing over the [skeleton knight] and could not help but feel angry. Triple digits might sound like great attack power to others, but this enemy was at level 12 and of the 1-star. That meant it had to possess a lot of HP. If he kept going at the pace he was going right now, it might take another five or eight hours before he defeated it.

[Blood Sacrifice!]

Because he wanted to defeat this creature faster, Adam did not hesitate to activate his new skill. Activating this skill felt odd. A strange heat surged through Adam's body, his skin turned blistering red like blood was coming to the fore of his flesh, and the muscles and veins in his arms all bulged. Not only did the visuals look unusual, but he could feel the strength flowing beneath the surface of his skin.

His health also dropped to +60, but he wouldn't let that concern him.

With his new skill activated, Adam charged in.

-320; -320; -320; -320; -320!

The amount of damage he dealt now was much better. With just five attacks, Adam delivered -1,600 points worth of damage. He didn't know how much HP this [skeleton knight] had, but he was certain it wouldn't take too long to defeat it now.

Like this, Adam attacked the [skeleton knight] with everything he had, constantly whittling away at its HP. When [Blood Sacrifice] entered a cooldown time, Adam dealt with this creature normally, dodging that massive sword it swung while delivering regular [slash] and [thrust] attacks.

-160; MISS; MISS; MISS; MISS; -160; MISS!

He did have to be careful. His HP kept getting chopped in half every time he used the [Blood Sacrifice] skill, bringing his HP from +120 to +60 to +30 to +15. His HP eventually dropped so low he was no longer able to use [Blood Sacrifice]… which sucked and made him realize he should have invested some money in potions. Once he left this place, Adam promised himself he would buy a crapton of [health potions] from Trader Wilkins.

While he eventually became unable to use [Blood Sacrifice], Adam still defeated the [skeleton knight] a lot more quickly than he had the [necromancer]. After the final [slash] struck the monster's chest plate, it toppled backwards, its bones scattering across the floor.

Ding!

[You defeated the 1-star enemy [skeleton knight]! Items dropped: [greater broadsword] and [steel greaves]. +5,000 experience points! +500 ability points!]

Adam gained quite a bit from killing the [skeleton knight], but he didn't level up again, and he didn't gain enough AP to upgrade [Blood Sacrifice]. That was the only skill he had left that he hadn't maxed out.

Instead of focusing on the experience and ability points, Adam checked out the two new items he had gained.

Item Name: Greater Broadsword	Item Type: Sword	Grade: Medium	Use require-ments: Can be equipped by a	Descrip-tion: A powerful sword that re-quires	Abilities: Physical Attack+100; Speed-5; 5%

			Warrior level 5 and above	two hands to wield, or a unique skill/ class to wield one-handed.	chance of caus-ing bleed status af-fect
Item Name: Steel Greaves	Item Type: Ar-mor	Grade: Medium	Use re-quire-ments: can be equipped by a Warrior level 5 and above	Descrip-tion: Well-made greaves that pro-tect a warrior's feet.	Abilities: Physical Defense+ 40

Both items were fairly good, so he decided to equip them. This brought his Physical Attack up to +245, though the cost for equipping this massive weapon was that his speed dropped to +6 again. His Physical Defense also increased to +70, which he had no problems with.

Now equipped with even better equipment, Adam left this chamber and traveled into the next room. It was just a stairwell. He walked down the round stairs for what felt like hours, eventually reaching the end, and entered another door. It was a hallway. Great. Another hallway. He wondered how many of these he would have to travel through before reaching the end. Finally, after who knew how far he had walked, Adam reached a door.

The moment Adam placed his hand on the rusted doorknob, a powerful shock traveled through his body, going from his tailbone all the way to his brain. He trembled for a moment as his instincts screamed at him not to enter this room. Something dangerous was on the other side. He didn't know what, but Adam had always been one to trust his instincts.

However, it wasn't like he could go back. The doors leading to the surface were all locked. All he could do was press on.

Adam opened the door and entered.

Far longer than it was wide, the room on the other side was brightly lit with torches, but he could not see to the end because a massive obstruction was blocking the way. It lay on the ground, a four-legged monster composed entirely of bones. A long neck with spiny ridges held aloft a skeletal muzzle with a distinctly reptilian appearance. It had a wide body, large legs, and was probably six times bigger than he was tall. As he stared at it, the creature lifted its head and glared at him with glowing red eyes.

The information above it told him it was a level 20 3-star [skeleton dragon].

Adam cursed. "Motherfucker! Who the hell designed this game?! FromSoftware?!"

THE RUSTED SPEAR

A dam died. There was simply no way he could defeat a level 20 3-star [skeleton dragon] at level 8 when his health had already been depleted to just +15 HP. After being swatted by the claws of the [skeleton dragon], everything went black and he woke up inside of the cathedral where players first appear.

The first thing Adam did was check his stats. He wanted to make sure his level hadn't dropped by being killed. Some games liked to impose penalties on players for dying. He'd even heard of one game where dying meant you had to start from the very beginning again.

Fortunately, it didn't look like his level had dropped here. That was good.

After confirming his level was unchanged, Adam left the cathedral and walked onto the dirt road. The Mayor looked up from what he was doing and caught sight of Adam. He blinked at the mask covering Adam's face. Then a wry smile appeared on his own face.

"You died?" he asked.

Adam rubbed the back of his head. "Yeah…"

"I've heard you otherworlders can be revived at cathedrals you've been to, and I have already seen a number of you come back." The mayor's expression of admiration made Adam a little uncomfortable. "I have always been envious of how you otherworlders can return from the dead. However, you should avoid dying at all costs. While you won't lose anything if you die in the Village of Beginnings, you will drop by at least one level every time you die after leaving. Please try not to be too reckless once you leave this island."

"Do not worry," Adam said with a nod. "I plan to be much more careful from now on."

After talking with the mayor, Adam went back toward the potion shop, a scowl marring his face. He'd been defeated by that blasted dragon, but there was no way he could leave things like this, no way he would be satisfied with his loss. Adam was out for blood now. He wanted revenge.

"Welcome," Trader Wilkins said when Adam entered the store. "What can I get for you—ah! It's you! Thank you so much for saving my son! I can never thank you enough for what you have done! This is not nearly enough to adequately compensate you, but please take these as payment."

Ding!

[You have received x10 [health potion], x10 [mana potion] and 300 gold coins from Trader Wilkins.]

Ding!

[You have completed the quest: [Find Trader Wilkins' missing son]! +5,000 experience points! +50 SP!]

It looked like coming back might have been a good thing after all. Adam didn't hesitate to put the +45 status points he had earned into his Strength stat, though he put at least +5 in his Constitution stat. Right now his health was abysmally low. One hit from that dragon would be enough to kill him. He didn't think adding some points to his Constitution would change anything right now, but even a little bit might help.

Plus more HP meant he could activate [Blood Sacrifice] more often.

His Physical Attack had increased a lot thanks to the additional +45 status points. Combined with the +100 Physical Attack offered by the Greater Broadsword attached to his back and the damage he dealt now would be much higher than before.

With that out of the way, Adam took a quick glance at the items he'd been given as a reward.

Item Name: Health Potion	Item Type: Potion	Grade: Low	Use requirements: None	Description: A low-grade health potion.	Abilities: Restores +100 health
Item Name: Mana Potion	Item Type: Potion	Grade: Low	Use requirements: None	Description: A low-grade mana potion.	Abilities: restores +50 mana

The potions weren't bad and restored a decent amount of HP and MP, but he didn't think he had enough. Adam sold all of the items currently clogging up his item pouch, then used all of the money on him and bought another fifty [health potions] and fifty [mana potions]. They were 10 gold coins a piece.

Now with sixty health potions and mana potions, Adam left the Village of Beginnings and began journeying back toward the cave that he had discovered. He already knew the way thanks to his perfect memory. All he needed to do was follow the route he took to get there previously.

He reached the forest in record time. As he began walking through the forest, Adam received a call. A window opened before him. The person calling him was named Changing_Fate.

He accepted the call.

"Fayte?"

"Adam! Hey!" Fayte said from the other end. She sounded excited. "I'm glad I was able to get through to you on the first try. I didn't know if you were one of those gamers who played solo on everything and never accepted calls."

"Well… to be fair to you, I normally don't accept calls, but I am making an exception for you, so feel free to call me whenever you want."

"That… actually makes me feel pretty special." While Adam could not see it, he could somehow tell from her voice that Fayte was blushing. That made him smile. Just a bit. "Anyway, Susan and I were lucky enough to wind up in the same Village of Beginnings, so we've been grinding together. We're both at level 5 right now."

"What is the average level of players right now?"

"Level 5. Some of the bigger players like the guild masters for the larger guilds and players who are listed on the International Power Rankings have already reached level 6, but there aren't many of them. The Power Rankings only consist of the top ten best players in the world." Fayte paused after answering him. "Can I ask what level you're at?"

"Level 8."

"WHAT?!"

Adam almost flinched when Fayte shouted in his ear. He didn't necessarily blame the woman for her response, but did she have to blow out his eardrum?

"How did you get your level up so quickly?! This leveling system is absolutely atrocious! After reaching level 5, the experience points required to level up becomes nearly five thousand."

Of course, Adam understood Fayte's shock. Leveling up in this game was really hard because the experience points required doubled after each level. This meant grinding was truly ridiculous in this game. Just to reach level 6 from level 5 required someone to spend at least ten to twenty hours grinding, which was why most people were still stuck at level 5. A level 7 [wolf] only yielded about +100 experience points at that level. That wasn't even mentioning how experience points were shared between members when people formed a party to grind. If two people at level 5 formed a party and killed a level 7 [wolf], they would only get +50 experience points each.

"I've been doing solo quests instead of grinding," Adam admitted. "There are a number of quests you can do in the Village of Beginnings that earn more experience points than if you just grind your level. The quest I'm currently doing right now also made me face several very powerful bosses that granted me even more experience points."

"So that's how you did it. All of us have just been grinding. I don't think the idea of taking on quests occurred to anyone since it's considered a rule of thumb that quests at the beginning of the game never yield good experience points. Maybe Susan and I should be doing that instead?"

"It certainly couldn't hurt."

Adam spoke with Fayte for the entire half an hour it took him to reach the underground passage. Once he reached the familiar cave entrance, he said goodbye and traveled inside.

None of the previous monsters he had defeated appeared to greet him, which meant it was a straight shot down to the dungeon room where the [skeleton dragon] was located. He was grateful. While those monsters yielded some good experience points, he really just wanted to destroy that blasted dragon.

Adam finally reached the room where the [skeleton dragon] was located and went inside. The door sealed shut behind him, meaning he was now trapped, but Adam had no intention of running. His blood was boiling. After suffering that humiliating defeat at this creature's hands—claws—he would not feel satisfied until he defeated it!

The [skeleton dragon] glared at him with its red eyes. It opened its mouth and unleashed a mighty roar as it once more tried to swipe at him with its clawed hand.

Adam ran forward and ducked low, letting the clawed hand pass over his head before he skipped back onto his feet and continued running. He reached the [skeleton dragon's] legs and struck them with a [thrust] and a [slash].

-600; -480!

He twitched. His current Physical Attack stat was at +300 thanks to the SP he gained from his last quest, which meant [thrust] did -600 and [slash] did around -480 damage, but he felt like that wasn't nearly enough. This enemy probably had even more health than the [necromancer] did.

He needed to find a way to deal even more damage.

With a snarl, he continued attacking it with [slash] and [thrust], but all of his attacks did the same damage, which was definitely not enough to put even a scratch in this creature's health. The [necromancer] had +30,000 health, and this thing was a dragon. A level 20 3-star [skeleton dragon]! Just how much health would this monster have? Adam wagered it was at least +50,000 if not higher.

As he attacked the [skeleton dragon's] legs, his massive foe tried to stomp on him. Adam ran away and leapt into the air as the stomp shook the ground. He thought he felt a shockwave push against him, but he couldn't be sure as he landed on the ground and kept running—only for the dragon's massive tail to come in swinging!

Adam cursed as he leapt sideways and barely avoided the tail, which slammed into the ground and shook the floor, walls, and ceiling. A crack spread along the ground where the tail smashed into it. He stumbled backwards but fortunately wasn't stunned. That would have been bad. However, the tail was now resting on the ground, which gave Adam an idea.

He leapt onto the tail and used the ridges of the [skeleton dragon's] spine to race up its body. As he did, he attacked numerous times with [slash] to search for a weak point.

-480; -480; - 480; -480; -480; -1,500!

Adam's eyes widened when he saw the -1,500 floating over the [skeleton dragon's] head. This attack had come after he landed on the creature's neck and began attacking its skull. It seemed the head was one of its weak points.

A grin appeared on his face.

[Blood Sacrifice]!

With [Blood Sacrifice] activated, Adam sacrificed half of his HP in exchange for two times more Physical Attack power for 30 seconds. He took an HP potion really quick and began attacking the [skeleton dragon] with numerous strikes to the head. Because he was on top of it, the [skeleton dragon] could not fight back since it didn't have any limbs that reached this far.

-1,500; MISS; -1,500; MISS; MISS; -1,500!

While Adam tried to stay on the [skeleton dragon] for as long as possible, the creature eventually wised up and began rampaging around like a bucking bronco. Adam was unable to maintain his balance. When the creature slammed its own body into a wall, he was flung off and landed on the ground, hitting hard and rolling for several yards.

-60!

"Ouch…"

While striking the ground like that hadn't hurt as much as it would have in real life, it was still very painful. His health gauge also dropped to +80, so he needed to take another health potion. Wincing as he stood to his feet, Adam stared warily at the [skeleton dragon] as it came stomping back over to him, its red eyes glowing with malevolence.

Actually, its red eyes did seem to be glowing a bit more than usual.

Adam's eyes widened.

"Shit! Shit, shit, shit! FUCK!"

Adam bolted like a frightened rabbit, and he was just in time to avoid the red beams fired from the eyes of the [skeleton dragon]. The beams tore into the stone floor, gouging two one meter wide trenches out of the ground. Not only did both trenches extend all the way to the wall, but they were a molten orange as if the beams were heat rays that could melt through stone.

An undead dragon was firing laser beams from its eyes?! What kind of crappy game was this?!

Because he didn't want to get caught by that attack again, Adam raced toward the [skeleton dragon] to once more engage it in close-quarters-combat. His goal was to climb onto its back and attack its head again. Of course, saying he was going to do that and actually doing it were two completely different matters. The [skeleton dragon] also seemed to understand what he wanted to do because it was doing everything in its power to stop him.

The [skeleton dragon] stomped onto the ground, unleashing earthquakes that caused a [stun] effect. Adam found himself stunned several times. He was lucky, however, because the [stun] effect didn't seem to work on him very well. It only lasted for a split second before coming undone. He didn't know what was going on, but he wasn't going to look a gift horse in the mouth.

-480; -480; MISS; MISS; MISS; MISS; -480; MISS; -480!

Adam had to dance around its legs constantly and wait for the [skeleton dragon] to use its tail, but it seemed reluctant to do that after what happened last time. It kept trying to squash him with its feet. He wondered about this monster's learning algorithm. It seemed far smarter than most enemies from other games, who all had very predictable attack patterns.

As the minutes wore on and the monster was unable to successfully attack him, it grew impatient and once more tried to swipe at him with its tail. That tail probably did the most damage out of all its limbs.

Adam timed the tail's movements and jumped two seconds before it reached him. He landed on the tail, grabbed the ridges to keep himself from being flung off, and waited for the tail to stop moving before he scrambled up it. He leapt onto the massive and bony back, ran up its body, and activated [Blood Sacrifice] before attacking its head again.

-1,500; -1,500; -1,500; -1,500; -1,500!

Now that he had worked out a strategy, the battle became a lot easier. Adam would race up the [skeleton dragon], attack its head after activating [Blood Sacrifice], and jump back down before it could throw him off. He would dodge the laser eye attack, go back in, and repeat the process.

Maybe it was a result of how realistic this game was, but the damage inflicted to the surroundings by the laser beams didn't disappear. They remained where they were. What's more, the trenches were still hot. Adam made the mistake of going near one, which caused his health to drop and pain to lance through his mind as the heat from the damage burned him. He needed to be careful and avoid those areas until the molten stone cooled.

This thing had a lot of HP. Adam had been counting the amount of damage he'd done, and he had already inflicted over -50,000 points worth of damage. To make matters worse, he didn't actually know how much health this thing possessed. It didn't have a health bar to show him. He only had those little numbers appearing above its head to let him know how much damage he was inflicting on it.

-1,500; MISS; MISS; -1,500; MISS; MISS; -6,000!

Adam smiled as he landed a critical strike on the [skeleton dragon]. His [Blood Sacrifice] skill deactivated after running its course, and Adam leapt off before it could buck him off and cause him damage. He consumed a health potion and a mana potion while in midair, landed on the ground, and kept running. He turned his head to look at the [skeleton dragon]. If it followed its normal procedure, then this would be the moment where it fired lasers from its eyes.

Except it didn't.

Adam became stunned when the [skeleton dragon] opened its mouth and unleashed a subsonic roar that created soundwaves. He didn't question how a creature without vocal cords could do that. Games like this didn't always have mechanics that made sense.

The moment those soundwaves struck him, he was forced onto his hands and knees as a scream tore from his mouth. Even though he only felt fifteen percent of the pain he would have experienced in real life, the pain of having a monster roaring into his ears like this was not something that could be underestimated. It felt like his eardrums were about to explode! He pressed his hands against his ears and tried to block out the sound to no avail.

The roar did eventually stop, but Adam could not move for several seconds. He felt sick, his ears were ringing, and his head was killing him. The pounding inside his skull made Adam feel like his brains were being squeezed out of his eyeballs. He just wanted to curl into a ball and squeeze his eyes shut. However, as a shadow appeared above his head, Adam realized there was no way he could curl into a ball right now.

He rolled across the ground as a clawed foot slammed into the floor where he'd been standing. Another chunk of stone was gouged out as the dragon foot crushed it. Adam grimaced when he saw cracks extending from underneath the foot. The amount of damage being done to the surrounding environment was ridiculous. What made him feel worse was that he hadn't been able to leave even a single scratch on this place. Maybe that meant you had to have a certain level of Strength or a high Physical Attack stat to damage an environment like this.

Adam once more began dodging its attacks and waited for it to use its tail. He waited for a long time. After what felt like an eternity, the [skeleton dragon] swept its tail at Adam, who leapt onto it one more time and began attacking upon activating [Blood Sacrifice].

MISS; -1,500; MISS; MISS; -1,500; -1,500; 1,500!

After inflicting another -6,000 points worth of damage, Adam was getting ready to leap off the [skeleton dragon] when he noticed that it was no longer moving. He glanced at the now-still body, then looked into the skeleton's eyes, which were growing dim.

Ding!

[You have defeated the 3-star enemy [skeleton dragon]. Items dropped: [dragon bone cuirass], [dragon bone gauntlets], and [dragon bone greaves]! +20,000 experience points! +4,000 Ability Points!]

Ding!

[Congratulations! You have leveled up! You are now at level 9! +30 HP! +10 MP! +5 SP!]

Ding!

[Congratulations! You are the first person to kill a 3-star enemy! Because you are the first player in the history of Age of Gods to kill a 3-star enemy, you have earned +10,000 Reputation. Reputation does not affect your status in any way. However, it does affect your standing among player and non-player characters. You may also be granted special privileges from non-player characters. Creating a guild also requires at least +100,000 Reputation. The more Reputation you have accumulated, the more easily recognizable you will be to shop owners and other important figures. Some shop owners may even give you discounts, and quest holders might be more

willing to give you higher level quests that are considered too dan-gerous for a player at your current level.]

Adam had never heard of Reputation being used in a game be-fore, but he guessed it was something like a person's fame. By ac-quiring a lot of Reputation, your acclaim within the game increased, which could offer some benefits like getting higher level quests from NPCs, creating a guild, getting store discounts, etc..

[Because you are the first person to acquire Reputation, you have been placed at the top of the Reputation Chart. You are cur-rently the only one on the Reputation Chart. An international an-nouncement will be made regarding your new status, along with your accomplishment of killing a 3-star enemy.]

Announcements like this were fairly common in virtual reality games. Because a lot of people, even people who didn't play video games, cared about who were the top ranking players, system wide announcements to list a specific player's accolades happened fre-quently, especially near the beginning of a game. He'd had several similar announcements made about him back when he was demol-ishing the top ranked players three years ago.

Ding!

[We have an international announcement to make! As of 3:32am Eastern Standard Time, the player Adam defeated the first 3-star enemy in the game and has earned +10,000 Reputation. Players with +100,000 Reputation are able to form Guilds. Please keep this in mind as you progress. We hope that all of you will strive your hardest to earn fame, fortune, and glory as you traverse the ancient and mysterious Forgotten Realm.]

It was a pretty standard announcement, all things considered. Adam didn't particularly care about his name being announced to the entire world. Actually, this fit rather well with his goals in the game. The more famous he was, the higher his reputation would become, and the better his chances would be of helping Fayte win her bet with Levon.

Since he had leveled up, Adam placed all of his SP into his Strength stat, upgraded [Blood Sacrifice] with the 4,000 AP he gained from killing the [skeleton dragon], and checked his stats to see how they looked now.

Name: Adam	Class: Warrior	Lvl: 9	SP: 0 AP: 1,200	Experience: 14,280/38,400 Reputation: +10,000
Strength: +105	Constitution: +15	Dexterity: +5	Intelligence: +5	Speed: +1
Physical Attack: +310	Health: 170/170	Hit-rate: 6%	MP: 60/60	Movement: +6
	Physical Defense: +95 Magic Defense: +15	Dodge-Rate: ???	Magic Attack: +5	

Resistance:	Blunt: 5% Slashing: 5% Piercing: 5%

Skill Name: Slash	Description: A basic skill where the	Current lvl: 5 MAXED	Ability: Causes 150% damage to enemy if it hits	MP consumption: 1	Cooldown time: 0 seconds

	player swings his or her weapon and attacks the enemy!				
Skill Name: Thrust	Description: A basic skill where the player thrusts his or her weapon at the enemy!	Current lvl: 5 MAXED	Ability: Causes 200% damage with a 5% chance at getting a critical hit	MP Consumption: 5	Cooldown time: 1 second
Skill Name: Blood Sacrifice	Description: By sacrificing 50% of your blood (HP), you have gained the ability to increase your physical attack power for a limited period of time! This skill is unique to the player Adam.	Current lvl: 4 AP needed to reach reach next lvl: 4,000	Ability: Causes Attack Power to rise 250% for 60 seconds Disregards skill cooldown times, allowing the user to attack with every skill without limit	MP consumption: 30 Special limit: Drops HP by half	Cooldown time: 30 seconds

He licked the inside of his cheek as he looked over his stats, nodded once in satisfaction, and switched to his item screen so he could check out the items that his enemy had dropped.

Item Name: Dragon Bone Cuirass	Item Type: Armor	Grade: 1-star	Use requirements: Can be equipped by Warriors level 10 and above	Description: This chest plate was made from the bones of a dragon. Not only does it look stylish, but it offers solid defensive abilities and resistance to elemental damage.	Abilities: Constitution+100 ; Physical Defense+200; +25% resistance to fire, earth, wind, lightning, water, and darkness damage
Item Name: Dragon Bone Gauntlets	Item Type: Armor	Grade: 1-star	Use requirements: Can be equipped by Warriors level 10 and above	Description: These gauntlets are made from the bones of a dragon. Not only are they stylish, but they offer solid defensive abilities and re-	Abilities: Constitution+10; Physical Defense+50; +10% resistance to fire, earth, wind, lightning, water, and darkness damage

				sistance to elemental damage.	
Item Name: Dragon Bone Greaves	Item Type: Armor	Grade: 1-star	Use requirements: Can be equipped by Warriors level 10 and above.	Description: Greaves made from the bones of a dragon. They are not only stylish, they also offer solid defense and resistance against elemental damage.	Abilities: Constitution+25; Physical Defense+75; +15% resistance to fire, earth, wind, lightning, water, and darkness damage.

It looked like he couldn't equip any of this armor until he reached level 10. That sucked, but he was confident he would reach level 10 soon.

Since he couldn't equip his new armor, Adam continued on. At the very back of the chamber was a small archway that led into another room. This room was much smaller than the one he battled the [skeleton dragon] in. The stone walls, floor, and ribbed ceiling weren't much to look at. However, there was a small platform in the center of this room, and embedded into a pedestal in the very center of the platform was…

"A rusty spear?"

Adam spoke out loud as he walked up to what was, indeed, an old and worn-looking spear. It was long at somewhere around seven feet in length, making it over a foot taller than him. The shaft was made of a worn out metal that glinted with a dull glimmer in the light. What's more, the spear point was equally dull and shaped like a simple triangle.

"I wonder what this thing is doing here," he muttered.

Given that this spear was located in a room immediately after a [skeletal dragon], Adam could only assume the dragon was guarding this weapon, but it didn't seem to have any unique attributes. It didn't even look like it could be used.

With a curious frown, Adam wrapped his fingers around the shaft. It was pleasantly cool. He offered a slight grunt before, straining his muscles, he pulled the spear out of the pedestal.

Ding!

[Congratulations! The weapon [Rusted Spear] has recognized you as its master! You are now the sole owner of the [Rusted Spear]. It cannot be equipped by anyone else, you cannot throw it away, and because you are now its master, you can no longer use any weapons aside from the [Rusted Spear]!]

"… Huh?"

Adam stared blankly at the announcement screen, which seemed to be saying something really idiotic right now There was no way this rusted, ugly ass spear could be the only weapon he was able to use now, right? Right?!

In desperation, Adam checked the weapon he currently had equipped. He opened his equipment window and stared at what he saw with ever widening and horrified eyes. He wanted to rub his eyes to make sure he wasn't hallucinating, but he felt like if he did that, he would feel even worse when he realized this wasn't a nightmare. That it was real.

Item Name: Rusted Spear Level: 1 Experience points needed to level up: 0/5,000	Item Type: Spear	Grade: ? ???	Use requirements: Can only be equipped by Adam Cannot be thrown away, cannot be given away, and cannot be unequipped	Description: This unknown weapon was found by Adam. It has recognized him as its master and cannot be used by anyone else.	Abilities: Strength +10; Physical Attack+10 Special ability: Sentient Growth
Item Name: Steel Greaves	Item Type: Armor	Grade: Medium	Use requirements: can be equipped by a Warrior level 5 and above	Description: Well-made greaves that protect a warrior's feet.	Abilities: Physical Defense+ 40
Item Name: Enchanted Steel Armor	Item Type: Armor	Grade: Medium	Use requirements: Can be equipped by Warriors level 5 and	Description: An enchanted steel chest plate. Grants increased	Abilities: Physical Defense+ 25; +5% resistance to slashing, blunt, and

			above	defense.	piercing damage

The [Rusted Spear] was the weapon now equipped. The [greater broadsword] he had equipped previously, which granted him +100 to his Physical Attack, was nowhere to be seen. Not only did this drop his entire Physical Attack stat by +100, but the [Rusted Spear] only offered a +10 to his Strength and Physical Attack, meaning instead of having a Physical Attack of +310 like he should have, he only had +240 because of his recent level up.

"No, no, no, no!" Adam shouted. "What the hell?! I don't want to equip this thing! Unequip! Unequip!"

Adam tried to unequip the weapon in his hand, but no matter what he did, the [Rusted Spear] remained locked firmly in his equipped status screen. Not even throwing it away worked. Every time he tried to throw it away, he would get an error message that said this course of action was impossible.

In other words, this piece of shit weapon was here to stay.

TITANIA

Adam did not know what to think. He now had a weapon that couldn't be unequipped and was incomparably terrible compared to his previous equipment. He couldn't toss it, sell it, or trade it away. He was stuck with it, and because he was stuck with it, he could no longer equip any other weapon.

What kind of terrible in-game mechanic was this?!

Because he didn't know what to think, he decided to just stop thinking entirely. Adam glanced at the rusty spear in his hand one last time, and then looked at the door on the other end. He hoped it would lead out. With everything that had happened, he no longer had any desire to remain in this dungeon.

The door was unlocked. As he grasped the handle, an oddly cool and refreshing sensation came over him, startling Adam a great deal. He shoved his shock to the back of his mind and opened the door.

On the other side of the door was a room, and not just any room. A soft rug sat in the middle of the room, made from a fabric that looked incomparably soft and had nature-esque designs stitched into it. To his left was a dresser. On his right was a bed. Both the dresser and bed looked like they were made from expensive wood. The rosy hue of the wood went well with the rug on the floor and the tapestries hanging from the ceiling, which contained the silhouette of a woman with wings. Everything about this place screamed posh and luxurious. There was just one aspect about this place that made him blink twice.

Everything was about four or five times smaller than they should have been. It was like someone had placed all of these in a shrinking machine, or like it was a doll house made for a little girl to play with her dolls.

As he walked further into the room, turning his head curiously to look at everything, a soft groan made him snap his attention toward the bed. There was a lump underneath the covers. It was wiggling. As he moved closer, the lump shifted some more, the covers fell away, and Adam became stunned.

A beautiful girl sat up in bed, yawning as she stretched her hands above her head.

The first thing most people should have noticed about this girl was her otherworldly beauty. Her skin was a soft peach color, perfect and unblemished, pliant and tender. It made Adam want to reach out and pinch her cheeks. It gave her a youthful look that made it hard to judge her age. She had a face like an angel, with perfectly symmetrical features that could only be created inside of a video game. Her body's proportions were likewise impossible in real life. Large breast. A small waist. A perfect bust to hip ratio.

Even Fayte did not have a figure like this woman did.

The second thing people should have noticed was probably her clothes. They were light and airy. The greens of her dress was very earthy and looked subdued on her beautiful figure. A slit ran up one side, showing off an expansive amount of her gorgeous leg. There was an odd sheer material covering the clothes as well. It gave her outfit a silvery emerald color. She didn't have any shoes, so her small and cute bare feet were visible as she wiggled her adorably tiny toes.

The third thing people should have noticed were the wings on her back. While partially translucent, each wing was beautiful beyond compare and looked extremely fragile, like the lightest touch would cause them to shatter. He thought they were fake at first, but then they fluttered a little, releasing small motes of sparkling dust into the air.

Of course, all this was secondary to one other, one very simple and astonishing aspect of this otherworldly woman's appearance.

She was only about one foot tall.

She was small enough to stand on the palm of his hand.

"Muuuu… nyaaaaaa…"

The woman let out an adorable yawn as she lowered her hands and rubbed her eyes, then tucked a strand of hair behind her ear, revealing that her ear, while small like a human's, came to a point near the tips.

"Haaa. That was a nice nap," the woman said to herself. "For how long did I sleep, I wonder?"

The woman spoke with a smoky and regal voice. It reminded him of a character from a movie he once watched with Aris. The movie had been about a monarch, a queen, and the way this woman spoke was exactly like the queen in that movie.

When Adam saw this woman, saw those features, and glanced at those wings, only one word came to mind.

"Fairy…"

While the word was only whispered, it felt abnormally loud in this minuscule room. The fairy most definitely heard it. She became alert almost instantly, her head snapping in his direction.

Their eyes locked.

"You there, remove that mask," the fairy commanded.

Adam bristled and thought about telling her off. No one told him what to do. However, this was very likely a story event, which meant it would behoove him to do what she wanted.

For now.

He removed his mask.

"You are… a human?" The fairy's eyes narrowed as she studied him. "A very attractive human." After confirming for herself that he was attractive, she glanced at the rusty spear in his hand. Her eyes widened as a lovely smile lit up her face, stealing Adam's breath. "A very attractive human who has been recognized by the spear. Tell me, young human, were you sent here by the goddesses?"

"Uh… no. I don't believe so," Adam said.

The fairy's brow furrowed. "Not sent by the goddesses? Then how did you acquire that spear?"

He shrugged. "Your guess is as good as mine."

"How odd. I was told to wait for the goddesses' chosen, but you say they did not choose you? Could something have happened? Maybe you were chosen and don't realize it, or perhaps... Hmm..."

Adam remained silent as the fairy tilted her head down and stared at her feet. She wiggled her toes and bit her lower lip, mumbling something to herself. He waited for a full minute before impatience got the better of him.

"Who are you?" Adam asked.

"Hmph. If you are going to ask someone for their name, then is it not common courtesy to introduce yourself first?" asked the fairy as she floated off the bed, then set herself down on the very edge. She crossed her left leg over her right one. The slit on her dress shifted, allowing him to see even more of her magnificent leg. Her small toes wiggled a little with surprising dexterity as she began bouncing her leg like she had attention deficit disorder.

"Considering the circumstances of our meeting, I think it would be more appropriate for you to introduce yourself first. Actually, I feel like you should have been waiting for me and introduced yourself before going into an exposition about what the hell makes this spear so special, don't you? Isn't that how these things normally work?" asked Adam, unwilling to let himself fall into this cliche.

"Ha ha ha! What an interesting human! You have wit if nothing else." The fairy wiped a few mirthful tears from her eyes, then gazed at him with those sky blue irises that seemed to contain a depth even more vast than the endless sky. "Very well. I shall introduce myself first. My name is Titania. I am the quee—er, no, I am the guardian of the spear now in your hand."

Since this fairy had introduced herself, Adam felt it was only appropriate he returned the gesture. "I am Adam. I'm a player who came down here because I was asked to find someone's son."

"A player? What an odd title." Titania tilted her head as she considered him. Then she decided that what he called himself didn't matter because she dismissed her inquisitiveness a second later. "Well, no matter. You may not be the goddesses' chosen hero, but you have been recognized by the spear, which means I am now free to leave this place."

"Before you go, could you at least tell me what you know about this spear?" asked Adam.

"Go? Ah. You seem to be under some kind of misunderstanding, but, well... hmm... I guess it would be best to talk about this now rather than later, would it not?" Adam had no idea what this woman was going on about, but Titania didn't seem to notice his confusion as she nodded several times like she had come to a decision. "Okay. Listen well, human. That spear in your hand has gone by many names. The Holy Spear, the Hero Spear, the Scourge of the Land, the Devil's Weapon. This spear has a long history of both incredible virtue and indescribable violence. Many people have wielded it in the past, but none have ever mastered it."

Adam listened, but the more he heard, the more confused he felt. Was this spear evil, or was it good?

"Are you confused?" Titania smirked. "This spear is neither good nor evil, but those who have wielded it have been both good and evil. The last time this spear appeared in the hands of man, it was wielded by a mighty and terrifying human whose name has been lost to history. He was responsible for the death of more than fifteen percent of the Forgotten Realm's population. His reign of terror and destruction was so bad that not only was all record of him stricken from history, but the goddesses decided this spear was too powerful and sealed it away until someone worthy could come along."

"I… see…" Adam was not quite sure he believed a spear with these terrible stats could do something like what this woman described, but he was not going to argue. "And what makes this spear so special?"

Titania's smirk grew even more smug. Adam wished he could wipe that look off her beautiful face.

"Have you not noticed? Why don't you look at its stats?"

Adam sighed, but he did as she asked and checked the stats again.

Item Name: Rusted Spear Lvl: 1 Experience points needed to level up: 0/5,000	Item Type: Weapon	Grade: ? ???	Use requirements: Can only be equipped by Adam. Cannot be thrown away, cannot be given away, and cannot be un-equipped	Description: This unknown weapon was found by Adam. It has recognized him as its master and cannot be used by anyone else.	Abilities: Physical Attack+10; Strength +10 Special ability: Sentient Growth

<table>
<tr><td></td><td></td><td></td><td>.</td><td></td><td></td></tr>
</table>

He considered the stats for a moment. The grade was unknown, its history was unknown, and its stats were terrible. except...

"Sentient Growth..." Adam murmured before looking at Titania again. "Is it because of the spear's special ability?"

"That is correct," Titania confirmed as she finally flew off the bed and fluttered over to him. The way she floated made it look like she was walking on air. "This spear is the only weapon in the entire world that has the ability to grow more powerful alongside its wielder. As you grow stronger and level up, the spear will grow stronger and level up with you. Your strength and abilities will determine how this weapon will grow. Your actions will determine whether this spear will become a force of good or evil."

So this spear was actually some kind of super special item. It sounded like one of those unique, one of a kind items people could acquire by doing something no one else had ever done. Once the item was acquired by someone, it could never be acquired by anyone else. He'd heard of these kinds of items before, but Adam had never gotten one when playing virtual reality games before.

"Okay. So this spear is terrible now, but it has the potential to become unstoppable later on," Adam said at last.

"That is exactly it. I'm so glad you are quick to understand." Titania really did seem pleased by him. There was a wide smile on her face as she fluttered in the air in front of him.

"Well, I guess now that I have this spear and know what makes it special, there is nothing more for me to do here," he said at last. "Guess it's time to go."

"Indeed, let us be off," Titania said as she fluttered over to his shoulder and sat herself on it. She didn't weigh much, so he barely felt her on him, but her actions were enough to startle Adam.

"Er… us?" Adam asked, shooing the woman off his shoulder.

Titania huffed as she fluttered before his face, placed her hands on her hips, and glared at him. "Of course. Us. Did you think I would let you go off on your own? I am the Guardian of the Spear. It is my job to remain by its side and watch over it at all times. Just because you are its master does not mean my job has changed."

Well… this was an interesting predicament. On the one hand, he did not know if he wanted a pint-sized woman tagging along with him everywhere he went. On the other hand, she seemed to be very knowledgeable about this spear, and if *Age of Gods* was like other virtual reality games he had played, then she probably had a lot of worldly knowledge as well. Bringing along such a fount of knowledge would definitely help him understand more about this world.

"I guess… it wouldn't be bad having you tag along with me," Adam said at last, speaking slowly as he reluctantly decided to let this happen. He knew how this worked. Even if he said no, it would just lead to pointless arguing, and this woman would win in the end.

A woman's persistence was a frightening thing.

"Hmph. You say that like you had a choice," Titania said with a triumphant smirk.

Adam's smile became strained. "So… since we are going to be traveling companions, I have to ask… do you have any special abilities that can help me out, or…?"

"Are you asking me if I will be useful to you?" asked Titania with a dangerous smile. Adam nodded. "Hmph. I should have known that was your concern. You may rest easy. Once you see my stats, you will understand that having me by your side will give you an incomparable advantage over other people. Indeed, I believe you will become so smitten with me that you'll never want me to leave your side again."

What an incredibly arrogant woman.

"We'll see about that…" He sighed, then recalled exactly what she said. "Wait. How can I see your stats?"

"Like this," Titania said before a window appeared in front of him.

Ding!

[Titania would like to join your party. Will you let her? Yes or no?]

Adam frowned at the screen before slowly pressing the "yes" button. He was still a little reluctant about letting this woman join him, but he was also curious about her and her abilities.

Once he accepted her into his party, a new screen appeared. This one looked very similar to his status screen. The difference was that it did not contain his statistics, but Titania's instead.

Name: Tita-nia	Class: Guardian of the Spear	Lvl: 1	SP: 0 AP:0	Experience: 0/100
Strength:	Constitu-	Dexterity:	Intelli-	Speed: +50

+10	tion: +10	+10	gence: +100	
Physical Attack: +20	Health: 100/100	Hit-rate: 10%	MP: 1,000/1,000	Movement: +50
Comprehension: +10	Physical Defense: +10 Magic Defense: +30	Dodge-Rate: 10%	Magic Attack: +200	Luck: +1

Skill Name: Song of Refreshing Rain	Description: A song that can only be sung by Titania. This song is refreshing and lovely, like light spring rain. It has an incredible healing affect.	Current lvl: 1 AP needed to reach next lvl: 20	Ability: Indefinitely heals +10 HP every 5 seconds for as long as Titania is singing.	MP consumption: 50 MP per second	Cooldown time: 30 seconds
Skill Name: Song of Vigor	Description: A song that Titania sings to increase the strength of her companions. When sung, this song will	Current lvl: 1 AP needed to reach next level: 20	Ability: Raises the Physical Attack and Magic Attack of all allies by 200% for as long as she is singing.	MP Consumption: 50 MP per second	Cooldown time: 30 seconds

	increase the Physical Attack and Magic Attack of every companion in her party.				
Skill Name: Song of Valor	Description: A song that Titania sings to increase the defensive abilities of allies. Defense and Magical Defense will increase for as long as this song is being sung.	Current lvl: 1 AP Needed to reach next level: 20	Ability: 200% increase for Defense and Magical Defense stat of all Titania's party members. Increase lasts for as long as Titania is singing.	MP consumption: 50 MP per second	Cooldown time: 30 seconds
Skill Name: Scan	Description: Titania can scan any enemy regardless of level and send that information to all members of her	Current level: MAXED	Ability: Reveals an enemy's stats. Can only be used on one enemy at a time.	MP Consumption: 10	Cooldown time: 5 seconds

	party.				

Adam stared at her stats for a good minute. He felt like his eyes were bulging from their sockets. He simply could not believe this little fairy could have such amazing abilities. Each skill except for [Song of Refreshing Rain] was just a buff, but they were probably some of the most amazing buffs he had ever seen in a video game. They were only at level 1 right now, but each of them increased a specific group of stats by 200%.

He could only imagine how powerful these would be with each level increase.

"I can see why you would boast about your abilities," he said at last as he closed the window and looked at the very smug fairy. "Those are some really amazing abilities."

"Indeed, they are. I am glad you can recognize just how incredible I am." Titania's chest seemed to swell with pride… or maybe her chest was just swelling. Those things were, after all, really big for a woman of her ridiculously diminutive stature. "And this is just the tip of the spear. Due to some unfortunate circumstances, I am only at level 1. You may have already realized that because I'm not very tall right now. Many of my greater abilities are currently sealed. However, once I regain my former glory, I will become an even greater asset to you during your travels."

So this woman had more abilities that were sealed at some point in the distant past because her level had decreased? Yeah. Okay. He could accept that. It was a very in-game type of lore. This reminded him of how some antagonists that joined your protagonist in RPGs were always at a lower level than when you fought them.

"Well, now that you and I are a party, why don't we get out of here?" Adam suggested.

"A grand idea," Titania agreed. "I have been locked away in this dungeon for far too long. It would be nice to get outside and finally see the sun after three thousand years."

Adam ignored the "three thousand years" comment. He didn't want to think about how this beautiful fairy who looked like an odd combination of young woman and little girl was actually thousands of years older than him. Well, this was just a game, so she technically wasn't older than maybe a few days, but he wasn't about to say something like that.

Game or not, a woman's wrath was not something he wanted to deal with.

However, just as he and his new companion were about to travel toward the door on the far side, an announcement screen appeared before him.

Ding!

[Congratulations! You have completed the hidden quest: [Master of the Spear!] +5,000 experience points. +100 AP! +1,000 Reputation!]

Ding!

Congratulations! You have completed the hidden quest: [The Maiden Fairy!] +5,000 experience points! +100 AP! +500 Reputation!]

Ding!

[You now have a single member in your party. Party members can be both player and non-player characters. Some non-player characters may temporarily join your party when you go on specific quests. Titania is a permanent member of your party and cannot be removed except during special circumstances. Not even Titania can remove herself from your party.]

Titania made a face as she saw the screen appearing in front of Adam and read the contents. It seemed she did not know what to make of this new phenomenon either. Crossing her arms, she gave the screen a scowl.

"What in the name of the Sun Goddess is this thing?"

"You've never seen an announcement screen before?" asked Adam.

"Obviously not. Announcement screen? What is that? Why are there so many messages popping up? Is this an announcement from the goddess?"

"Don't know," Adam said. He wanted to say something else, but before he could, a loud noise pierced the atmosphere, causing Titania to shriek in surprise.

Ding!

[We have an international announcement to make! As of 5:19 am Eastern Standard Time, the player Adam became the first person to complete a hidden quest. He completed the hidden quests [Master of the Spear] and [The Maiden Fairy] and has earned +10,000 Reputation. In honor of being the first person to complete a hidden quest and completing two hidden quests at the same time, we are gifting Adam an extra +1,000 Ability Points. We hope these rewards

will motivate other players to try their hardest to earn fame, fortune, and glory in the mysterious Forgotten Realm.]

Adam waited until the announcement ended, then scratched his head. He guessed this was technically a good thing. He did just earn +10,000 experience points, which meant he only needed about +14,120 more to reach level 10. That was definitely a good thing. He also earned even more Reputation, which was also good, since it meant his reputation was increasing. Since he was helping Fayte with her bet, that was very good indeed, but at the same time, he felt like a large target was being painted on his back.

Well, he had been prepared for this to happen eventually. He just didn't expect it to happen so soon!

"What was with that speech?" asked Titania. "Was that a goddess speaking to the world? Since when did they do that? And why do I not recognize her voice?"

"Have you never heard these announcements before?" asked Adam.

"Would I ask about them if I heard them before?"

"I guess not."

"Then there is your answer. Now, tell me more about these 'announcements.'"

As Adam and Titania finally began moving, taking the door on the other side of the room, which led to a large staircase, Adam tried to explain what these announcements were to Titania. But no matter how hard he tried to explain it to her, the several thousand year old fairy just couldn't understand.

✳✳✳

His mask was back in place as he climbed ever higher. The staircase was a lot longer than even Adam suspected. It took nearly an hour to reach the top. That was enough to make him wonder how deep underground this dungeon went. He hadn't noticed it when he was traveling down, but now that he had nothing to do but climb stairs, he realized this dungeon was probably the equivalent to a ten or fifteen-story building.

"The sun! Finally! Sun Goddess be blessed!" Titania fluttered through the air as they entered the forest via a door embedded into a rock wall. She stretched her arms above her head and smiled as the sunlight peeking through the canopy of leaves warmed her face. "You never know how much you take something for granted until it is gone. I have missed the feeling of the sun on my face far more than I ever realized was possible."

While Adam was still pretty shell-shocked over everything he had learned and everything that happened while in that dungeon, he couldn't stop himself from smiling at the little fairy. Titania noticed this and coughed into her hand as she fluttered over to him. She sat down on his shoulder. Her weight was oddly comfortable, like his shoulder was just the place where she belonged.

"What is the plan now?" she asked.

"I need to reach level 10 before I can leave the Village of Beginnings," Adam explained. "So now we are going deeper into the forest, where there are higher level monsters for me to kill."

"I see. So you need experience points," Titania said with a nod. "Very well. I shall help you acquire the experience you need to level up. I also need to gain some experience points myself. It is utterly appalling that a woman of my stature is only at level 1."

"A woman of your stature, huh?" Adam muttered, glancing at the tiny female with an odd look.

Titania narrowed her eyes. "You were thinking something rude just now, were you not?"

He looked away. "Of course not."

"Do not think you can hide your thoughts from me! You were thinking about how short I am!" Titania crossed her arms and glared at him as Adam walked through the forest, her tiny feet bumping against his shoulder. "Do not let yourself be fooled by my current size. Before I was sealed away in that dungeon to become the Guardian of the Spear, I was even taller than you."

"Is that so…"

"You do not believe me?"

"Of course I do."

"Do not lie to me! If you are not lying, then lock me in the eyes when you say that! Do not look away from me!"

"It's kinda hard to look into your eyes when you're sitting on my shoulder like that."

Adam and Titania continued to bicker as they traveled ever deeper into the forest. It was odd, but the strangely non-antagonistic banter felt very familiar to him, like he'd done this all before. No, maybe rather than familiar, it would be more accurate to say it felt right. He felt like this odd relationship he had with the little fairy on his shoulder was something he should have.

While he was walking, an alert suddenly informed him that someone was calling. It was Fayte. She was the only person who could be calling him since she was the only person on his friend list.

"Fayte?"

"Adam!" Fayte suddenly shouted in surprise. "What is with all these announcements?! First person to defeat a 3-star enemy? First person to earn Reputation? First person to complete two hidden quests?! Just what exactly are you doing?!"

While the loud voice made Adam wince, he still managed to chuckle a little as he heard the woman's shocked exclamations. He kind of enjoyed surprising her.

"It's just like those announcements said. I accepted a quest to help someone find their missing son and ended up entering a dungeon, where I fought a 3-star [skeleton dragon] and completed two hidden quests. I'll tell you more about it when I log off and we meet in the real world. Oh! You might be pleased to know that I am also at level 9."

"You are?! That's great! Susan and I just reached level 6 not long ago."

"Is that the level most people are at?"

"I think so. The more important members of the larger guilds are at level 7 now, and I hear the Spear God is at level 8, but level 6 is the average."

Adam spoke with Fayte for a little while longer, but he eventually hung up because Titania was giving him an odd look.

"What was that about?" she asked.

"Sorry. I was talking to a woman called Fayte. She is… a friend," he decided at last. Yes, he could consider Fayte to be a friend after spending more than a week in her company. At the very least, he liked her enough to consider her one.

"I had not realized you knew telepathy," Titania muttered.

"Telepathy? You mean the player chat feature?" asked Adam.

"Player chat? What is that?"

"… Never mind."

Adam decided that explaining the concept of the player chat function to a non-player character was futile, so he did not bother. Titania huffed as he remained silent.

It took several minutes, but Adam finally came across an enemy. It looked like a wolf, but it was about three times larger than the standard wolf, had a horn on its head, and its bristling fur was a silvery blue instead of midnight black. Titania cast [scan] on it to reveal its stats.

Name: Storm Wolf	Description: A wolf that was struck by lightning but survived. Now it has the ability to manipulate lightning.	Class: 1-star	Lvl: 15	Health: 15,000/15,000 MP: 1,500/1,500
Physical Attack: +300	Constitution: +200	Dexterity: +100	Intelligence: +50	Speed: +250

Rend: A physical attack that deals incredible damage. Ability: Causes 200% damage to enemy if it hits. Has a 10% chance of causing bleed. MP consumption: 100 Cooldown time: 0 seconds	Storm Wolf Howl: The Storm Wolf unleashes a loud howl that stuns its opponent. Ability: Has a 25% chance of causing stun. MP Consumption: 150 Cooldown time: 30 seconds	Storm Blast: The Storm Wolf generates a large amount of lightning on the tip of its horn and launches it at its enemies. Ability: Causes 500-600 lightning damage to multiple opponents. Has a 50% chance of causing stun if it hits. MP Consumption: 1,000 Cooldown time: 60 seconds		

Adam could not stop himself from grinning as he saw the stats appear on a screen in front of his eyes. This would be so useful when battling enemies. Now he no longer needed to worry about not knowing what kind of attacks his opponent's could do or how much health they had. Knowing was half the battle, which meant he'd now half-won every battle he would ever find himself in.

… This would have been so useful when he was battling that stupid dragon.

"Shall I aid you in this battle?" asked Titania.

"Not yet. Hold back a bit," Adam said. "I would like to see how well I can wield this spear. It's been a very long time since I held one."

"Very well. I will merely watch and see how you do."

As Titania flew back a little, Adam advanced on the [storm wolf], which noticed his presence and began snarling. Since it saw him, there was no need to hold back. Adam activated [Blood Sacrifice] and raced forward to attack. The [storm wolf] clawed at him with a basic [rend] attack, but Adam slipped around its massive paw, spun the spear in his hand, and used [thrust] to impale the monster through its stomach, then swung his spear and activated [slash].

Bright damage marks appeared on its skin when his spear struck it.

-960; -768!

Adam frowned as he saw how little damage he was doing, but he now understood it was because his spear's level wasn't high enough. If he wanted this weapon to truly become formidable, he simply needed to raise its level.

Falling back into the style he had learned so long ago, Adam moved across the ground on the balls of his feet as though he was hopping around. The [storm wolf] attacked with a claw swipe to his face. He flitted around the attack like a rabbit. His enemy howled in frustration and swiped again, but he once more dodged, then switched stances, slamming his left foot against the ground before rushing forward and thrusting out his spear like it was the horn of a rhinoceros.

-960!

He changed stances once again. His movements became erratic and skittering like a spider walking around on eight legs. His attacks became fierce and poisonous, but not in the literal sense. They were deceptive, meant to slip around an enemy's guard and attack the weak points, though he couldn't figure out where this wolf's weak points were, so he just released a relentless barrage instead.

-768; -768; MISS; MISS; MISS!

Once more, Adam shifted stances, this time lunging forward like a serpent. His spear pierced the [storm wolf] through the nose, but the creature moved fast enough to avoid being completely stabbed through. His attack also missed. Adam was not bothered by that as he lunged again, his actions very much like those of a coiled snake springing forth.

-960!

The battle with the [storm wolf] continued, and Adam whittled away at its health while Titania watched from the sidelines, her arms crossed as she observed him with keen eyes. He had managed to reduce its HP to +1,000. However, just as he was getting prepared to finish it, something happened.

"Oh. My. God! It's a 1-star enemy!"

"Sweet! We finally found a 1-star enemy!"

"Hey! Who is that guy fighting it?"

"Don't know. I can't read his stats. He must have them hidden."

"Who the hell cares about that guy?! Let's kill this thing! Ha ha ha! All I care about is getting the experience and AP from defeating this monster!"

Nearly a dozen people had arrived. All of them were dressed in basic clothes. A few had armor and some were wearing mage robes, but none of them had anything Adam would have called great equipment. Two of the people present were Mages, two were Archers, one was a Priest, and the rest appeared to be Warriors. While the Mages and Archers stayed back and prepared their arrows or magic, the Warriors charged in to attack the [storm wolf] with their swords.

A chill entered his eyes as his thoughts grew cold.

These people were trying to steal his kill!

MERCILESS

Adam glared at the Warrior closest to him. It was a man with a head shaped like a walnut, thick eyebrows, and a ferocious grin on his face. He was wearing basic player clothes that all players wore when they first arrived, so he was probably low on the hierarchy of whatever guild he belonged to.

Not that Adam cared. This man could have been the guild leader, and he still would have done what he did.

-384!

Adam only used the basic [slash] skill on the Warrior, but it was more than enough. This man was only at level 5, and according to Titania's [scan] skill, he only had 150/150 health. He also didn't have any defensive equipment.

The [slash] carved a deep furrow in the man's body, though there was no blood, no gore. It was a bit odd for Adam, who was used to seeing people's internal organs spilling out when he carved them open with an attack like that. A scream erupted from the man's mouth. It only lasted for an instant. Adam's attack had taken away all of his HP. The Warrior died mere seconds after being hit, his body striking the ground with a heavy thud.

This single action caused the other twelve members of whatever guild had shown up to stop what they were doing and stare at Adam and their now fallen comrade. They were so shocked that they couldn't do anything when the [storm wolf] unleashed [storm blast] into the group. A massive bolt of lightning flew from the horn on its head, striking the ground and unleashing several lightning chains that struck two of the remaining six Warriors. Both Warriors screamed as their HP was reduced to zero and they died.

Seeing an opportunity, Adam activated [Blood Sacrifice] again, then attacked the [storm wolf] with [slash] and [thrust]. His attacks whittled down the remainder of the monster's health, reducing it to zero and killing the creature before any of the other players could even launch a single attack.

Ding!

[You have defeated the 1-star monster [storm wolf]! Items dropped: [storm pelt] and 500 gold coins. +2,000 experience points! +100 AP!]

Ding!

[Titania has leveled up! She is now at level 2. +20 HP! +1,000 MP! +10 SP!]

Ding!

[Titania has leveled up! She is now at level 3! +20 HP! +1,000 MP! +10 SP!]

Ding!

[Titania has leveled up! She is now at level 4! +20 HP! +1,000 MP! +10 SP!]

Ding!

[Titania has leveled up! She is now at level 5! +20 HP! +1,000 MP! +10 SP!]

Adam felt the satisfied smile appear on his face as he received the experience and ability points from killing the [storm wolf]. He was also surprised to see that Titania had leveled up so much, but then he remembered she was only at level 1, and if her level up system was the same as his, then the experience points required to level up would be double that of whatever you needed to reach the previous level. She could level up so many times in a row right now because her level was low and didn't require many experience points. It would become harder as time went on.

Still, the fact that she had leveled up so much after a single kill made him pretty happy.

Of course, the people around him could not see the smirk he wore thanks to his mask, but they must have sensed the smug satisfaction he felt. The remaining nine players bristled and shouted at him.

"Who the hell do you think you are?!"

"You think you can kill our guild members and get away with it?!"

"Let's kill this motherfucker!!"

The four Warriors remaining surrounded Adam as the Priest used some kind of buff magic on them, the Archers knocked back their arrows, and the Mages got ready to cast a spell.

Adam glared at the people surrounding him and was just about to attack the nearest Warrior to break the encirclement, but mere seconds before he could, a flash of light flew down from above and began floating next to him.

This flash was, of course, Titania.

The fairy's sudden appearance caused everyone getting ready to attack to pause. Uncertain expressions crossed the faces of the players surrounding Adam. They looked at each other, then at the fairy, then at each other again.

"W-what is that? An enemy?"

"She's so beautiful…"

"Is she a fairy?! She looks like a fairy!"

"What?! No way! What would a fairy be doing in the Village of Beginnings?!"

Titania eyed the people surrounding Adam as they talked up a storm, then looked at him with a bold smile.

"It seems you are in trouble. Now may I help you?" she asked.

"Please do," Adam said.

The first thing Titania did was use [scan] on the nine people surrounding him. All of them were at level 6. The Warriors had health ranging between +110-160, with a Physical Attack stat of +40-60 because their overall stats were more balanced than his own and they didn't have any good equipment. The Archers also had +110-160 health, but their Physical Attack was even lower. The Priest and Mages had the lowest health, but they also had the highest MP, and their Magical Attack was nothing to scoff at.

Even so, Adam was not worried.

Immediately after casting [scan] several times, Titania clasped her hands in prayer and began to sing [Song of Valor], which increased his Physical Defense and Magic Defense by 200%. This meant his +95 Defense was now +190 and his +15 Magic Defense was +30. That might not seem like a large defensive increase, but if a person's Physical Attack was only +70, then they would not be able to damage him.

Adam did not bother activating [Blood Sacrifice] since it wasn't necessary to deal with these people. Before they even had time to recover from their shock at seeing a fairy, he attacked them, using [slash] to insta-kill the Warrior nearest him. His attack went from that person's left shoulder to their right hip. After the Warrior screamed and died, Adam spun around and used [thrust] on a Warrior about two feet from him.

"What the fuck?!" That Warrior shouted seconds before Adam's spear impaled him through the chest. Once again, there was no gore, no blood. Even so, the man released a shrill scream of pain before his HP was reduced to zero and he died. Adam yanked his spear from the Warrior's chest and went on to attack the next one.

There were only two left.

"Fuck! This little shit just killed three of our people "

"Kill this bastard!"

"Mages! Fire your magic! Priest! We could use some magic buffs here!"

The Mages were startled, but it seemed they had experience with VR gaming because they recovered from their shock quickly and opened fire. The magic they cast was a basic [energy bolt] spell.

It was non-elemental magic that fired a bolt of pure energy and had an attack power of +120. Had anyone else been struck by these attacks, they would have been killed instantly.

-90; MISS!

"What?! What is going on?! Why did our attacks do so little damage?!"

"What the hell?! Fuck! I just used [scan]! Check out this guy's stats! He's at level 9!"

"WHAT?!"

The knowledge that Adam was at level 9 sent a shockwave rippling through the remaining members. Adam used that momentary distraction to take a [health potion], then kill the last two Warriors. He sliced one of them through the throat with [slash], then impaled the other one with [thrust]. His actions of taking out the last two Warriors sent fear racing through the two Mages, the Archers, and the Priest.

"Dammit! Fire! Hit him with your arrows!" the Priest shrieked.

The archers were shaking as they knocked back their arrows and fired them at Adam, but he dodged to the side, avoiding the arrows with incredible ease. Compared to bullets, these arrows were moving in slow motion.

"Shit! How is he dodging us?!"

"He must have real life combat experience! God damn it! Why did we have to run into this fucker?! Why couldn't Daniel be the one who ran into him?!"

Adam didn't know who Daniel was, but he didn't care. He raced toward the Archers, who screamed and tried to flee, cutting them down before they could move too far.

-384; -384!

The Archers were both killed, their bodies dropping. During the time Adam was slaughtering them, the Mages and the Priest managed to run away. He noticed them in the distance and thought about chasing them. After a moment, he decided it was not worth the effort and turned toward the battlefield.

It was a bit odd seeing a battlefield with no blood. Adam was no stranger to violence. His hands were stained in so much blood that he could no longer see what color his skin was.

Of course, he had not killed in years, not since meeting Aris, but that did not change the facts. And the fact was that seeing a bunch of corpses that weren't bleeding was just odd.

Corpses in Age of Gods didn't remain there forever. Even as he stared at them, the players' bodies disappeared into particles of light. The players would revive at the cathedral. He knew the moment they were revived, they would tell their boss about him, which could invite some trouble, but that just meant he needed to reach level 10 quickly.

"Those people were pretty weak," Titania said as she fluttered down to him.

"That's what happens when you join a party like that. You have to split the experience points, so of course their levels are going to rise slowly, and they won't gain as much. Their equipment was also the same equipment they had when they first began playing," Adam said.

Titania tilted her head when he said "first began playing" like she couldn't understand what he meant, but then she nodded. "So those people are otherworlders like you. I should have realized that's what they were."

"You know about otherworlders?" asked Adam.

"But of course. This is not the first time otherworlders have come to our lands. Long ago, when the world was in chaos, a kingdom that existed long ago used a forbidden summoning ritual to summon a hero from another world to slay an ancient evil. The ritual has since been forgotten. However, it seems many otherworlders are appearing in our world now. Oh! I should mention the ancient hero was someone who wielded this spear previously. According to legend, he was a very righteous man. This happened about two thousand years before my time."

So there was an in-game lore about hero summoning. He'd heard the "summoning a hero to another world" theme was really popular near the beginning of the twenty-first century. The genre had gone out of style after awhile, but maybe the creator for *Age of Gods* was a fan of it and decided to incorporate it into his game's lore.

Well, it wasn't like that mattered. It was just in-game lore.

"It looks like you leveled up quite a bit," Adam said to change the subject.

"It's just five levels," Titania said as though gaining three levels after killing a single enemy wasn't anything special, though

Adam could see the way she puffed out her chest. "It isn't that big of a deal."

"Where'd you allocate your status points?" he asked.

"Into my Intelligence obviously," Titania said as if it was a matter of course. "We fairies gain the largest benefits from having a high Intelligence. Of course, having more health and a higher defense would also be useful, but we won't gain many benefits from increasing our Strength or Constitution. I also used sixty of the ability points I gained to level up all my current songs. Now they are all level 2."

Adam nodded. He was tempted to look at her stats, but he didn't think now was the time.

"Let's keep moving," he said. "I would like to reach level 10 before I log off tonight."

"Log off?"

"Er… before I go back to my own world for the day. I can't stay here all the time."

"Oh? I did not know it was possible to so easily return to your original world."

Since he wanted to level up fast, Adam did not hesitate to leave this area and travel deeper into the forest. Those +12,000 experience points he needed to level up were not going to earn themselves.

✳✳✳

Daniel Frost was a mage and the leader of the Rising Phoenix Alliance. While he understood that he was not the most powerful person in the virtual world, he also knew that he was not a small fry either. Very few people would go out of their way to anger him. Those few who did often suffered incredibly harsh consequences.

That was why, when several of his people came to him with stories about how one man killed more than half their party, he could not help but feel like he was being lied to.

"Did you really get wiped out by one player?" he asked.

They were in the middle of the forest. Daniel was with his party of five, which was a standard party for players. He was the Mage, but they also had a Warrior, an Assassin, an Archer, and a Priest. This standard party lineup was used the most in online multiplayer games because it offered the most stability.

He was a level 7 Mage. Level 7 was the current highest level anyone in the game had outside of Lin Akamine, the current number 1 player in the entire world.

"We don't have any reason to lie to you, Guild Master," the Priest said. This man and two Mages had run all the way over here after escaping from that madman who had killed their party. "We were just minding our own business and fighting against a 1-star [storm wolf] when this guy named Adam came along. Not only did he steal our kill, but he began attacking us!"

The two Mages by the Priest's side nodded.

Daniel felt like gravity was tugging his mouth into a frown. He crossed his arms and ignored the battle going on a little ways off. His party members were currently attacking a level 7 [wolf], but they were doing an excellent job without him. The Warrior was acting as their tank by drawing the [wolf's] agro, while the Assassin dealt incredible damage with [throat slit]. Meanwhile, the Archer was taking potshots using [dead eye] and the Priest was healing them. It wouldn't be long before the enemy was killed.

He didn't see a reason to intervene.

"It's possible this person didn't realize who he was messing with," Daniel said at last. "None of the guilds have been officially established in-game. He was probably just an opportunist looking to steal your kill without knowing you belonged to my guild. Even so, we cannot let someone get away with killing our members. Our guild has a reputation to uphold. We'll let every member know to keep an eye out for this guy. If we see him, don't attack. Just report on his whereabouts to me."

"Yes, Guild Master!"

The Priest and two Mages saluted him before heading off. They also needed to grind their own levels. As he watched them go, Daniel turned his back on the battle that had just finished and thought about this Adam player who had killed several members of his guild. He certainly would not let this go unpunished. If he ever found that man, he would definitely make him wish he was dead.

***

The deeper into the forest Adam went, the higher each monster's level became, and the more experience points he earned for each kill. Of course, regular monsters did not grant him much in the way of experience anymore. There was also a level cap on the monsters here. After reaching a large mountain that he guessed acted as the border for the Village of Beginnings, the highest level monster was 10.

The level 10 [brown bear].

Name: Brown bear	Description: A bear that roams the forest. Brown bears are very aggressive and will attack anything that comes near it.	Class: Regular	Lvl: 10	Health: 2,000/2,000 MP: 100/100
Strength: +500	Constitution: +50	Dexterity: +10	Intelligence: +10	Speed: +20
Skill Name: Slash Description: With just one powerful swing, the brown bear can rend the flesh from his enemy's bones. Ability: Deals +1,000 damage MP consumption: 5 Cooldown	Skill Name: Roar Description: The brown bear can unleash a ferocious roar that stuns the enemy! Ability: 10% chance of causing stun MP Consumption: 5 Cooldown time: 10 seconds			

time: 0 seconds				

Its stats weren't bad, but they were nothing compared to the monsters he'd fought down in that dungeon. This wasn't even talking about the [necromancer] and the [skeleton dragon]. Even the regular skeletons had been stronger than this guy.

-528; MISS; MISS; MISS!

Titania was already chanting [Song of Vigor] to increase his physical attack power, which caused the damage he did to increase from +240 to +528. Unfortunately, his Hit-Rate still wasn't very good. Three of his first four attacks missed. To make matters worse, one of his missed attacks had been [thrust], which would have dealt even more damage than [slash].

Meanwhile, the [brown bear] tried to use [roar], but it only had a 10% chance of stunning him and it didn't work. When [roar] did nothing, the [brown bear] attacked with [slash]. Adam, however, merely hopped from side to side like a rabbit as he backed away, allowing the claws to miss him.

[Blood Sacrifice]!

Because he wanted to finish this quickly, Adam activated his unique skill and attacked the [brown bear] with even more vigor than before.

-1,440; MISS; MISS; -1,440!

He only needed to land two attacks before the [brown bear] was killed. The creature unleashed a pained roar that sounded more pathetic than frightening as it fell backwards, hitting the ground so hard the earth shook.

Ding!

[You defeated a [brown bear]! Items dropped: [bear fur] and 100 gold coins! +100 experience gained!]

Adam sighed as he looked at his stats. He'd killed fifteen enemies in the past three hours, but all that amounted to was a measly +1,500 experience points. The amount of experience points he needed was still over 10,000. He really wanted to know who the frack designed this game. The leveling up system was seriously messed up.

At least Titania had leveled up again. Her current stats were fairly decent.

Name: Titania	Class: Guardian of the Spear	Lvl: 6	SP: 0 AP: 0	Experience: 800/1,600
Strength: +10	Constitution: +10	Dexterity: +10	Intelligence: +145	Speed: +50
Physical Attack: +20	Health: 180/180	Hit-rate: 20%	MP: 4,300/4,300	Movement: +250
	Physical Defense: +20 Magic Defense: +30	Dodge-Rate: 20%	Magic Attack: +290	

Skill Name: Song of Refreshing Rain	Description: A song that can only be sung by Titania. This song is refreshing and lovely,	Current lvl: 2 AP needed to reach next lvl: 40	Ability: Indefinitely heals +15 HP every 5 seconds for as long as Titania is singing.	MP consumption: 50 MP per second	Cooldown time: 30 seconds

	like light spring rain. It has an incredible healing affect.				
Skill Name: Song of Vigor	Description: A song that Titania sings to increase the strength of her companions. When sung, this song will increase the Physical Attack and Magic Attack of every companion in her party.	Current lvl: 2 AP needed to reach next lvl: 40	Ability: Raises the Physical Attack and Magic Attack of all allies by 220% for as long as she is singing.	MP Consumption: 50 MP per second	Cooldown time: 30 second
Skill Name: Song of Valor	Description: A song that Titania sings to increase the defensive abilities of allies. Defense and	Current lvl: 2 AP Needed to reach next lvl: 40	Ability: 220% for Defense and Magical Defense stat of all Titania's party members. Increase	MP consumption: 50 MP per second	Cooldown time: 30 seconds

	Magical Defense will increase for as long as this song is being sung.		lasts for as long as Titania is singing.		
Skill Name: Scan	Description: Titania can scan any enemy regardless of level and send that information to all members of her party.	Current level: MAXED	Ability: Reveals an enemy's stats. Can only be used on one enemy at a time.	MP Consumption: 100	Cooldown time: 0 seconds

Her health was still abysmal, but her magic was impressive. It also didn't really matter if her health was low since she didn't pull any agro from enemies. The only thing they would have to worry about was if they fought against players, who were far more intelligent than the monsters they'd been battling.

"All right. I think I'm logging off—erm, returning to my original world. I should be back in a few hours," Adam said at last.

"Very well. I shall be waiting for you here," Titania said with crossed arms and a somewhat putout look on her face.

Adam gave her a strained smile before he logged out. He opened his eyes to find himself inside of his bedroom in Fayte's apartment. The clock informed him that it was 1:45pm, meaning he'd been playing inside of that game for about ten or eleven hours.

He stood up and stretched as he made his way out of the bedroom and into the shower. He stripped off, took a quick shower under the cold water to wake himself up, redressed himself, and headed into the living room. Fayte was not there. He assumed she was either still in *Age of Gods* or had gone out.

Adam made himself a simple sandwich and ate while watching the news. Most of the news was discussing *Age of Gods*, which seemed to have really rocked the world. It had barely been a day since it's release, but it already had 5.7 million players.

The world after World War III had been ravaged. Over 1 billion people had died during World War III and another 1.5 billion died from Mortems Disease immediately after WWIII, and more were dying from that disease each day. The Earth's current population was only about 4.3 billion. That might sound like a lot, but it was a far cry from the 7.4 billion people there had been before World War III. While 5.7 million was still a drop in the bucket, that was a lot in a world that had been ravaged by war.

Adam suspected more people would join *Age of Gods* as the game went on. More than 70% of the world's population played virtual reality games these days. Some people spent all their time playing and earned their living through gaming, while others were just casual players who played to earn some extra pocket money. Once the money exchange system for *Age of Gods* became active, even more people would pick up the game.

The sound of footsteps reached his ears just as Adam finished eating his sandwich. He looked at the hallway to find Fayte walking into the living room with a tablet in hand. She was dressed in simple pajama bottoms and a spaghetti strap shirt. While the outfit appeared casual, on her, it looked amazing.

"I see you're finally out of the game. You missed breakfast."

Fayte's gentle smile as she sat down beside him remained the same as when he first saw it. The couch shifted to accommodate for her weight. She sat close enough that he could have reached out and touched her.

Adam nodded. "I know. I got caught up trying to level up. I'd really like to reach level 10 soon and leave the Village of Beginnings."

"I think that's something everyone wants," Fayte admitted with a giggle. "Who could have imagined leveling up would be such a hassle?"

"What level are you at?"

"Still at level 6." Fayte's smile widened as she studied him with her keen eyes. "I checked the forums not long ago. The Rising Phoenix Alliance posted a message on the forums about a guy named Adam who reached level 9. It was more of a rant than a message. According to them, this 'Adam' killed most of their party by himself. Daniel Frost has offered a reward for anyone who finds out more information about you."

"And Daniel Frost is…?"

"He's the leader of the Rising Phoenix Alliance," Fayte said. "The Rising Phoenix Alliance is a powerful branch of the Pleonexia

Alliance. They are consistently ranked within the top fifty guilds owned by the Pleonexia Alliance. You'll probably want to be cautious whenever you log into Age of Gods again, but knowing you, you'll be fine."

Adam had not realized those people were members of the Pleonexia Alliance, which was the most powerful guild in the American Federation. They were part of the Pleonexia Family. The guild master for the Pleonexia Alliance was none other than Levon Pleonexia, the heir to the Pleonexia Family and its future leader

He cursed. If Adam had known those people were part of the Pleonexia Alliance, he would not have let those two Mages and that Priest escape.

"I'll keep that in mind, though I don't think it will matter right now," Adam confessed. "I'm planning to reach level 10 either later tonight or early tomorrow morning. Once I have, I will leave the Village of Beginnings behind."

"If you do that, you will become the first person to leave a Village of Beginnings." Fayte hummed thoughtfully. "It's been estimated by some specialists that the highest level players won't be able to leave for another four days. It will probably take everyone else around seven or eight days. Of course, those people don't know you are at level 9."

"Who has the highest level after me?" asked Adam.

"Lin Akamine of Japan," Fayte said. "She's currently at level 8."

Adam knew of Lin Akamine, but he mostly knew her reputation. They had never met in person and only met a few times in the game world. Back when he was participating as an independent player to earn money for Aris's treatment, he had fought against her twice and won both times. Their battles were still occasionally talked about in online forums and chat rooms.

Adam continued talking to Fayte for another hour before she said she was leaving to meet with Susan in real life.

"I will have to introduce you to her some time, but we'll want to wait until she gets to know you in the game. Su is shy and doesn't take to meeting new people very well."

"We'll see," Adam said. "I think I told you before that I'd prefer not meeting anyone in real life to avoid complications, but who knows what the future will hold, right?"

Fayte understood why he might not want to meet Susan, so she just shrugged before slipping on her boots, bundling up in that ugly overcoat of hers, putting on her veil, and slipping out the door.

Once she was gone, Adam put his plate inside the dishwasher, then headed into Aris's room. He sat down without ceremony and began telling Aris about his fight with the [skeleton dragon] and how he met Titania. He would not log onto *Age of Gods* until 7:30pm after eating dinner with Fayte.

AMBUSH

Ding!

[You have defeated a level 10 [wolf]! [Wolf] has dropped the items [wolf pelt] and 60 gold coins. +100 experience points!]

Ding!

[You have defeated a level 10 [brown bear]! [Brown bear] has dropped 120 gold coins. +100 experience points!]

Ding!

Ding!

Ding!

Adam sighed as he killed what felt like his ten thousandth enemy and watched the blasted experience bar on his status screen barely rise. He'd been killing monsters since 4:00am this morning. He didn't know what time it was, but at least two or three hours must have passed by now. At present, his experience was at 28,730/38,400. That wasn't bad, but he still needed around +10,000 experience points to level up.

"I feel like this is getting us nowhere," Adam said with a sigh.

"Speak for yourself." Titania wore a very pleased smile as she spoke. "I have leveled up quite a bit." Then she sighed, fluttered over to sit on his shoulder, and placed her chin on the butt of her hands and elbows on her knees, looking depressed. "That said, I feel like I should not be happy to only be at level 8. Back when I was at the peak of my power, I was at level 90. For me to feel joy at reaching level 8 makes me feel pathetic."

Adam wasn't sure he believed her when she said she was at level 90, but she also didn't have a reason to lie to him. She didn't gain anything by it. He'd also learned that Titania, while arrogant, wasn't really a braggart. She simply had a strong belief in herself and her own abilities.

At the moment, Titania's stats looked like this:

Name: Titania	Class: Guardian of the Spear	Lvl: 8	SP: 0 AP: 200	Experience: 1,200/12,800
Strength: +10	Constitution: +10	Dexterity: +10	Intelligence: +170	Speed: +50
Physical Attack: +20	Health: 200/200	Hit-rate: 20%	MP: 17,000/17,000	Movement: +250
	Physical Defense: +20 Magic Defense: +30	Dodge-Rate: 20%	Magic Attack: +340	

Skill Name: Song of Refreshing Rain	Description: A song that can only be sung	Current lvl: 2 AP needed	Ability: Indefinitely heals +15 HP	MP consumption: 50 MP per second	Cooldown time: 30 seconds

	by Titania. This song is refreshing and lovely, like light spring rain. It has an incredible healing affect.	to reach next lvl: 40	every 5 seconds for as long as Titania is singing.		
Skill Name: Song of Vigor	Description: A song that Titania sings to increase the strength of her companions. When sung, this song will increase the Physical Attack and Magic Attack of every companion in her party.	Current lvl: 2 AP needed to reach next lvl: 40	Ability: Raise the Physical Attack and Magic Attack of all allies by 220% for as long as she is singing.	MP Consumption: 50 MP per second	Cooldown time: 30 second
Skill Name: Song of Valor	Description: A song that Titania sings to increase	Current lvl: 2 AP Needed to reach	Ability: 210% for Defense and Magical Defense stat	MP consumption: 50 MP per second	Cooldown time: 30 seconds

	the defensive abilities of allies. Defense and Magical Defense will increase for as long as this song is being sung.	next lvl: 40	of all Titania's party members. Increase lasts for as long as Titania is singing.		
Skill Name: Scan	Description: Titania can scan any enemy regardless of level and send that information to all members of her party.	Current level: MAXED	Ability: Reveals an enemy's stats. Can only be used on one enemy at a time.	MP Consumption: 100	Cooldow n time: 0 seconds

"It would be nice if we could run into a 2-star enemy," Adam said as he began walking. "I'd even take running into a 1-star enemy right now."

They were once again surrounded by trees. The scent of the forest filled the air. It was the scent of wood, dirt, and flowers. A canopy of leaves blocked out most of the sunlight and created geometric shapes on the ground, though the shadows moved as a soft breeze caused the trees to sway.

Adam had always marveled at how realistic this video game was. Even now, he could hardly tell this world wasn't real. The soft breeze against his skin, the smell of the forest, the feeling of grass crunching underneath his boots, all of it felt so real. So vibrant.

It was honestly a little scary.

"Hmph. The very fact that you think 1-star and 2-star enemies are worth anything is sad," Titania muttered.

"Hey, don't forget I'm new to all this. Running into a 2-star enemy would give us a huge level boost. They give more experience points than regular enemies, and they give us ability points as well. If we could get some abilities points, we could upgrade your skills."

Adam poked the little fairy on his shoulder with his index finger, but she swatted his finger away. She didn't seem irritated. At the same time, he knew it bothered her when he did this, which was why he did it every time she complained.

"I am aware of that," Titania muttered with a tired sigh.

Adam had currently maxed out all three of his skills, so he didn't have any use for the ability points at present, but he believed they would be useful later on. He was certain there would come a time when he could either learn new skills or class up. New classes often provided more skills. Of course, learning new skills from items like scrolls was another common trope in video games.

They traveled around a little more, but Adam only gained about +2,000 experience points and didn't run into 1-star or 2-star enemies.

They decided to go back to the Village of Beginnings and sell all the items they had acquired from item drops. Adam's inventory said he had 200 [wolf pelts] and 150 [bear furs] plus a variety of other items which now filled his inventory. He was at full capacity. If he went to the item shop, he could sell the [wolf pelts] for 5 gold coins and the [bear fur] for 10 gold coins.

Adam soon reached the area where level 8 monsters congregated. The scenery hadn't changed, but the monsters went from [brown bears] to [wild boars]. They only gave him +50 experience points, so they weren't worth his time. He cut them down when they attacked. However, if they avoided him, he was content to not attack.

Ding!

[You have defeated a [wild boar]! Items dropped: 20 gold coins! +50 experience points!]

Just as Adam finished slaying a [wild boar] with a single [thrust] of his spear, a gentle ringing in his ears let him know that someone was calling him through the player chat function. Of course, there was only one person currently who had him on their friend list.

"It's that Fayte girl again," Titania said, tilting her head. "When are you planning on introducing me to this child?"

"When we meet in the game world," Adam said as he accepted the call. Titania furrowed his brow when he said "game world" like she didn't understand, but he barely paid her any attention. "Fayte? What's going on?"

"Adam! I reached level 7!" Fayte's excited voice came over the player chat.

It sounded like it was coming from everywhere at once, but only he and Titania could hear it. Oddly enough, while Titania could hear Fayte speak, she could not speak back. Adam wondered if that was because she was a non-player character, or if it was because Fayte was not a member of Adam's party, or if maybe she couldn't talk because she was not involved in the call.

"That's great!" Adam was truly excited for Fayte. However, he felt like what he really enjoyed when she contacted him like this was the joy in her voice when she accomplished something. "Is that the standard level right now?"

"There are a few people who are at level 7, but they're all leaders of large guilds like the Frost Knights, Hell's Blaze, and the Rising Phoenix Alliance. There are also some exceptionally gifted solo players like Mist who reached level 7, but he's also a VR gamer who is listed at number 6 on the International Power Ranking Chart. I heard Levon Pleonexia is currently at level 7 too."

Adam clenched his hands when he heard the name Levon, but he kept his tone light as he continued talking to Fay. "Who else is at level 7 right now?"

"Hmmm… there's Daggerfall of the Daggerfall Dynasty and his two brothers. All three of them reached level 7 a few hours ago. There is also their bodyguard. The Spear God. I read on a forum that he actually reached level 8 around the time you reached level 9. Not sure what level he's at now."

So there was someone like that who could quickly level up? Adam wondered if this Spear God had gone on any quests like he had. That was the most plausible explanation since leveling up by grinding simply didn't give you that many experience points right now. It was easier to level up by taking on quests.

"Of course, these are just the players in the American Federation who have reached level 7. There are some players in European Union and Asia who have reached that level too. There was even an article I read today that said Lin Akamine reached level 9 this morning."

Adam felt a moment of shock. He hadn't realized there was someone who had reached the same level as him. That was impressive. *Really* impressive. Adam spent at least 12 hours a day playing, so he could well imagine how much time and effort it took to reach this level.

"I guess I should get my butt in gear and level up then," Adam joked. "I can't let anyone beat me."

"You definitely cannot. My livelihood is depending on you," Fayte said, laughing.

As Adam spoke with Fayte, the little fairy on his shoulder crossed her arms and glared at him like he'd committed a crime against her. She often got like this when he spoke to Fayte for a prolonged period of time. He didn't think Titania was jealous so much as she disliked it when he didn't pay attention to her.

As their call continued, several people walked out from behind the trees and surrounded him. He stopped walking and eyed these people. They were all players. He didn't recognize any of them, but he would have been surprised if he did since Adam never paid attention to people who did not interest him. There was a mix of Archers, Assassins, Mages, Warriors, and Priests. A quick headcount revealed there were five Archers, two Assassins, four Mages, six Warriors, and two Priests, making for a total of nineteen people.

"Hey, Fayte? I'm gonna have to call you back," Adam said.

"Huh? What's wrong? Did something happen?"

"I'm surrounded by bad guys. Talk to you later," was all Adam said before disconnecting the player chat. He frowned, but kept calm as he firmly gripped the spear in his right hand. "You know, it's pretty rude to ambush people while they're taking a stroll through the forest. I hope you all have a good reason for it."

One of the four Mages stepped forward as Adam spoke. He had sandy blond hair that was curly, messy like a bird's nest, and blue eyes. His pale skin looked a little unnatural, like he hadn't gotten enough sun. That was a fairly typical gamer problem They spent so much time indoors that they didn't get enough melanin. He assumed this man played games for most of the day. Unlike many of the people surrounding him, who all still wore the outfits they started playing in, this one wore the black robes of a Mage.

"There's a fairy on his shoulder. Is this the guy?" he asked another Mage behind him.

"That's definitely the guy who nearly wiped out our entire party!" the other Mage said. "I could never forget this man and the mask he wore!"

Nearly wiped out their entire party? Adam narrowed his eyes as he looked at the Mage that just finished speaking, which caused the other man to break out in a cold sweat. The frown on Adam's face increased as he tried to place this guy within his memories.

"You… who the hell are you?" he asked.

"Are you saying you don't even recognize me?!" the Mage snapped. He looked shocked and angry, his face blistering red. "You almost killed me the other day!"

"Hmph. You say that like I should care," Adam snorted.

Titania giggled, which caused all the attention to shift to her. Despite the fact that she was barely a foot tall, she was still a gorgeous woman who had the face of an angel and a body that seemed like the embodiment of sin. The men around them became absent-minded. Even the Mage who had first stepped over to him flushed bright red. His nostrils flared like a bull seeing red after really getting a glimpse of the beauty sitting on Adam's shoulder.

"Do you really not remember this man? He was one of the people who tried to steal your kill," Titania said.

"Ah. Right. That did happen, didn't it?" Adam nodded. "Yes, I do remember some dickweeds who tried to steal my kill when I was fighting a 1-star monster. So that was you, huh? Don't tell me you wanted revenge and decided to get reinforcements?"

It was obvious to Adam that was exactly what had happened. He was currently surrounded by nineteen people who were armed to the teeth. What could they possibly want if not to shake him up and kill him to get revenge for killing several members of their group?

"The other day, you killed seven members of my guild," the Mage said in a cold, slow voice. It seemed he had recovered from Titania's beauty. "I'm not exactly sure what went down, and honestly, I don't really care. You killed members of my guild, and I can't exactly call myself the leader of a guild if I let my people get killed without even getting retribution for them."

Titania snorted. "You are an idiot."

"What?!"

The Mage looked shocked that an NPC was insulting him. And it wasn't just him. The other members of his party also wore flabbergasted expressions as the tiny woman on Adam's shoulder called their leader an idiot.

"Those men of yours committed the crime of trying to steal another person's kill. Adam only did what any person would do in that situation and punished them. As the leader of this group, you should be reprimanding those people for acting like reprehensible brigands so they will learn not to make such a grievous error in judgement again, but you are instead trying to punish a man who only did what you yourself would probably do in a similar situation." Titania was giving the Mage an imperious look as she lectured him, like she was a queen looking her nose down at a disobedient subject. "How can I not call you an idiot when you are acting so stupid?"

The Mage's face turned so red Adam was surprised steam didn't begin rising from his head. Not only was his face burning with anger, but his arms were shaking as he clenched his hands into fists. The staff in his right hand made an odd creaking sound as if the wood was being placed under a great amount of duress.

"You... do you know who I am?! I am Daniel Frost of the Rising Phoenix Alliance! My guild is one of the strongest branch guilds of the Pleonexia Alliance! How dare you insult me like that, you worthless NPC!" the man, who Adam now knew was called Daniel, shouted.

"En pee see?" Titania questioned with a tilt of her head. "Adam? What is this en pee see? Is that some kind of otherworlder insult?"

"Oh? So you are members of the Rising Phoenix Alliance, are you?" Adam asked, his tone and eyes growing cold.

"Don't ignore me!" Titania snapped, but that was exactly what Adam did. It wasn't like he could answer her when they were surrounded by hostile people.

"That's right," Daniel said. "We are from the Rising Phoenix Alliance, and I am their guild master. As their guild master, it is my responsibility to seek retribution from those who would sully our name and kill our members. That is why I'm going to kill—"

-440

Daniel's rant was cut off after Adam used [slash] to kill him in a single attack. The Mage's body dropped to the forest floor with a dull thud. This action was so fast that none of the other players could react. All they could do was stare at the corpse of their leader. No one made a move. No one said anything. They had all been stunned by Adam's swift and decisive action.

Adam grinned as he launched himself at the nearest Warrior, a man who was standing in front of the remaining three Mages. His [slash] once more killed another player in an instant, dealing -440 damage instead of his typical -480 thanks to the armor his enemy was wearing. It was still enough to kill him. As the man's body dropped to the ground, Titania flew into the air and began singing [Song of Valor] to increase his Physical Defense and Magic Defense as Adam reached the shocked Mages and killed two of them in less time than it took to blink. One of those Mages was the guy who got away last time.

It was only after the third Mage was killed that the other players reacted.

"Holy fucking shit! This dude just insta-killed our leader!"

"What do we do?!"

"What do you mean, what do we do? Don't ask something so stupid! We obviously need to kill this bastard!"

The Warriors were the first to respond, and they quickly tried to hem him in, but Adam did not fight against them yet. When being attacked in a group with a combination of long and close-range attackers, the most important thing to do was kill those who fought at long-range first, so they couldn't take shots at him while he was distracted by the other enemies. That meant killing the Mages and the Archers. Since the Mages were all dead, Adam bypassed the Warriors with fleet feet and attacked the two Archers.

"Damn it! He's too close for me to fire at him! Ahhh!"

"Shit! He just killed Mendez—Aaack!"

-480; -460!

Two [slash] attacks removed two of the five the Archers, who could have potentially threatened Titania. The other Archers were located on the opposite side of the battlefield. They had split up so he couldn't attack all of them, which was admittedly a good tactic. He praised Daniel for his sense of tactics if not his sense of diplomacy.

-0; -0; -0!

Adam felt the sting of three blades slashing into his back because he wasn't fast enough to dodge, but even though he could feel the attacks, no damage was done thanks to Titania's [Song of Valor] doubling his Physical Defense. Once the three Warriors finished attacking, it was his turn.

He used [slash] on one of them, swinging his spear so fast it appeared to be nothing more than a blur. His attack went from the Warrior's left hip to his right shoulder. Had this been in real life, he would have been sliced apart, his entrails spilling to the floor as he died instantly. This was not real life, however, so all that happened was he lost -364 of his health. Of course, he only had about +200 HP, so Adam's attack killed him instantly.

Spinning around on the balls of his feet, Adam thrust his spear forward and impaled another warrior through the throat. [Thrust] was activated. The man choked as the attack penetrated his flesh. No blood came out, but a big -374 appeared over his head. When Adam removed the spear tip from his throat, the Warrior fell backward.

"Damn it! What kind of monster is this?! Could he really be at level 9 like Axel said?!"

"This isn't the infamous Spear God, is it? Shit! We picked the wrong guy to mess with!"

Adam almost smiled. Because of how quickly he had struck, the Mages did not have time to use [scan] on him, which meant they knew nothing of his level or his abilities. What's more, because he had placed almost all of his status points on his Strength stat, his Physical Attack power was high enough to kill all these people in a single hit. He didn't even need to activate [Blood Sacrifice].

Now there were only three Archers, two Assassins, and three Warriors.

Speaking of the Assassins…

Adam felt his instincts warn him of danger and leapt backward as something struck the ground he had been standing on It was one of the Assassins. As masters of quick killing, they had the highest Physical Attack stat in any game, but their true ability lied in their stealth attacks. If they could catch their opponent by surprise, they could do critical damage, which could double or even triple the damage done.

Since his attack failed, the Assassin tried to disappear into the trees, but he was caught by Adam's [slash], which killed him in a single stroke. Adam didn't pay attention to the man as he fell to the ground and instead turned on his heel and charged through the remaining three Warriors. He swung at two of them with [slash], killing them both before they had time to put up a defense, and then broke through their line and attacked the remaining three Archers.

Ever since this battle had begun, Adam noticed that all of his attacks were hitting their targets, which surprised him at first. It was only after thinking about it that he realized his attacks were hitting because these people were players. Their Dodge-Rate was low like his Hit-Rate, which made it easier to hit them.

Titania had not once stopped singing the entire time. The [Song of Valor] continued to echo across the battlefield, granting him increased defense. It was odd, but he actually felt empowered when she sang, like her singing did more than just raise his stats but made him feel physically sturdier than normal.

He wondered if it was all in his head.

The Archers had been trying to shoot her down, but while Titania's greatest ability lay in her high Intelligence stat, her second greatest talent was in her Speed stat. She was far faster than the Archers. Dodging their attacks was easy even if her Dodge-Rate was low. All Dodge-Rate did was determine how often attacks missed rather than whether or not someone could dodge. She flitted through the air faster than they could knock arrows back and fire them. They were so busy trying to shoot her down that they never noticed Adam until it was too late.

-480; -480; -470!

The three last Archers died, the Mages had already been killed, one Assassin was gone, and five of the six Warriors lay dead on the ground. That meant there were only two people left. One Warrior and one Assassin. While Adam could not see the Assassin, who was no doubt hiding and waiting for the perfect moment to strike, the Warrior was in front of Adam and shaking in his boots.

"I-I'm sorry." The man dropped his weapon to the ground and raised his hands in surrender. "I'm really sorry! I didn't want to attack you! Honest! I was forced to by my guild master! He said if we didn't attack you, he would kick us out of the guild!"

Adam kept a wary eye out for the Assassin as he walked over to the man who had surrendered. He was certain this was an attempt at distracting him. At the same time, he gave the man what he hoped was an understanding smile and nodded several times.

"Hm. Hm. I understand completely. It is very hard to go against your guild master. After all, he controls the guild you belong to, so he has the power to command you to do whatever he wants," Adam said.

"T-that's right! That's totally right!" The Warrior could not nod fast enough. "He's always working us like horses to grind levels, but then he steals the kill and gains the most experience points. That's how he was able to level up so fast! If not for that, I would already be at level 7 instead of level 6."

"Don't worry. I understand how you feel." Adam's words made the man's eyes brighten with hope. That hope disappeared moments later after Adam's next words. "But, you know, even if I understand how you feel, that doesn't mean I'm going to let you off. After all, would you let off the bastards who ambushed and tried to kill you?"

"Wait—"

-480!

Before the man could plead with him more, Adam claimed his life. His spear tore through the man's body, causing it to spin like a top before he fell to the ground with a heavy thud and didn't move.

Immediately after he killed the last Warrior, the Assassin swooped down from above and tried to attack him by plunging his dagger deep into Adam's head, but he only took a single step back and used [thrust] as the Assassin landed on the ground. The man was so surprised he missed that he could do nothing as the spear plunged into his head.

-1,440!

"Oh? It seems hitting the head of a player can cause a critical hit," Adam said as he pulled his spear from the corpse. The body fell to the ground. A few seconds later, the assassin he had just killed and all the other players vanished into particles of light.

"Hmph. These otherworlders were truly foolish," Titania said as she landed on his shoulder. He felt her small hand as she placed it against his cheek and leaned on it like she was leaning against a wall. It felt... odd. He'd never had such a tiny hand touch him before. It made him sort of think of a barbie doll, but Titania's hand was soft and warm and certainly not made of plastic.

Adam shrugged, mindful of Titania's presence. "Not every player can be smart, though I feel like the master of a guild should have more intelligence than this. Perhaps I am giving guild masters too much credit."

"You most certainly are. By the way, have you checked out the stats on your spear? It should have leveled up quite a bit by now."

"Er... no, actually. I have not. Let me do that now."

Adam opened his equipment screen and selected the [Rusted Spear] to display its stats.

Name: Rusted Spear Lvl: 4 Experience points needed to level up: 1,700/40,000	Item Type: Weapon	Grade: ? ???	Use requirements: Can only be equipped by Adam. Cannot be thrown away, cannot be given away, and can-	Description: This unknown weapon was found by Adam. It has recognized him as its master and cannot be used by anyone else.	Abilities: Physical Attack+40; Strength +40 Special ability: Sentient Growth

			not be un-equipped.		

It looked like his spear really had leveled up a little; his Strength and Physical Attack both had a +40 added to them. That explained why his attacks were doing more damage than before. He'd thought that was odd but hadn't paid much attention because he'd been busy.

The weapon he had been using before this had +100 for just Physical Attack, which was good but not great. Now that he was thinking about it, being able to add both points to both his Strength and Physical Attack was more beneficial than the other weapon he had been using. His Physical attack rose by +2 for every +1 point added to his Strength. At +40 Strength, his Physical Attack gained an additional +80, meaning the [Rusted Spear] was currently boosting his Physical Attack by +120.

"It hasn't leveled up much yet," Adam said, sighing when he saw how many experience points it needed to reach level 5. "I don't know who invented this level system, but that is just ridiculous. +40,000 experience points to reach level 5? That's hardly fair."

Titania shrugged and sat herself back on his shoulder. As they began walking again, she started speaking, telling him more about the world he was in.

"There is a story passed down in the Fairy Clan that speaks of the creation of this world. Our world was created by the four goddess. Gaia, Goddess of the Earth; Aqua, Goddess of Water; Stella,

Goddess of the Sun; and Luna, Goddess of the Moon. The one who created the leveling system was Luna. If you have any complaints about the difficulty leveling up, you should take them to her." Titania gave him a smug look. "Not that it would do you any good."

"Hmmm…"

He'd already heard this story from the mayor, though he hadn't known everything Titania was telling him, like how the Moon Goddess created the level system. That was a new one to him.

Adam went back to the Village of Beginnings and sold his pelts, furs, and everything else he didn't need at the item shop. The shop owner was an older woman named Ms. Romelda. She looked like she might have been a beauty in her youth, but now her hair was gray, wrinkles lined her face, she had a stooped back, and her breasts were sagging in her shirt, making him wonder if the woman knew what a bra was. Still, she was a nice old lady. Adam sold all of his spoils and received 1,200 gold coins.

With the additional coins he received from the lady, he now had a hefty sum of 26,500 gold coins, which wasn't a small amount. Most of the money he earned came from his kills. Level 10 monsters usually dropped around two to five hundred gold coins depending on what type of monster it was. [Brown bears] usually offered the most money from their drops.

He wondered what the exchange rate between in-game currency and real world currency would be when the Money Exchange System finally came out.

"By the way, Ms. Romelda, you wouldn't happen to have any tasks you need help with, would you?" Adam asked. A quest would be so much better than simply grinding away. He hated level grinding, especially in this game where it would take him whc knew how many hours just to reach level 10.

"Now that you mention it, I do have something I could use some help with, if you'd be willing," Ms. Romelda said, her eyes lighting up as if she'd been hoping he would ask this question. "A few days ago, my wedding band went missing. I don': know what happened to it. I checked my entire house and couldn't find out. However, about one day ago, the lumberjack, Cabal, said he saw some goblins heading south and one of them was wearing a ring that looked just like mine."

Adam had only ever headed north, which was where the forest lay. He didn't know what was to the south.

"What's south of here?"

"If you keep traveling south, you will eventually reach the ocean," Ms. Romelda replied. "There are several beaches south of here. Us villagers don't go down that way because cf the monsters, but I hear there are a lot of caves located near the cliffs down south."

Ding!

[You have been offered a new quest: [Find Ms. Romelda's Wedding Ring!] Will you accept? Yes or no?]

"Don't worry, Ms. Romelda. I will do my best to find your ring," Adam said as he pressed "yes."

Ms. Romelda's eyes teared up. She sniffled several times as she raised her hand to wipe the tears from her eyes.

"Oh… thank you so much, young man. I truly appreciate this. That wedding ring is the last memento I have of my dearly departed husband."

Ding!

[The quest: [Find Ms. Romelda's Wedding Ring!] has been accepted!]

LEVEL 10

"So that was one of the so-called Village of Beginnings," Titania said.

"You know of them?" Adam asked.

"I have never been to one myself before now, of course, but everyone has heard of them. Long ago, the people who grew tired of the constant wars and strife that plagued the world moved away from the four main continents and established these Villages of Beginnings to avoid the constant killing. The reason they are called the Village of Beginnings is because everyone who lives inside them is incredibly weak."

"So there was in-game lore like that…"

"What does 'in-game' mean?"

"Uh… never mind."

Adam and Titania kept a constant stream of chatter going as they traveled south. The rolling hills were filled with players seeking to level up. Most of the players this close to the village were new. Their levels were only at 1 or 2. Adam watched as a pair, one man and one woman, took turns attacking a [wild rabbit] before turning away from them and continuing on.

"Have you ever been to the ocean?" asked Adam.

"Who do you think you're talking to, young man? I traveled all over this world for over five hundred years and saw all there is to see before I was tasked with becoming the Guardian of the Spear. Of course I have been to the ocean."

Titania was, as always, sitting on his shoulder. It seemed to be her favorite place. The only times she left was when he logged off and when they were in combat.

The salty scent of the sea reached Adam seconds before they arrived at the beach. Waves gently lapped at the sandy shore, a few seagulls flew in the blue sky above, and the waters were so blue it was hard to judge where the ocean ended and the sky began.

Adam saw no signs of goblins, but Ms. Romelda said they were near the cliffs, which were further east. He could see them in the distance and judged them to be about one mile from where he stood. Spear in hand, he marched toward the cliffs.

"What can you tell me about goblins?" asked Adam.

"Goblins are disgusting and vile creatures," were Titania's first few words. "They are short and smelly, and their skin is the color of puke."

"I see you really like goblins, don't you? Tell me what you really think."

"They are a mischievous, violent race. They like to pretend they are harmless at first. Whenever they arrive in a new village, they will play what could be construed as pranks. Thievery, vandalism, and the like. However, this is all a ploy to make villagers lower their guard while they learn the lay of the land. Once the goblins know everything they need to, they launch an attack on the nearby village. The men are slaughtered. The women are used to make babies. There are no goblin women, so they must procreate with other races, but what sane woman would sleep with a goblin?"

"So they're like a race of murdering rapists? That's just great."

These goblins sounded like a nasty piece of work.

Adam did not know much about goblins beyond what he knew from stories and video games, and there was never any real lore about them in those games. Well, there might have been, but if there was, he had never paid it much attention.

It wasn't long before they arrived at the cliffs. There were no caves near the beach and no method of climbing up the cliffs, so Adam had to travel further inland and loop around Most of the monsters in this area like the [wild hog] and the [crystal snake] were only at level 5. Adam didn't even see a goblin until Titania called out to him.

"Look over there. [Goblins]."

Adam turned his head and saw that, indeed, there were several goblins just a little ways off. They were, just as Titania had said, short humanoid creatures with green skin, bald heads, and gangly arms and legs. The clothing they wore was threadbare, obviously stolen. None of it matched. One goblin might be wearing overalls several sizes too big, while another might have a too large shirt and too small pants.

They looked like very awkward creatures.

"Any ideas? Kill them or follow them?" asked Adam.

"You should definitely follow them," Titania said. "If there are goblins here, then there is a nest, and if there is a nest, the people living in the Village of Beginnings will be in danger. Better to take them out now."

Adam did not consider himself a hero. His hands were far too stained with blood for that, but he didn't mind doing some pest control. He was actually hoping that if he exterminated this entire nest, he would finally reach level 10.

"What do their levels look like?" he asked.

"One moment," Titania said as she used [scan] and sent him the information.

Name: Goblin	Description: Goblins are vile and evil creatures who like to pillage, rape, and murder members of the Races of Light.	Class: Regular	Lvl: 11	Health: 600/600 MP: 10/10
Strength: +80	Constitution: +40	Dexterity: +10	Intelligence: +5	Speed: +5
Abilities: Bash Description: The Goblin hits someone with a cudgel				

Causes Strength * 2 damage to whoever gets hit MP Consumption: 5 Cooldown time: 0 seconds				

The [goblins] seemed pretty weak for level 11 monsters. Those creatures down in the dungeon where Adam rescued Trader Wilkins' son had been a lot stronger, and they were only at level 10.

Adam followed the [goblins] as per Titania's suggestion, keeping behind the trees and using his talent at moving silently to avoid being spotted. He was not an Assassin-class player and therefore didn't have any skills related to stealth. However, this game was surprisingly realistic and allowed him to use skills brought over from the real world in this one. Adam was almost certain no Assassin-class player could defeat him in stealth except for maybe Lilith.

The goblins never even looked back.

They eventually led him to a cave located not far from the ledge of the cliff. It looked like the mouth of a giant monster emerging from the ground. The [goblins] jabbered at two other [goblins] guarding the gate before disappearing deeper into the caves. Adam couldn't understand what they were saying. It sounded like gibberish to him.

"Okay. Let's move," he said, gripping his spear tightly as he broke into a sprint.

As Adam burst through the treeline, Titania flew off his shoulder and began chanting [Song of Valor], which increased his physical and magical defense by 210%. Meanwhile, Adam quickly activated [Blood Sacrifice] to double his attack power.

The [goblins] noticed him before he could reach them. They jabbered and squawked before readying their makeshift clubs. Both [goblins] looked angry, like he was a vile fiend for intruding on their territory. He could see the rage in the whites of their eyes, which were now bloodshot with anger and blood lust.

Adam reached them and thrust out his spear. The [thrust] skill activated and stabbed the first goblin through the throat. Because he had [Blood Sacrifice] active, his attack did -1,108 points of damage, which was more than enough to one-shot the [goblin]. The creature released a loud death gurgle as it fell backward.

The other [goblin] tried to attack him, swinging its club with reckless abandon, but Adam stepped back, shuffled sideways along the ground, and swung his spear in a motion that drew a line from the goblin's left shoulder to right hip. As always, he felt the resistance of his weapon digging through flesh, muscle, and bone.

-1,039!

The goblin went down in a heap.

Ding!

[You defeated two [goblins]! Items dropped: [club], [wedding ring], and 120 gold coins. +600 experience!]

Adam took out the [wedding ring] from his inventory and looked it over. It was a simple wedding band made of silver. It didn't have any embellishments on it, but it was well-crafted. He assumed this was Ms. Romelda's wedding ring, which meant his quest was technically complete and he could go back to the village.

But that might not net him enough experience points to level up.

Without even glancing in the direction of the Village of Beginnings, Adam stepped into the caves and began descending. Darkness almost immediately engulfed him. The deeper he traveled, the darker it seemed to become, until he could barely see two feet in front of him.

"It's a good thing I have a torch," Adam muttered as he brought a torch from his inventory and lit it up.

"This Village of Beginnings certainly has many problems surrounding it," Titania muttered.

"Speaking of the Village of the Beginnings, how did you and this spear end up on this island?" asked Adam.

"I am unsure," Titania said. "When I was sealed away with that spear, I did not know where I was being sealed."

"And who sealed you?" asked Adam.

"..."

Adam sensed Titania's reluctance to speak and sighed. "It's fine if you don't want to tell me."

"I apologize."

Adam glanced at Titania out of the corner of his eye to see the tiny woman looking a little odd. She wore a conflicted expression. Perhaps some part of her did want to tell him about how she was sealed away with that spear, but the rest of her was resistant to the idea.

Well, they had just met. He would find it more odd if she trusted him enough to tell him something so important right off the bat.

Some noise up ahead caused Adam and Titania to quiet down. They slowed their pace to a crawl and readied themselves for combat. [Blood Sacrifice] had already worn off, but Adam was not worried about that. Even without it, he'd only need two swings to take the life of a [goblin].

Around the next corner was the band of [goblins] who had entered ahead of him. It didn't look like they had noticed him, but that could change if he made too much noise. Adam slowly crept along the cavern floor, once more using his real life talent for stealth to close the distance without them noticing. Once he was in range, Adam stabbed his spear forward and activated [thrust].

-528!

His first attack came so close to killing his target that he almost swore, but his next attack disposed of it. While he managed to kill the first [goblin] before it could retaliate, the other two that were with their now dead companion turned toward him and angrily advanced on him with clubs drawn. They released garbled words that made no sense. However, one didn't need to speak goblin to know what they were saying.

Adam didn't hesitate. He twirled the spear in his hands several times and activated multiple [slash] attacks. Rather than just attack at random, however, Adam danced around his opponent, shuffling his feet against the ground in what, had someone been looking at him from a bird's-eye view, would have looked like the petals of a sakura blossom.

MISS; MISS; -528; MISS; MISS; -528; MISS; -528; -528!

Each goblin was hit with [slash] twice, which reduced their health to zero, killing them in less time than it took to blink. Adam stepped over their corpses and continued on.

Ding!

[You have defeated three [goblins]! Items dropped: [wooden club], [silver necklace], and 240 gold coins. +900 experience points!]

"You are quite skilled with a spear. Are you a spearman in your world?" asked Titania.

"I'm actually an assassin in my world," Adam admitted with a sardonic laugh. "However, when I was younger, the girl I loved was a talented spearman. She was the one who taught me how to wield a spear."

Adam went silent after that as memories played out in his mind. The angelic face of a young girl who couldn't have been more than eight or nine years old, framed by locks of black hair, and possessing the most stunning green eyes, appeared within his mind. She wore a brilliant grin filled with confidence. He almost choked as the memories returned to him.

"Adam! Look at my new technique! I just learned it today!"

"You don't know how to read?! That's okay. I can teach you."

"Adam... my parents... they said I can't be with you anymore, but don't worry! I don't care what they say. I'm not going to stop seeing you."

"Adam... hic... I don't want... to ever leave you. Let's run away together... I don't want to be my father's daughter anymore... I just want to be with you..."

Adam placed a hand against his chest, clutching it as an almost physical pain pierced his heart. He stumbled forward. Ignoring Titania's surprised shout, he took several shuddering breaths and shunted those unwanted memories away. He didn't... need them anymore. He didn't want them anymore. These memories only brought pain.

"Lexi is gone," he whispered. "Aris is the only person I need now."

He nodded once. Yes, Lexi wasn't around anymore. She had disappeared from the face of this world without a trace, and he could never find her no matter how hard he searched. She was probably dead. The only person in his life who mattered now was the girl he was living with.

Titania said nothing. Her eyes were pools of unknown emotion as she stared at him.

They continued on, traveling deeper into the cave. There weren't many [goblins] at first, but their numbers increased the further Adam and Titania descended. At first, they would run into groups of two, then three, and then four. The amount of experience points Adam gained by the time they reached the bottom was +3,600.

The bottom of this cave was vast and connected to the ocean. A large body of water sat not several yards away from the cavern entrance, flowing in through a passage that overlooked a small bay. The water looked dark, though Adam was sure it was just his eyes playing tricks on him due to the lack of light.

There were several [goblins] near the shore. They were dumping something in the water, and it took Adam several seconds to realize those strange chunks were actually body parts. His lips thinned when he saw the hand of what looked like a young child hitting the water with a splash.

"Let's kill them quickly and leave," Adam said as he stepped out of the passage and into the cavern.

Titania once more began singing [Song of Valor] as Adam activated [Blood Sacrifice]. He charged toward the group of four [goblins], who didn't notice his presence until he was nearly right on top of them.

-1,108!

His first attack impaled a goblin through the chest. He yanked his spear out of the now dead [goblin's] body, spun the blade around, and used [slash] to cut another [goblin] down before it could recover from its surprise.

-1,039!

While he managed to take out the first two [goblins] quickly, the other two recovered and attacked at the same time He was fortunate their attacks were so clumsy. Adam skipped backward to avoid their downward swings, then [thrust] his blade at the [goblin] on his left, killing it in one shot. The other went down when he performed [slash] two times to form an X-pattern on its flesh.

Ding!

[You have defeated 4 [goblins]! Items dropped: x4 [wooden clubs], [ladies undergarments], and 1,000 gold coins. +1,200 experience gained!]

Adam sighed as he looked at the amount of experience points he had gained. It wasn't bad, but he still needed about +7,000 more to level up.

He looked around and saw that there was no one present, no more enemies to slay, which meant he couldn't level up here.

"Let's go back and complete this quest," he said. "With luck, we will earn enough experience points for me to reach level 10... Titania?"

Titania had not spoken to him in awhile, which Adam realized was because she had been staring at the waters this entire time. He frowned and wondered what she was doing. Just as he was about to ask her, she screamed at him.

"MOVE!"

Adam didn't ask questions as he leapt aside seconds before something burst out of the water, struck the place where he had been standing, and cracked apart the rock floor. It was a long, black tentacle. It must have been at least two feet thick, and was covered in barnacles and warts. Even as he watched, the tentacle retracted back into the water.

"What the hell was that?!" asked a shocked Adam.

"Let me [scan] it for you," Titania said.

Name: Giant Octopus	Description: A one-thousand year old octopus that has grown to be several dozen feet large. It has been relying on the goblins to feed it human flesh.	Class: 2-star	Lvl: 20	Health: 40,000/40,000 MP: 900/900
Strength: +600	Constitution: +1,600	Dexterity: +100	Intelligence: +50	Speed: +500
Abilities: Tentacle Slam Description: Slams enemy into the ground with a tentacle MP required: 10 Cooldown time: 0 seconds	Tentacle Sweep Description: Sweeps away all enemies with tentacle 100% chance of knocking enemies off their feet MP required: 20 Cooldown time: 5 seconds	Needle Shot Description: Shoots needles from its mouth 50% chance of poisoning someone who is hit MP required: 100 Cooldown time: 10 seconds		

So he was up against a [giant octopus] that shot poisonous needles from its mouth? It was a 2-star enemy and at level 20?! This was...

"This is great!" Adam shouted. "I was worried because we haven't earned enough experience points to level up, but it looks like I'll be able to level up after I kill this thing!"

"That's what you're happy about?!" Titania snapped. "This is a 2-star enemy, you know! You're only at level 9!"

"So?" Adam laughed. "Who cares about that? Just help me kill it!"

"You..."

Titania seemed shocked that Adam was so gung-ho about fighting this [giant octopus], but that was because she hadn't seen him fight and kill both the [necromancer] and the [skeleton dragon] back in the dungeon where she and the [Rusted Spear] had been sealed.

Adam activated [Blood Sacrifice] and asked Titania to sing [Song of Vigor]. His first skill increased his Physical Attack from +330 to +660, and Titania's song further increased his stat to +1,452. It was an impressive number that made Adam grin.

With adrenaline pumping through his body, Adam threw himself to the side as another tentacle slammed into the ground and leapt at it. He used [thrust] and [slash] seconds after each other, spinning his spear around several times to attack the tentacle as many times as possible before it could retract. His feet formed the shape of a sakura blossom against the ground as he maneuvered himself around the tentacle during his all out assault.

-2,323; -2,178; MISS; -2,178; MISS; MISS!

While Adam missed three times, his constant attacks still brought the original +40,000 HP down to around +33,321. A loud squeal of pain erupted from somewhere in the water as the tentacle retracted. Adam had to wait again for the tentacle to come back.

He almost missed the second tentacle coming in from his other side to sweep him away. Adam leapt into the air, avoiding the tentacle, then slashed at it as he came back down. He only managed one hit, but it sapped another -2,178 off his enemy's health.

At that moment, [Blood Sacrifice] reached its time limit, and Adam had to wait for the 30 second cooldown time to end before he could activate it again. He took a health potion to restore his HP, dodged the tentacle attacks from the [giant octopus], and launched numerous attacks at it before it could recover.

MISS; MISS; -990; -990; MISS!

MISS; MISS; -990; -990; MISS; MISS; MISS!

Adam realized he was missing more attacks than normal, but he thought that might have something to do with the [giant octopus] rather than his ability to hit something. Maybe these tentacles were simply so slippery they had a higher than average Dodge-Rate.

The [giant octopus] must have gotten frustrated with its inability to hit him as well. Several tentacles shot out of the water and tried to pierce his body. He danced through the hailstorm of tentacles, which punctured the ground as if the rock floor was made of toilet paper. At that moment, the cooldown time for [Blood Sacrifice] ended, so he activated it again and began attacking the tentacles with reckless abandon.

-2,178; MISS; MISS; -2,178; -2,178; MISS; -2,178; MISS; MISS!

Adam hated how much HP these 2-star monsters possessed. As he constantly whittled away at the [giant octopus] and its stupid amount of health, he tried to think of a more efficient way of killing this thing. He didn't just want to keep attacking tentacles. There must have surely been another method that would let him end this fight quicker.

As more tentacles attacked, Adam continued to dodge and attack in turn, not stopping even after [Blood Sacrifice] ended again. Fortunately, Titania and her beautiful singing voice could go on until she ran out of MP.

Speaking of…

"I'm out of MP!" Titania shouted at him.

Adam reached into his pouch and pulled out a [low-grade magic potion] as he dodged backward, until he was standing right next to Titania.

"Here!" he said as he held out the potion.

Because she was so small, Titania could not hold the potion herself. Adam cracked the top open and tipped it back so Titania could drink it. They were out of the tentacles' reach right now. He watched as several tentacles futilely slammed into the ground in front of him.

When Titania finished the MP potion, she began singing again while Adam activated [Blood Sacrifice] once more and dashed forward to renew his assault on the [giant octopus].

- 2,178; MISS; MISS; -2,178; -2,178; -2,178; MISS; MISS; - 2,178; -2,178!

The battle continued. When the [giant octopus] had less than +10,000 health, the water bulged like skin swelling up after someone was bitten by a mosquito. Something broke the surface. It was a monstrous head with glowing red eyes, an ugly mouth with puckered lips, and odd protrusions that looked like warts all over its skin. The fact that it was breaking the water's surface could only mean one thing.

It was going to use [Needle Shot].

Adam ran away from where he had been standing. His reaction time was quick. The needles were launched from the creature's mouth barely a second after he moved, hundreds of needles clinking against the stone floor. While they all missed, this seemed to enrage the monster, who once more tried to slam him into the ground with a tentacle.

And that was when Adam got an idea.

The tentacle crashed into the ground, and Adam leapt onto it and ran along the tentacle, activating [Blood Sacrifice] as he used his inborn grace to race across the slippery surface. He reached the [giant octopus'] head in record time and used [slash] over and over again.

-6,534; MISS; MISS; MISS; MISS; -6,534!

His attacks quickly brought the creature's health down to zero. The [giant octopus] thrashed hard like it was spasming. Adam yelped as he was thrown off its body, hitting the water with a hard splash. Coldness filled his veins as he sank, but he kicked his legs and quickly broke the water's surface, gasping for breath. He looked around and was just in time to see the [giant octopus] disappearing into the dark water. The last thing he saw was one of its tentacles sinking beneath the surface.

Ding!

[You have defeated the 2-star monster [giant octopus]! Items dropped: [unknown key], [Water Trident], [unknown map], and 1,200 gold coins. +10,000 experience points! +1,600 ability points! +5,000 Reputation!]

Ding!

[Congratulations! You have leveled up. You are now at level 10! +30 HP! +10 MP! +5 SP!]

Ding!

[Congratulations! Titania has leveled up! Her level is now 9! +20 HP! +1,800 MP! +10 SP!]

Adam listened to the announcements as he swam to the shore, then put his newly gained SP into his Strength stat and equipped the [Bone Dragon Greaves], [Bone Dragon Cuirass], and [Bone Dragon Gauntlets]. Now that he had reached level 10, he could finally equip this excellent equipment, which boosted his stats to an unbelievable degree.

Name: Adam	Class: Warrior	Lvl: 10	SP: 0 AP: 1,700	Experience: 3,080/76,800 Reputation: 26,500
Strength: +150	Constitution: +150	Dexterity: +5	MP: +5	Speed: +6

Physical Attack: +380	Health: 200/200	Hit-rate: 6%	MP:90/90	Movement: +6
	Physical Defense: +435 Magic Defense: +150	Dodge-Rate: ???	Magic Attack: +5	

Resistance:	Fire: 50% Water: 50% Earth: 50% Wind: 50% Lightning: 50% Darkness: 50% Slashing: 50%

Skill Name: Slash	Description: A basic skill where the player swings his or her sword and attacks the enemy!	Current lvl: 5 MAX MAXED	Ability: Causes 150% damage to enemy if it hits	MP con-sumption: 1	Cooldown time: 0 seconds
Skill Name: Thrust	Description: A basic skill where the player thrusts his or her sword at the enemy!	Current lvl: 5 MAX MAXED	Ability: Causes 160% damage with a 5% chance at getting a critical hit	MP Con-sumption. 5	Cooldown time: 1 second

Skill Name: Blood Sacrifice	Description: By sacrificing 50% of your blood (HP), you have gained the ability to increase the damage you do.	Current lvl: 5 MAXED	Ability: causes 300% attack power for 60 seconds Disregards skill cooldown times, allowing the user to attack with every skill	MP consumption: 20 Special limit: Drops HP by half	Cooldown time: 30 seconds

Name: Rusted Spear Level: 4 Experience points needed to level up: 11,700/40,000	Item Type: Spear	Grade: ? ???	Use requirements: Can only be equipped by Adam. Cannot be thrown away, cannot be given away, and cannot be unequipped.	Description: This unknown weapon was found by Adam. It has recognized him as its master and cannot be used by anyone else.	Abilities: Physical Attack+40; Strength +40 Special ability: Sentient Growth

Item Name: Dragon Bone Cuirass	Item Type: Armor	Grade: 1-star	Use requirements: Can be equipped by Warriors level 10 and above	Description: This chest plate was made from the bones of a powerful dragon. Not only does it look stylish, but it offers solid defensive abilities and some special stats.	Abilities: Defense+200; Constitution+100; 25% resistance to slashing, fire, earth, wind, lightning, and darkness damage.
Item Name: Dragon Bone Gauntlets	Item Type: Armor	Grade: 1-star	Use requirements: Can be equipped by Warriors level 10 and above	Description: These gauntlets are made from the bones of a powerful dragon. Not only are they stylish, but they offer solid defensive abilities and resistance to elemental damage.	Abilities: Defense+50; Constitution+10; 10% resistance to slashing, fire, earth, wind, lightning, and darkness damage.

Item Name: Dragon Bone Greaves	Item Type: Armor	Grade: 1-star	Use requirements: Can be equipped by Warriors level 10 and above	Description: Greaves made from the bones of a powerful dragon. They are not only stylish, they also offer solid defense and resistance against elemental damage.	Abilities: Defense+ 75; Constitution+ 25; 15% resistance to slashing, fire, earth, wind, lightning, and darkness damage.

Thanks to his new equipment, Adam's stats had skyrocketed, especially his Constitution and Defense stats. Now when he leveled up again, he would gain a lot more HP because his Constitution stat was so high. He also had a Physical Defense stat that was so solid most monsters living near the Village of Beginnings would not be able to damage him. Other players wouldn't be able to hurt him either.

"I think we're good," he said with a cheerful smile. "Let's get going."

Adam began walking off, only to realize that Titania was not following him. He turned around and looked at the tiny fairy.

"What's wrong?" he asked.

"There is nothing wrong," Titania said, snapping out of her stupor and flying over to him. She landed on his shoulder and huffed. "I am merely beginning to realize how abnormal you are."

"Well, thanks. I'm happy to know you think I am odd."

"Hmph. Odd does not even begin to cover it. A normal person at level 9 would never be able to defeat a level 20 2-star monster no matter how talented they are."

Adam couldn't say anything to that. All he could do was shrug.

They made their way out of the cave and back to the Village of Beginnings, where Adam delivered Ms. Romelda's ring to her in exchange for +1,000 experience points, +100 ability points, and x10 [health potions] and [MP potions] respectively. It wasn't a bad haul all things considered.

Once Adam finished delivering the missing ring, he went to the Mayor.

"You already reached level 10?!" The mayor seemed shocked as he wiped his sweaty face with a handkerchief. "My word, but you otherworlders are impressive. Or maybe it is simply that you yourself are impressive."

"This human is my companion. Of course he is impressive." Titania's chest swelled with pride as if she herself was the one being complimented. It was almost like she hadn't been calling him abnormal barely half an hour ago.

"A-a-a-a fairy! It's really a fairy! I can't believe there is actually a fairy here… why is she so little?"

"… Do you want me to curse you?"

The mayor's response surprised Adam, but he soon learned that fairies were considered an extinct race. According to the mayor, a fairy had not been seen for at least five-thousand years, which surprisingly coincided with when Titania had been sealed away alongside the spear. This knowledge seemed to depress Titania, who grew quiet and contemplative.

"A-anyway," the mayor got back on track, "now that you have reached level 10, I assume you wish to leave? We do have a ship that will take you to the mainland. We can give you passage right now if you'd like, but please be warned that once you leave, you will not be able to return. If you have anything you would like to accomplish before leaving, now is the time to do it."

"I would like to leave," Adam said.

"In that case, please follow me," the mayor said with a gesture.

Adam did not hesitate to follow after the mayor as the older man walked off. There was nothing more for him to do in this Village of Beginnings. It was time to leave.

~To Be Continued...

AFTERWORD

Hello one and all. This is Brandon Varnell speaking. I sincerely hope you enjoyed Man Made God 001. If you did and have the time, please consider writing a review on Amazon. Reviews are imperative for an author's growth and help readers make decisions on what books to read. Amazon also does this magic trick where books with over one-hundred 4 and 5-star reviews are shown to more readers.

While I have done one other series that has a leveling system, Man Made God is the first gamelit series I have ever written. I remember going on Amazon and reading a crap ton of gamelit stories in preparation to write this, including The Land, Ready Player One. Sword Art Online, The World Book, Stonehaven League, Death March Rhapsody to a Parallel World, The Completionist Chronicles, New Era Online, and quite a few other best selling RPGlit series. I have no real experience with leveling systems or gamelit, so I wanted to make sure I did a good job.

Creating a leveling system was much harder than I expected. I ended up making Adam level up to 10 twice after writing three books and had to redo his entire level progression from volume 1.

I also wanted to see how other authors wrote their characters into a video game world. During my reading, I discovered that there were a few ways in which characters entered a game. This list contains what seems to be the most used methods based on my research:

1. A hot new game comes out. The protagonist grabs a copy, loads it up, and finds himself/herself trapped inside of a death game with thousands of other players.

2. A terminally ill patient/convict on death's row is offered a way to avoid death, but the catch is their subconscious will be converted into polygons and downloaded into a brand new game that some sketchy scientists are testing.

3. The protagonist gets isekai'd to a world that has a leveling system just like his favorite video game!

4. The protagonist just wants to live another life in this new VRMMO, but something happens after he/she is loaded into the game, and he/she learns that this game is much darker than it first seemed.

These methods were used the most in the forty or so books I read. I'm sure there are many more. I also know that Japan has released a string of slice-of-life gamelit light novels about cute girls playing VRMMOs for fun.

Out of all the books I read, the one where a loved one is terminally ill and the protagonist is offered a chance to save them was the least used. A story called Shura's Wrath was what influenced the beginning of this series. I only read one dozen chapters before I learned something disturbing about the protagonist that made me quit, but I really enjoyed those first few chapters, enough that I wanted to create a similar premise for the beginning my story.

You'll notice right off the bat that Adam Lancer is very much an alpha protagonist. I usually like my protagonists to start out as a more anime archetype character, but I didn't think that would work here. I felt like a character who was action-oriented, decisive, and strong would make the story more compelling.

Before I leave you all, I would just like to give some last minute thanks.

Thank you Abby for editing my story. I made quite a few small mistakes that slipped through the cracks during beta reading and self-edits, so I am glad most of them were caught before I hit publish.

I would also like to thank Lonwa_A for his artwork. He did the cover art for Swordsman of the Rift 1, and I thought his more realistic art style would fit the Man Made God narrative better than a more anime art style. His art is very gorgeous.

Finally, I would like to thank you readers for continuing to support me. Authors need readers to thrive. Without you, we would be nothing, and I am so glad to have you all here with me. I sincerely hope you will join me for Man Made God 002.

~Brandon Varnell

BRANDON VARNELL IS
WRITING STORIES AND
CREATING COMICS ON
PATREON!

HAVE YOU EVER EXPERIENCED ONE OF THOSE LIFE-CHANGING INSTANCES? AN EVENT SO MOMENTOUS THAT, YEARS LATER, YOU'RE STILL MARVELING AT HOW IT CHANGED YOUR LIFE?

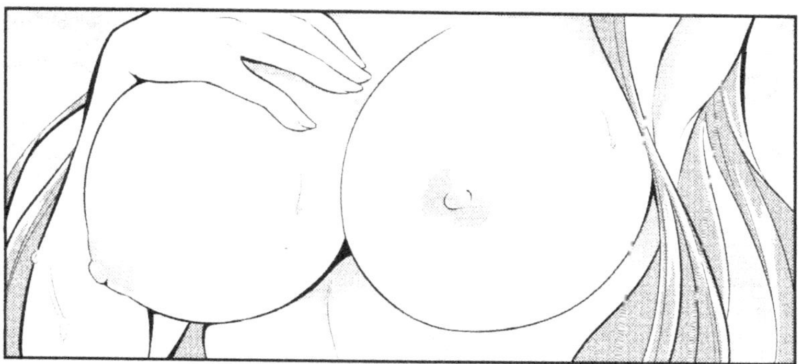

I HAD ONE OF THOSE. IT HAPPENED A WHILE AGO

EVEN TO THIS DAY, THROUGH ALL THE CHANGES THAT HAVE HAPPENED, THROUGH ALL THE EXPERIENCES THAT I'VE BEEN THROUGH, I STILL CAN'T BELIEVE HOW THIS ONE MOMENT CHANGED MY LIFE FOREVER.

NO MATTER WHAT CAME AFTER, OUR FIRST MEETING IS SOMETHING THAT I'LL ALWAYS REMEMBER.

ESPECIALLY SINCE, AT THE BEGINNING OF THIS TALE, I THOUGHT SHE WAS NOTHING BUT AN ORDINARY FOX WITH, UNORDINARILY ENOUGH, TWO BUSHY RED TAILS.

IT HITS YOU WHEN YOU LEAST EXPECT IT TO.

COMING SOON!

Hey, did you know?
Brandon Varnell has started a Patreon
You can get all kinds of awesome exclusives
Like:

1. The chance to read his stories before anyone else!
2. Free ebooks!
3. exclusive SFW and NSFW artwork!
4. Signed paperback copies!
Er... maybe we don't want that last one, but the rest is pretty cool, right?

To get this awesome exlusive conent go to:
https://www.patreon.com/BrandonVarnell
and sigh up today!

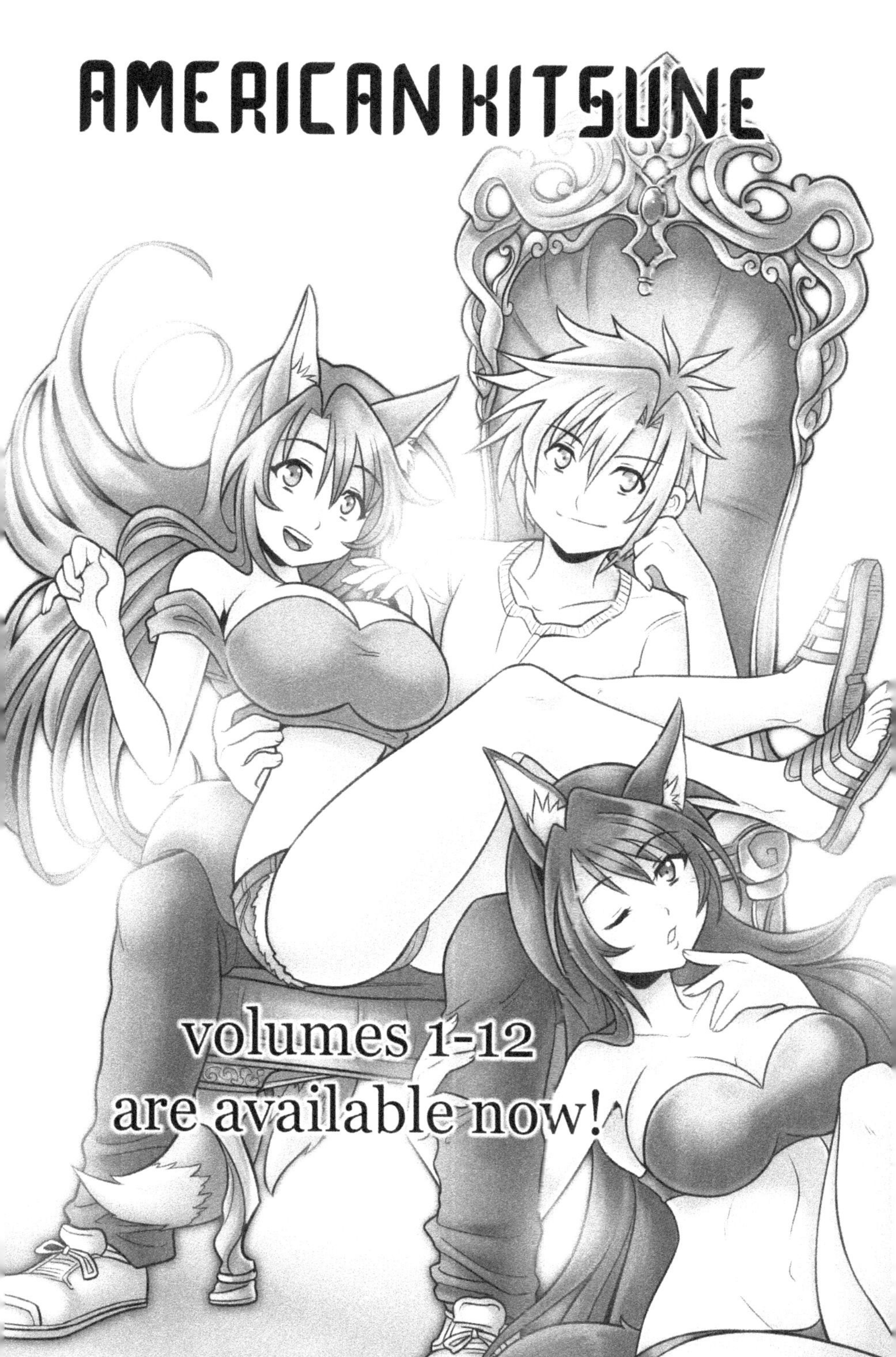

AMERICAN KITSUNE
volumes 1-12
are available now!

catgirl doctor
Buy volume 1 on paperback, kindle, and Kindle Unlimited!

Volumes 1-7
are available now!
A Most
Unlikely
Hero

INCUBUS
VERTICAL
BUFFET
volume 1 is available on paperback, kindle, and kindle unlimited!

Arcadia's IgnobleKnight
Volumes 1-7
are available now!

The Complete Series is available now on paperback and Amazon Kindle!
JOURNEY of a BETRAYED HERO

Volumes 1 & 2 are available on
paperback,
Amazon,
and Kindle Unlimited

Swordsman
Of the
Rift 2

The Executioner Series
The complete series
is available now!

Want to learn when a new book comes out?
Follow me on Social Media!

 @AmericanKitsune

 +BrandonVarnell

 @BrandonBVarnell

 http://bvarnell1101.tumblr.com/

 Brandon Varnell

 BrandonbVarnell

 https://www.patreon.com/
BrandonVarnell

www.ingramcontent.com/pod-product-compliance
Lightning Source LLC
Chambersburg PA
CBHW070752190726
48292CB00002B/513